27 Truths

**THE TRUTH ABOUT LOVE SERIES
AVA'S STORY, BOOK 1**

Also By MJ Fields

The Men of Steel Series

Forever Steel
Jase
Jase and Carly
Cyrus
Zandor
Xavier
Momma Joe

The Ties of Steel Series

Abe
Dominic
Eroe
Sabato

The Rockers of Steel Series

Memphis Black (Memphis and Tallia)
Finn Beckett (Finn and Sonia)
River James (River and Kianna)
Billy Jeffers (Billy and Madison)

LRAH Legacy Series (These families' stories are intertwined starting with The Love series, they move to the Wrapped Series, the Burning Souls series, and end in Love You Anyways. Many more series will spin off from these characters already written and each will be a standalone series but for those of us who love a story to continue I recommend reading in this order.

The Love Series
(Must Be Read In This Order)

Blue Love
New Love
Sad Love
True Love

The Wrapped Series

Wrapped In Silk
Wrapped In Armor
Wrapped In Always and Forever

Burning Souls Series

Stained
Forged
Merged

LRAH Legacy Additions

Love You Anyway
Love Notes

The Truth About Love Series
27 Truths

**The Norfolk Series
(Must Be Read In This Order)**

Irons 1(Jax and Frankie, book 1)
Irons 2 (Jax and Frankie, book 2)
Irons 3 (Jax and Frankie, book 3)

The Caldwell Brothers Series (co-written w/ Chelsea Camaron)

Hendrix
Morrison
Jagger

To The Reader

There is a moment that your breath is taken away. You feel a connection, one that you know is only made for two people. A moment you are so frightened of losing that words are lost. So, without reason, you allow that beautiful once in a lifetime moment to be felt, but you never put it into words.

A moment like that deserves words.

Moments like that deserve so much more than a memory you will relive in your mind forever as the time you fell in love with the person you know you were meant to spend eternity with.

I am sure I am not alone in this observation. But love isn't only a feeling. So many things come into love's equation.

The scent of love is distinct. It's not covered in store-bought aromas that are flowery or musky. It is a scent that you never forget yet can't describe. It is a smell that, when it wafts through the air and tickles your nose, you will instantly remember the first time you encountered it. Yet, instead of trying to understand it, you simply bask in it and pray for its return.

The look of love is not two dimensional; it's not even three dimensions. There are endless sides, different depths, and it can change in the blink of an eye.

The truth about love is that the fall isn't the most beautiful part. It's the whole story: the beginning, the middle, and everything in-between. It doesn't end.

The truth about love is that there aren't just two people. People bring their pasts with them. They bring their pain, their joy, their wounds, their experiences, their knowledge, and their desire to make it work.

The truth about love isn't easy to tell. It isn't black and white.

You love someone, and they will surely love you. If you give of yourself selflessly enough, so will they.

In each chapter heading is a truth about love given to me

by a friend, family member, or reader just like you. It does not necessarily introduce the chapter.

This book doesn't end with a typical HEA, but it is about love's truths and tragedies.

It is about the beautiful and the broken.

XOXO
MJ

LEGACY SERIES
— FAMILY TREE —

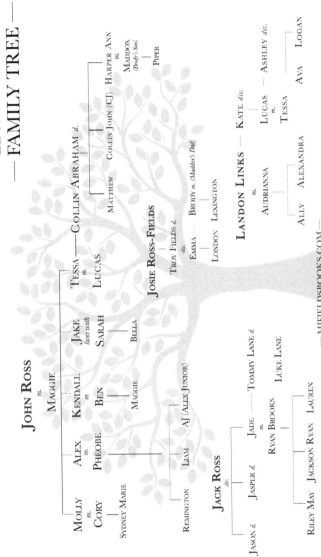

JOHN ROSS
m.
MAGGIE

MOLLY
m.
CORY

SYDNEY MARIE

ALEX
m.
PHEOBE

LIAM   AJ (ALEX JUNIOR)

REMINGTON

KENDALL
m.
BEN

MAGGIE

JAKE
lives with
SARAH

BELLA

TESSA
m.
LUCAS

COLLIN ABRAHAM *d.*

MATTHEW   COLLIN JOHN (CJ)   HARPER ANN

MADDOX
(Brody's Son)

PIPER

JOSIE ROSS-FIELDS

TROY FIELDS *d.*
liv.

EMMA   BRODY *m. (Maddox's Dad)*

LONDON   LEXINGTON

LANDON LINKS — KATE *div.*

AUDRIANNA
m.

ALLY   ALEXANDRA

LUCAS — ASHLEY *div.*
m.
TESSA

AVA   LOGAN

JACK ROSS
div.

JASON *d.*   JASPER *d.* — TOMMY LANE *d.*

JADE
m.
RYAN BROOKS

LUKE LANE

RILEY MAY   JACKSON RYAN   LAUREN

Prologue

You can't run or hide from love. Love will always find you.
— H. Scully

Seven Years Ago

FOR AS FAR BACK AS I can remember, I have loved Luke Lane.

Luke's father, Tommy, was my father's best friend. Dad and Tommy went to school together, played football together—they did everything together. They planned to play football in college together, but Tommy Lane fell in love with Jade Ross, and Jade fell in love with Tommy.

From the stories I have been told, they were the happiest high school couple ever. They shared a love story for the ages.

One night during their senior year in high school, they went to Syracuse. Tommy was driving with Jade by his side. My father and Ryan, a friend of theirs, were in the back seat. A drunk city bus driver ran a red light, hit the vehicle on the driver's side, and Tommy was killed. They were all rushed to the hospital where Jade found out she was pregnant.

My father did what he knew Tommy would do for

him. He helped Jade in any way he could. And when Jade's son was born, he was named after my father, and my father became his godfather.

My father is not particularly close to his own parents. The Ross family became his family, even after the breakup with his high school girlfriend, Tessa Ross. They still loved him and included him in nearly everything. By default, my brother Logan and I were part of that family, as well.

Even when Jade married Ryan, my father was still a huge part of their lives. He loved Luke Lane like he was his own. He loved Luke Lane because he was Tommy's son.

I love him because I know that we are meant to be together.

Growing up next-door to him, we saw each other often. With our families being so close, I saw him even more often. Holidays, birthdays, cookouts, pool parties—we even vacationed together.

Luke Lane was taller than me, bigger than me, older than me, and there was always a part of him that was protective of me. He watched out for me, much like my father watched out for him.

When all the kids would choose teams for beach volleyball or kickball, I was always the last chosen. Luke once told me that I should stop wearing my tutu and my crown all the time, and then they might take me a little bit more seriously as an athlete. I told him, when he was captain, he should choose me, anyway, because that's what people who love each other do. I was young, very young, and he was ... Luke. He nodded and said, "Fine."

From then on, I was always his second pick. I understood that he needed to make sure his team had a chance to win, and he understood that I was still going to wear my crown and tutu.

There are pictures of him and me in abundance: me on his shoulders in the pool, me tagging along behind him, me at his football games, him at some of my dance competitions, and hundreds of photos at get-togethers. There are more pictures of the two of us than me or him with anyone else.

Those things don't just happen; they are signs. A sign that Luke Lane and Ava Links are meant to be together forever.

When I went through my "awkward phase"—you know the one: body changing, boobs growing, things like that—he no longer put me on his shoulders in the pool. He no longer picked me to be on his team when we played games. Instead, he distanced himself.

At first, it hurt.

At school, when I told my best friend Harper, his second cousin, that I had been reading magazine articles on how to make a guy fall in love with you, she laughed.

I didn't think it was funny at all.

"Oh, I'm sorry, Ava. I didn't mean to hurt your feelings. It's just …" She stopped, and I waited.

Harper Abraham was that girl you wish you could be. She was the top of our class academically; any sports she played, she excelled at; and she was a friend to all, kindness pouring out of her. She did not do drama, and she smiled often. As a result, when she laughed at my teenage heartbreak, it pissed me off.

"Just what?" I asked, packing my book bag full of magazines and books.

"Ava, don't be mad. He's just … I don't know, older and, like, family," she finally said.

"*You're* his family; I'm not."

Harper and I went through a rough time after that.

3

I left the library and never mentioned his name to her again. I hid my love for Luke for a while. When she brought it up, I shot it down. She didn't get it. He was mine, I was his, and that was the way it was. Harper wasn't the kind of girl who dreamed of her Prince Charming, though. She was too worried about spreading kindness and helping the less fortunate. (Seriously, she is that perfect.)

When Luke started dating, I accepted it. He didn't love those girls. I mean, what was there to love? They didn't know him, and he didn't know them.

Harper was right. Our age difference was an issue, but someday, it wouldn't be. Until then, I had to believe that true love would prevail.

And it would.

Luke joined the Army. The day I found out, my heart broke.

"Why?" I asked him when no one else was in earshot.

"Why, what?" he asked, also looking around to make sure no one could hear me, including his bimbo girlfriend.

"Why are you doing this? Leaving me?" I waved my hand around. "Leaving us?"

He looked at me and crossed his arms over his chest. "I'm a man, Ava. Until you grow up, you won't understand this, but I need to make my own way."

Tears immediately sprung to my eyes. My emotions were all over the place: hurt that he saw me as a child, sorrow because he was leaving, and anger because he just didn't get it.

Then he hugged me.

"Someday, you'll understand, okay? I'll be back."

You'll be back for me, I thought. *For me.*

I prayed for Luke Lane every night. I prayed for his safety. I prayed for his return. I prayed for his love. God knew he was made for me, and so did I. That was all that mattered.

He came home on leave in time for graduation. His brother Jackson, Harper, his cousin Liam, and I all graduated that year. A few days after graduation, there was a party celebrating his safe return. And like every time he came home, there was a girl waiting. She was not me. She was physically my opposite: tall, big boobs, and red hair. I am short and dark-haired with less than average sized breasts and an ass that brings attention that I'm undetermined whether I like or not.

Alexis was also a complete bitch. Bitches come in droves, so that bitch brought her mini-bitches. The mini-bitches and queen bitch ate, drank, and were merry. They clearly enjoyed their time poolside, strutting around with their plastic personalities and plastic-enhanced body parts.

I overheard a conversation they had about how hot he was and "obviously he could do better than being a soldier in the Army because his family clearly could afford to send him to college."

It happened to be a day when I was liking the size of my ass. I had snuck a few drinks and decided to go plant my butt amongst the bitches.

"I'm Ava." I smiled nice and big, getting comfortable. They all clammed up. "So, I heard you talking shit about Luke."

They gasped and vice bitch, the one closest to Alexis, rolled her eyes. "We were just saying he could do better." She waved her hand about. "I mean, look at this place. It's not like he has no other options. Clearly, he could take better care of Alexis if he just worked for his family."

I pulled my shades down and looked over at them. "He's busy taking care of a country. And what exactly is she doing? No, never mind, I heard. She quit school."

"So she could be available for him," vice bitch snapped.

"Then what does she do the other eleven months out of the year? Sit around and bitch to you guys about needing a man to take care of her?" I hold my hand up. "Never mind. Don't give a shit. You're all trifling ass bitches, anyway."

"And who the hell are you?" one of them gasped. "Some teenage trust fund baby?"

"No, bitch. I'm going to be a woman who will make damn sure I can take care of myself and my man. The only sucking off him I'll be doing is—"

"Ava, I need your help," Harper said, grabbing my arm and yanking me up.

"But—"

"Now."

"Bitches," I grumbled as I walked away.

"Fat ass," one said behind me.

I tried to yank my arm away as I turned around. "Your boyfriend liked it."

"Ava," Harper snapped, pulling me into the garage.

"What a bunch of cu—"

"You're loaded," Harper gasped.

"So?" I huffed. "At least I'm not a cu—"

"Ava, everything okay?" Luke's brother Jackson asked, snickering.

"Bitch told me I have a fat ass." I turned around and bent over. "It may be fat, but it's a nice fat ass, right?"

"Everything okay in here?"

I looked back as Luke walked in the garage.

They all said everything was good, all except me.

"Do you think my ass is fat?" I asked.

His eyes locked onto mine. There was something different in them, something that heated my body in the center and spread into every cell.

"Answering a question like that can get a man in trouble," he said, his nostrils flaring a bit.

"Trouble is my middle—"

"Ava's had too much to drink," Liam interrupted, coming in behind Luke.

After that incident, the crowd thinned. My parents stayed to help Jade and Ryan clean up. I did, too. Then Mom and Logan left before Dad and I got in the pool to cool off from the drunken cleaning in ninety-degree heat.

Luke's brothers, Riley and Jackson, were in the pool with their girlfriends. Lauren, his sister, was walking in the house with Jade.

I was on an inflatable floating tube, and Luke was standing by the edge of the pool. He was shirtless, his arms crossed over his expansive chest, wearing black board shorts hanging low on his hips, exposing the small trail of hair leading beneath his waistband. He was so beautiful it was almost painful to look at him. I swore he could have made my eyes bleed. His jet black hair was cut short on the sides, his full lips completely kissable, and his deep, dark blue eyes were cast down.

He looked up as if he could sense me looking at him, his face unreadable. I wondered what he was thinking. God, I wished I knew what he was thinking.

He squatted down and put his hand in the water as if to test the temperature. When he looked up at me again, he lifted his hand and curled his finger, beckoning me.

I pointed to myself because I was unsure he was truly referring to me.

The side of his lips curled up, and he looked around then back at me with his eyebrow raised and nodded.

I let out a very slow breath that was held as I looked

around. We were alone. Everyone had left. Totally alone.

I paddled toward him, my eyes not leaving his, his never leaving mine, as I reminded myself to breathe. Just breathe.

It seemed like it took forever to get to him, but if it truly did, it was okay with me. He was looking at me, and it was so very different than it had ever been.

As I swam closer, I expected him to stand, but he didn't.

"Water's too cold for you, Ava."

"I'm not cold," I said, my voice sounding different, sexier.

"No?" He shook his head back and forth as he said it.

"As a matter of fact, I'm kinda hot," I told him, sounding much more confident than I felt.

"I think you should come up out of that water," he said, reaching out his hand for me.

I took it, and he pulled me up. Before he had a chance to pull it away, though, I took his hand and placed it against the base of my neck.

"Do you think I feel cold?"

His body tensed, and he shook his head.

I kept his hand in place and looked around. "No one else is here." I looked back at him and watched his eyes dart between my lips and my eyes. "So, tell me; do you think my ass is fat?"

He didn't respond.

I took my hand away from his, but he left it on me.

My chest rose and fell faster, so did his.

"What does your boyfriend think?"

"Don't have one," I responded quietly.

"So no one has touched you?" he asked as he started to pull his hand away.

I quickly covered it with mine, not wanting him to remove it.

"I'm not a virgin if that's what you're asking."

"No?" His hand started to move up my neck slowly.

"No. I'm not a child, either."

"Don't appear to be," he said, focused on his hand that was gently gripping my neck as his thumb slid up and down my jawline.

He was touching me, and my heart was nearly pounding out of my chest. Luke Lane was touching me.

His thumb brushed across my lower lip, and I closed my eyes and ran my tongue slowly over it. Then I wrapped my lips around it and sucked gently.

"I have a girlfriend," he grumbled.

I tipped my head back, letting go of his thumb, opening my eyes, and looking into his. "You could do so much better."

He didn't confirm or deny. I knew he was aware it was true.

"Can't do this with you," he said as his lips hovered centimeters from mine.

My mouth was watering. My legs were trembling. My body's core was on fire. I wanted him more than I had ever wanted anything in my life, and I was so close to having his lush lips on mine.

I had to kiss him. I was terrified that, if I didn't take this opportunity—one given by fate—I would never have it again.

"Then don't," I whispered as I grabbed his waist with one hand and the back of his neck with the other.

Then I kissed him.

The sound that escaped him when our lips met came from a place of unmeasurable depth. Every ounce of courage it took to kiss him was swallowed up in its complexity. I trembled when his arm wrapped around me and pulled me tightly to him.

If he let go, I feared I might fall or pass out.

He didn't.

His kiss intensified. Hands in my hair, his tongue caressing mine, he kept his other hand holding me securely against him.

I couldn't breathe. All I could do was feel, and the feelings were so overwhelming I swore all control was not just gone; it was shattered.

He pulled his mouth from mine, and I couldn't help grabbing his face.

"Don't stop," I pleaded softly.

"Ava …" he whispered and closed his eyes.

My name had never sounded so beautiful and tormented all at the same time.

"Please …" I begged, bowing my head until it touched his chin.

"I'm not the man you need," he said gruffly, and the sadness in it didn't go unnoticed.

"I don't need a man," I said, daring to look up at him. "I'm going to law school; you're going back to Kentucky. I know that."

"Then why?" His brows furrowed.

"Because I have wanted you my entire life," I said out loud, while inside, I told him it was because I loved him. *I love you so much.*

"We've both had way too much to drink." He stepped back.

"Luke …" I started, my hands trembling for a completely different reason.

"I have a girlfriend," he repeated.

I shook my head as I told him, "She doesn't deserve you."

His eyes penetrated mine, and we were silent, but

it wasn't awkward. In the silence, there was a force field keeping us both in the same place, not letting us move.

I closed my eyes and said again, "She doesn't deserve a man like you."

"You don't deserve a man like me, Ava. All those romantic notions you have about me are not reality. When you tell me you want me, I know damn well you want what you think I am. You sure as hell don't want me."

"Do so," I said and quickly realized I sounded like a spoiled little girl.

"I'm a soldier. I fight. I breathe for my country, and I will die for my country if need be. It is who I am. I am not walking away from who I am to play house with a girl who thinks she knows me when, in reality, I never knew who I was until the United States Army brought it out of me."

"I'm not a stupid girl," I told him.

"Never said you were. But if I fucked you, it would be a fuck, not a relationship. No wedding bells or picket fence. If I fuck you, Ava, it's purely physical."

"What about your girlfriend? Do you love her?"

He shook his head. "Don't know. I loved the promises she made to me when I got home and that, if I wanted her to come with me, she'd come. I loved the letters she wrote when I was in the field, loved that she would marry me tomorrow."

"But …"

"I don't anymore. She doesn't want me to stay in. She's doing nothing here with her life. The first time I came home, I told her she needed to do her thing, that I had changed. She didn't listen."

"Then why not just break up with her?"

"I like having someone at home. I like getting

letters in the field." He looked back up. "I'm a fucking asshole."

I shook my head. "You're not. She's stupid."

He sighed and shrugged.

"I'm not stupid. I'm going to be so busy at school for seven years, Luke. Seven. Break up with her. I'll write you."

"Ava …" he said in a tone that made me feel like he thought I was stupid or maybe not worthy.

"I write you letters, anyway," I told him immediately. "And when you come home, I'm always here."

"This won't always be home for me."

"Pft, like it will be for me," I said, acting like it was no big deal. And it wasn't. He was my home. He just didn't know it yet.

"Sex isn't a once a year thing," he told me.

"So?"

"So tell me you'd be okay with me fucking you and others."

No, but after me, you'll want no one else, I thought to myself.

"As long as you're okay with the same," I told him.

His eyebrows shot up as he studied me.

"What? I'm not ready to settle down. I have goals and dreams and aspirations."

He turned and started to walk away.

"Where are you going?"

He stopped and looked back. "If I come back out here and you're gone, it means you're smarter than I am. If I come back out and you're still here, I'll know you mean what you said. If we do this, it's physical, Ava. That means you don't tell anyone—"

"I won't," I said almost too enthusiastically.

"Not even Harper," he said.

"Of course not Harper," I huffed.

He looked me up and down again. "You should be gone when I get back."

"You should break up with that bitch before you come back out."

The corner of his mouth quirked up, and he nodded.

One

Every relationship has peaks and valleys
— E. Clinton

Present Day

I LOOK OUT THE WINDOW as the plane takes off out of LaGuardia. The city lights are always beautiful in the evening from up here. The lights at Christmastime are even more beautiful, especially as the falling snow eclipses them momentarily. It's as if they are dancing, waving good-bye to the travelers like me who are leaving the hustle and bustle of city life to return home to family and friends for the holidays.

When the dancing, twinkling lights can no longer be seen, I lean forward and remove my new black Louis Vuitton Heritage high boots then lean down and grab my Louis Keepall 45 Bandouliere graphite, digging through it until I find the little black pouch my ruby red patent Tieks are in. They are the most comfortable pair of shoes a girl could wear. I also pull out the pink blanket I have had since birth, Bingo.

I'm going to the place where I am from, a place where I have always felt adored and loved—home. I have always been my dad's princess, and I still hold that title. I'm going home to a place where I can walk outside, take a deep breath, and smell the fresh country air. I'm going home to a place I can laugh at things that are not politically correct, that I can say whatever I want and not worry what others think. They don't judge me, because they know me. They know my heart. I'm going home to the place where I have no ladder to climb or egos that require stroking, because they know me, and I don't need to prove that I am who I say I am.

The seat is big enough for me to fold my legs up beside me. I place Bingo against the cabin wall and lay my head against it as I lean back in my seat.

I just celebrated Christmas with my Mom, her new husband Robert, and my brother Logan. Watching the two of them literally trip over themselves to try to outdo my father is almost sickening. It was no Christmas.

Unlike my brother, I actually try to ignore and push away the hurt that comes from a family being torn apart by lies and infidelity. "They didn't divorce us; they divorced each other," I always tell Logan, just like Dad has told us on several separate occasions. It's honest. It's real. It is their truth. It doesn't make it hurt any less. It doesn't mean it's our truth.

My younger brother Logan and my truth is that, after the initial shock and pain wore off, the two people—our parents—we thought were deeply in love weren't. They hadn't been for years. We sought out a reason because it didn't make sense.

That truth about love is even more painful because it involves the same two people, the ones who taught us what love is, who unknowingly lied to us and changed a part of us that should never have been changed, because in truth, there should be no lies. In love, there should be no hate. In life, when you come home, it should be a place where you don't feel yourself being torn apart.

Even as a young adult, it's hard to juggle life between parents, so I decided to forgive the lie and try not to judge them, while Logan chose to deal with it in his own way, which is bed hopping. Boys, ugh.

I know she tried to act like it wasn't a big deal when Logan and I decided Christmas should be the 22nd this year, but it must have been. Regardless, I can't imagine waking up on Christmas and not having my father's childlike excitement almost screaming from his eyes when we walk down the stairs in the morning. I can't imagine not waking up to him overdoing it while insisting that, yes, there is a Santa Claus, and yes, he actually was here last night as Logan tries every year since he was in sixth grade to convince him otherwise. Dad never cares, and I love him even more for it, whereas Logan totally calls him a dork.

I hold the blanket to my nose and inhale. The scent that I know is just a memory gives me a feeling of calm, of home, of love.

I'm going home for two weeks, and I am going to enjoy it. Not just enjoy it, I am going to love it.

I always do.

I close my eyes and picture Luke as I saw him last summer. I know he will look different now. He always does. He gets bigger, more defined, stronger. His eyes are more intense yet never show or tell me anything more than he wants me to know. His touch is less gentle every time I see him. Nothing like that first night at the pool, the first time Luke and I made love. I tell myself it's need, desire, and love. We have never exchanged those three words, but it doesn't mean they aren't there.

He asks me if I have been safe with my other

partners, and I tell him what he wants to hear. I tell him yes. When I ask him, he nods. What he doesn't know is there has been no one else in my bed or inside of me.

I've made out with other men and have been on dates, but no other man has been inside of me. I use them to get what I don't get from Luke … yet.

When he leaves, he never says good-bye. I go through some type of sadness, but not a depression. After all, I know he loves me, and someday very soon, I am going to say those words to him, knowing when I do, he will return them.

Over the past seven years, I have kept my promise—well, except the part about telling Harper. When I told her I had slept with him, she and her now husband were going through a rough time. I did it because she was a mess, and I wanted her to see she wasn't alone.

The other promise I kept was writing to him. At first, it was every week. Then, when he didn't return a single one for four months, I sent one every two weeks. I was hurt when he still didn't return my letters, so after a year, I sent one a month and continue doing so.

Every time I get upset about not getting one in return, I remind myself that he's busy. He's in the middle of some conflict or a war zone somewhere—he doesn't have time to write.

Now that I have passed the bar exam, I have decided that, when I see him this time, I'm going to tell him how I feel. I'm going to tell him I want to be with him and will go wherever he wants me to go. I'm going to tell him I love him, and I always have.

In my daydreams, he smiles, hugs me, kisses me, and when he is finally inside of me, when we are physically connected, he tells me he loves me, too.

I should be nervous, but I'm not, not one bit. I know what our love is, and it is real. So real I can close my eyes and he is right there with me. And I know he can close his eyes and feel the same.

Two

Love is worth fighting for, even if it hurts.
— C. Stalker

"THERE'S MY BABY GIRL!" I hear Dad's voice boom through the airport as soon as I round the corner and walk toward the security glass wall.

I wave as he grins from ear to ear and waves back. Logan is next to him, rolling his eyes. He only stayed one day at Mom and Robert's penthouse apartment overlooking Central Park before he flew home.

I hurry toward my dad, and as soon as I am near enough, he snatches me up in his big old arms, hugs me, and yes, spins me in a circle. I love the way my father's hugs make me feel.

"My princess," he says before planting a kiss on my cheek and setting me back on my feet.

"Daddy, you look amazing. Must be a Tessa thing," I wink, and he shakes his head. "Married life treating you good, huh?"

"Tessa is wonderful." He gives me a look that tells me not to push, takes my bag, throws his arm around my shoulder, and then we walk toward the exit.

"Where is she?" I ask. Normally, she would be with him.

"There is a houseful of people making Christmas

cookies. You two up for that, or do you want to go home?"

When my parents divorced, Dad kept the house we were raised in. He chose not to sell it even after he and Tessa got married and moved in together. He said we had great memories in that house, and he wanted us to be able to come home whenever we wanted.

It was our home. Every holiday, birthday, and memory we had all through school seemed to center around it.

"Are they at your house or Harpers?" Harper is my best friend and lives in the house she was raised in. Dad and Tessa live up the lane about a quarter of a mile.

"Harpers." He nods.

"Sounds good to me. How about you, Loggie?"

He nods. "Sure."

Dad throws my bag in the back of the SUV, and then we are off. We pull out of the airport and take a right. We pass the automotive factory then hang a left, following the path I have traveled a million times toward home.

Once we're on Route 34, it starts to snow. I look up at Dad, and he smiles at me in the rearview mirror.

"Had to beg for that to happen, kids. You're welcome."

I giggle from the back seat and lean up, tapping Logan on the shoulder. He looks back.

"Santa's coming soon, Loggie. What did you ask him for in your letter this year?"

Dad laughs while Logan rolls his eyes and says, "Aren't we a little bit too old for that shit, Ava?"

I gasp and cover my mouth. "Daddy!"

Dad nods. "We're believers, Logan. Do you need a reminder?"

"No," he says immediately.

"Ava, I think he does." Dad winks at me.

Logan threatens, "I swear to you, I will jump out of this—"

Dad and I start singing, "*Oh, you better watch out, you better not cry...*"

"Oh, for God's sake," Logan grumbles as we continue singing Christmas carols all the way home.

We pull down a dirt road lined with tall pine trees. Every third or fourth one is lit up with dancing, multi-colored Christmas lights.

"No white lights this year?" I ask Dad.

"Nope, Piper wanted colored ones, and whatever Piper wants, she gets," he chuckles.

Logan looks back at me and snickers. I know he thinks I may be bothered by this. I'm not.

I roll my eyes at him and look at Dad. "She's almost three now. It's crazy that my best friend has a three-year-old."

"It's crazy that Dad's a grandfather." Logan laughs.

"Kind of," I say, thinking I see a flash of hurt in Dad's eyes through the rearview mirror.

Dad and his wife Tessa were high school sweethearts. Apparently, they had a rough go and broke up. Tessa met Collin Abraham and married him shortly after. They had three children—twin boys and Harper, my best friend. Our families were always close.

Collin was shot and killed. Then my mother's secret affair was exposed. We found out shortly after that Dad had and always would love Tessa. True to a man with my father's character, he went after what he loved, and he did it knowing he would have her back.

What should have been an awkward situation—your father marrying your best friend's mother—was far from it. We all knew each other. Hell, we vacationed together, played sports together, did so many things together.

"Does she call you grandpa?" I ask, hoping to make him smile again.

He smirks. "Pop-pop."

"That's adorable," I say, and it is.

Driving past Dad and Tessa's house, I see a nativity set lit up in the yard.

"Baby Jesus needs a coat, Dad. This isn't Jerusalem." Logan snickers. "Oops, no he doesn't. He's God's son; he's probably warm."

"It was his father who put him on the cross," I remind him.

"How jacked up is that?" Logan laughs.

"Right?" Dad laughs, too.

We pull down the road and turn onto the paved driveway toward Harper and Maddox's house. It's lined with cars, most of which I recognize, all family and close friends. I don't see Luke's truck, but he will be there.

"Damn," Logan sighs.

"It's cookie time, Loggie," I joke.

"Remember, Santa loves snickerdoodles," Dad says, looking at me in the mirror.

I shake my head. "He likes cut-outs."

"Not anymore," Dad says as he parks the SUV. "He likes snickerdoodles."

When we walk through the front door, we are greeted by the noise that surrounds the Ross family— laughter, talking, some music in the background—and it hits me. These people have always been my family.

Logan shrugs off his coat and hangs it up on one of the twenty or so hooks lining the wall of the back entry then helps me with mine.

"I raised a man." Dad pats him on the back.

"And a princess." Logan nods at me.

"Ha, ha." I smile and nudge him with my elbow.

When we walk into the expansive kitchen, Jade, Luke's mother, is the first person to see us.

"Ava!" She is the first of many to hug me, and I hug her back.

"You've done something different," she says, looking me up and down.

I shake my head. "No, nothing."

"Hey, Ava," London, Harper's seventeen-year-old sister-in-law hugs me.

"Damn, girl," I gasp. "You look different. More grown up."

She grins. "I graduate this spring."

"Braces are off," I comment.

"Thank God." She groans.

After hugging Tessa, Harper, and Maddox, I try to hug their daughter Piper, who apparently is going through a Mommy stage and wouldn't let me. Then I hug Maddox's parents, Tessa's parents, and then Tessa's brothers and sisters.

Tessa wraps an apron around me. "You ready to get down to cookie business?"

"Sure am," I tell her, pulling my hair free from the apron strap and tying it up in a bun on top of my head.

Everyone is chatting, laughing, and drinking homemade wine. Christmas music plays in the background as we roll dough, cutting cookies into Christmas tree, snowman, Santa Claus, and star shapes.

"Harper, where is everyone?" I ask quietly.

"You missed most of them. Liam, Remington, Jackson, and …" She pauses.

I smile. "And …?"

"Luke. They all had dates."

I smile back as I feel my spirit being crushed and my heart breaking. "Well, good for them."

"Good for who?" Jade asks as she reaches for the wooden rolling pin.

"The boys and their dates," I answer.

Jade looks at me and shrugs. "I suppose it's time they all started thinking about their futures. Hopefully, Luke will find someone who keeps his butt here. He says he's reenlisting again."

His sister Riley groans. "I don't get it. Hasn't he sacrificed enough?"

"Some people are born to be soldiers," Jade says sadly. "I just wish he'd stop volunteering to go to war."

"I just wish he'd stay away from that skank. God, how long has it been? How many times has she been married?" Luke's youngest sister Lauren chimes in.

Every one of them looks alike: black hair and blue eyes. But Luke is taller, bigger, and less talkative.

"Twice," Jade and Riley say at the same time then laugh.

I hold it together for an hour before I tell them all I'm exhausted. Dad immediately feels my forehead like I'm five years old, and Tessa smiles when she sees him doing it.

For some reason, I take comfort in their exchange. Their love is timeless.

§

I LIE IN MY CHILDHOOD bedroom with my head at the foot of the bed so I can look out the window and see when Luke returns. If he returns. God, my stomach hurts. I feel physically sick knowing he's out with that bitch Alexis.

I try to remind myself that he loves me. I know he does. Then I wonder if someone told him about me and T, the drummer for Harper's husband Maddox's band. We never slept together, just kissed, talked, laughed, and spooned.

I decide that he's probably trying to prove a point to me. I decided he is trying to make me jealous. I decide I understand. And I decide, when I tell him I love him and he tells me he loves me back, I will forgive him because, after those three little words are exchanged, nothing will ever keep us apart.

I look at my phone. It's midnight, and he's still not back, but neither are his brothers.

I get out of bed and crack the window so I can hear when he pulls in. Then I lie back down and close my eyes, knowing this sick feeling in my stomach will be gone as soon as I see him look at me the way he does. The way he stiffens when I smile at him, like he is forcing himself to hold back all the lust and desire he has for me, knowing once we touch, he can't control his need to kiss me, make love to me. The way his eyes dance between my lips, my eyes, and back to my lips. The way he says, "You still in this, Ava?" and my heart beats faster and harder. Knowing what comes next makes my core turn from fire to lava. The words come out raw, needy. They sound like gravel, and I internally cringe until I hear, "Let's fuck."

The way he grabs the back of my neck and pulls me toward him. The way his hungry mouth takes my lips so fiercely they feel bruised for days. The way his other hand cups me, and I can't hold back the cry that leaves my throat.

"Hurry," I say as he pulls my shirt up while kicking off his shoes and I unfasten his belt.

"Hurry," I plead as he one-handedly unhooks my bra and yanks it from my body.

"Hurry," I whimper as he pulls off my pants and thong, both in one swift move.

"Hurry," I say as my hands pull his shirt over his

head and throw it to the ground.

"Hurry," I say as he pushes his pants down far enough to roll on the condom as I run my hands up his biceps, his shoulders, and link them together behind his neck.

"God, I've missed you," I say as he lifts me up, and I wrap my legs around his hips.

He thrusts inside me fully, holding nothing back.

"Yes," he hisses as he pushes me up against the wall and takes me hard and fast with urgency and need.

"Been too long," he grunts as he moves his body, taking what he needs from me, giving me what I need from him.

"Can't hold back," he grunts as his pace hastens.

"Don't you dare," I whimper.

He stills. It's over too quickly, but I know round two is minutes away.

§

I WAKE BECAUSE I AM freezing cold and look at my phone. It's three in the morning, and I still can't see his vehicle. I know it has to be there. I get up and try to get a closer look, but still, I can't see. The sound of his engine and the lights in his truck must have been muffled by my dreams.

I look down, hoping to see his footprints below my window, but I know the falling snow would have covered them.

I close the window and decide it's best if he thinks I ignored the pebbles or one loud whistle he's always used to get my attention. Then he will know I am not okay with him dating here in our hometown. I'm not okay with him being with her of all people.

I lie back down, still sick to my stomach, and try to fall asleep. I lie there for three hours before deciding to take a walk. It's cold, and hopefully, when I come back in, the heat will help me sleep.

I will see him today. It's Christmas Eve.

I throw on an Under Armor shirt and long underwear, layering them with sweatpants and a sweatshirt. Then I pull on wool socks and head downstairs.

I look out the window to see that dawn has broken.

I pull on my thin North Face ski jacket and shove my feet in my winter hiking boots then walk out the door.

I don't hate the cold, but you don't just go for a walk at six in the morning on December 24th in Central New York. It's bitter cold, the roads are crappy, and living in the country, there are no sidewalks, so you're on the curb. I know this since I've lived here all my life, but clearly, I wasn't thinking when I decided to get up and take a leisurely stroll by Luke's house to rid my anxiety that he isn't home, try to expunge the nervous energy, and freeze enough to put myself to sleep. It makes no sense, but here I am, a twenty-five-year-old woman making a ridiculous decision because why? Because I am in the most complicated relationship in the history of relationships. Is it worth it? Yes.

My steps quicken as I near his driveway, needing to see his truck. Then I need to keep walking so I don't look like a foolish little girl if he happens to see me walk by. As much as I would like to turn around and possibly jog home and jump back into bed, it can't and won't happen.

When I walk quickly past the house, I see his truck isn't home, and I feel emotions boil up in my throat as tears tease my eyes. I am hurt, sick to my stomach, and angry. My steps come more quickly as I make my way down to the end of the road.

When I'm almost at the stop sign exactly half a mile from my house where I planned to turn and head back,

I see a Chevy turn off at Tollgate Hill Road toward me. It's Luke.

As he nears me, I look at the ground to avoid the awkward nod, wave, or even more awkward, him possibly not waving at me, which would be heartbreaking. But maybe he just got up early.

He slows down as he passes, and I speed up my pace. Then I hear brakes, a transmission shifting gears, and the tires crunching as he backs up and is now literarily right beside me.

He rolls down his window. "Need a ride?"

I try to get a good look at him. I try to see if he's an early riser or if he is just now getting home from a late night.

I smile and shake my head. "I need the exercise."

His eyes go from my lips to my eyes and back again. "Get in the truck, Ava."

Three

Love is ugly and love can heal.
— M. Sanchez-Cortez

I LOOK UP, AND OUR eyes meet, blue to blue.

He runs his hand over his head and sighs, "It's too early to be taking a walk. Too shitty out, too."

The words register, but I'm so damn busy trying to stop myself from feeling like I want to kiss him one second and slap him the next. He's clearly been out all night. He looks exhausted.

"Ava, get in the damn truck."

He swings his door open, steps out, picks me up, all but throws me inside, and jumps in behind me when a snowplow whizzes past us.

"What the fuck are you doing?" he snaps.

I immediately look away from him. I feel stupid, so damn stupid.

"Ava?" The way he says my name is cold and has never sounded worse.

"I was walking," I snap back, scowling.

He throws his truck in drive and heads toward my house. "Bad fucking idea, kid."

When he passes his house and then mine, I look at him.

He senses it immediately and looks over at me. "My

family will be up soon. Passed your brother heading into Ithaca, so I'm gonna assume he's going to the gym, but can't be too sure. Safer to get a hotel."

"Didn't you get enough last night?" comes out snippy and immature.

He slows down and looks at me. "You and I have a problem I don't know about? If we do, say the word and I'll take you home." His eyes do that thing, going back and forth between mine.

It's been too damn long, and I have planned the next two weeks out to a T. I need to tell him I'm ready to move forward with what is going on between us.

I'm crushed that he may have been with her, but that's my fault, too. I have played this game with him and been just fine with it because, in being a player in this game for two, my end goal has always been to win his heart.

When I don't say anything, he says, "Good." He nods. "You all bundled up?"

I nod back, not wanting to say anything because I am nervous, more so than I ever have been in my life.

"I thought maybe you'd gained some weight. You think you could lose some of the layers before we get there, Ava?" he says with all the directness Luke brings whenever we are together.

I start with my jacket and very slowly remove my sweatshirt. The way he watches me makes my pulse quicken and my mouth get drier. It's as if every sense heightens, including my sense of need.

He hops out of his truck and heads inside the Super Eight in Dryden, the next town over. He is gone long enough for me to become more anxious and far less brave than I felt when he was in the truck. The thought brings clarity.

With him, I feel stronger.

When he comes out, he opens my door and steps back. I reach out my hand for him to take. He helps me out and then releases my hand so he can hit the key fob and lock the door. Then he turns and walks toward the door.

I follow him.

As soon as I walk through the door, he turns, wraps his arm around my waist, lifts me, and shuts the door.

My heart is pounding against his, his against mine. I look into his eyes, and my breath is lost. I have to look away.

"With me?" he asks as he gives my hips a squeeze.

I nod. Then I glance up into his eyes.

They show signs of age and sadness. That's new.

I can't help myself from reaching up and rubbing my thumbs along the sides of his eyes.

"You worry too much."

He pulls away from my touch slowly and loosens his grip, allowing my body to slide down his until my feet hit the floor.

"Let's fuck." The words come out just as raw and needy as they do every time we're together. The sound of his voice, like gravel, lightly scratches my insides like it always has.

He grabs the back of my neck and pulls me toward him. His hungry mouth takes mine fiercely, and I groan into his. With his other hand, he cups me, and I can't hold back the cry that leaves my throat.

He breaks our kiss and grabs the hem of my shirt, pulling it up.

"Hurry," I quietly beg.

We both kick off our shoes as he unhooks my bra, and I unfasten his belt.

"Hurry," I beg a bit more loudly as I allow my bra to fall from my arms and immediately unfasten his belt then push down his pants and boxers.

My body is seconds from falling apart, and he isn't even inside me.

I whimper as he pulls off both my sweatpants and thong in one swift movement.

"Hurry," I close my eyes and beg as he pulls his sweatshirt free.

Keeping my eyes closed, I hold his hips and try to slow down my pace as I run my hands up his strong body.

"Hurry," I say as I run my hands up his biceps, his shoulders, and link them together behind his neck.

God, I've missed you, I think as he lifts me up, and I wrap my legs around his hips.

He thrusts inside me fully, holding nothing back.

"Yes," he hisses as he pushes me up against the wall and takes me hard and fast with urgency and need.

"Damn you, Ava," he curses the pleasure he gets from me as he moves his body, taking what he needs from me, giving me what I need from him.

"Can't hold back," he grunts as his pace hastens.

"Don't you dare," I cry as I meet his thrusts.

I wrap my arms around his neck and hold on to him more tightly than ever before, feeling his body calling mine to release almost immediately.

I bite down on his shoulder, and my back hits the wall as he fucks me harder, faster, and without restraint or apology.

We come together, and to me, it's a sign that the universe has finally aligned. This is our time. His and mine, mine and his. And I know the minute I tell him I love him, everything will be as it should.

When my legs stop trembling, I unhook my ankles from behind him, and he pulls out of me.

"Need a couple minutes," he says, avoiding eye

contact as he walks to the bed.

His ass is magnificent: hard, tight, muscular.

I watch as he kicks off his pants and sits at the end of the bed then sighs before looking at me. "You need to clean up?"

"Oh." I nod. "Yeah, I should."

I walk quickly into the bathroom and take care of our...love?

Wow, that's a first. How does one broach that subject? Do I even need to? He wouldn't put me in harm's way any more than I would him. I'm sure it's fine.

After cleaning up, I grab a towel and walk out of the bathroom toward the bed.

He's lying on his back with one hand behind his head, the other over his eyes. His lower body is uncovered, giving a sinful view.

I slide in next to him, not touching him. He makes the first move, always.

"Give me ten," he states.

I lie back, look at the ceiling, and start counting to six hundred.

§

I WAKE TO THRASHING, UNDISTINGUISHABLE curses, and low pain packed with sorrow-filled noises that sound almost like a cry.

I sit up quickly, realizing where I am and the noises are coming from Luke.

I grab for his hand to try to wake him, but as soon as I touch him, I am flying backward off the bed.

"I'll kill you!"

I jump up and see him jump off the bed.

I run to the doorway yet remember I'm naked and my clothes are near him. Therefore, I run into the bathroom and shut the door, locking it behind me.

I am not afraid of Luke, but I have read enough on PTSD to know the man who threw me from the bed was not Luke, not my Luke. This Luke is fucking frightening.

"Ava! Open the fucking door," he says in an angry yet regretful tone.

"You okay?" I ask through the door.

"Ava," he sighs.

Now that's Luke. My Luke.

I open the door and smile. "Bad dream?"

The way he looks at me makes me wish I hadn't opened the door. I think it's disgust, disdain. Regardless, it's not happy. Not happy at all.

"Am *I* okay?" he half-laughs, half-snaps as he reaches up and touches the corner of my eye.

Ouch, I think.

He walks past me and turns on the faucet. "Ten minutes, Ava, ten. Not"—he pauses and looks at his watch—"two hours. Two hours, dammit!"

Before I have time to say anything, he holds a cold washcloth against the corner of my eye.

"Fuck!"

I hold my hand over his. "You had a bad dream. You didn't mean it. That's why they call it an accident."

"Don't. Don't make fucking excuses for me."

"Luke, you've been in war zones for—"

"Don't do that, either. Don't pretend to know what the fuck goes on over there."

I feel like I'm making everything worse, so much worse. But dammit, I know he didn't mean it. And I sure as hell know I will not let the man who has put his life at risk for this country, the man I love, think that he is alone. I am with him.

"I won't pretend to know, Luke, but you need to know I am so proud of you for all that you do."

"Don't, Ava. I know how you all feel about my decision to reenlist."

"*You all*?" I ask, shaking my head. "I see you, and I see me. And you've known me since birth, so you know there is no way in hell I can stop myself from saying what's on my mind, and on my mind is me being proud of you."

"Ava ..." He shakes his head.

I hold my finger up to his lips. "I'm not done."

His eyebrows shoot straight up.

"It was a damn accident."

He sighs.

"Two hours, though?" I give him the uh-oh look.

"Right, we need to go." He looks at me like he wants to say something yet doesn't.

When he turns, I grab his hand. "We're okay, right?"

He stiffens and turns back. "Meaning?"

"No protection," I whisper as if someone may hear me.

"I don't know, are we?" He acts annoyed.

"Clean on my end." I grin like a stupid kid and immediately regret it when he rolls his eyes slightly, almost causing me to lose my courage.

Almost.

"Luke, I need to tell you something else."

"We need to get dressed and go," he says, yanking my hand and pulling me behind him. "Does your brother stay at the gym for two hours?"

"Depends on what kind of ass is there." I laugh.

He looks back at me. Again, it's like he has something to say yet doesn't.

So I do.

"Speaking of ass, yours is rock hard, Luke. I really love your ass." I use the word love to test the waters.

He nods and drops my hand as he grabs his clothes.

"I think you should have my name tattooed on it."

He whips his head around and huffs, "Yeah, right."

Ouch.

I'm not a quitter, so I continue, "You have the flag over your heart, so that part's taken. So, I figured—"

"Damn right it is," he agrees. "My one true love is my country."

Double ouch, but Daddy didn't raise a quitter.

I position myself in front of him, use both hands to grab his face, and look him right in the eyes. "The flag is a beautiful thing, but that chest, that heart, I think they're big enough that you could probably love someone else, too."

"Don't have time for round two, Ava." He gently grabs my wrists, but I hold tight.

"I'm done with school. I'm a grown woman, and you are definitely a grown man, Luke Lane. We've been playing this game for seven years in hiding, and I would rather play it out in the open—"

"Ava." His tone is one that begs caution.

"I love you, Luke. Always have, always will," I say with a smile. "I know you feel—"

"That's fucking it up!" He pulls my hands free of his face and steps back. "You all think you know me, but you don't. You don't know the real me. Not one of you."

"I know everything I need to know in order to stand here, bare, looking at you just the same, and saying it a second time. I. Love. You."

"No, Ava!" My name isn't said with need wrapped in sinful intent like he normally says it. My name is cold and sounds loathed.

At this moment, I hate the name my parents gave me.

"You don't know me. None of you do. The whole

bunch of you think this little pissant town means everything when, in reality, it isn't shit. Nice place to visit, but there's no fucking way I'd make a home here."

And then the final blow…

"The world doesn't begin here, nor does it end here. And I hate like hell to say it, but the same goes for being between your legs."

Silence. Deadly, ugly, excruciating silence.

§

WHEN HE PULLS INTO MY driveway, he finally looks at me, "I thought things would be cool with you and me. I thought you were grown enough to separate physical and emotional feelings, Ava. Guess I was wrong." He sticks his hand out to fucking shake mine, "Life lesson, kid."

I don't shake his hand. Mine are shaking so badly I couldn't if I tried.

When I can't get my seatbelt unfastened because of the shaking, I could swear I see hurt in his eyes. When he tries to help me, I manage to bat his hand away without crying. Again, I think I see some sort of emotion, but I know that's a lie.

In fact, everything I thought I felt, everything I told myself about mine and Luke Lane's … fated love, everything I believed with all my heart, all my soul—it was all a big fat lie.

How stupid am I? How pathetic am I? How childish am I?

When I finally get my seat belt unfastened and jump out of his truck, I turn and open my mouth because I am Ava fucking Links, and I may be stupid, naive … both, but there is one thing for certain: I damn well don't let people get the best of me.

What comes out? Not what I expected.

His name breaks my voice. The embarrassment of that breaks the dam holding back the flood of emotions I have been fighting to keep bottled up. Then, by some miracle, my legs regain feeling, and I turn and bolt like a child runs from a snake or an angry dog in fear.

As soon as I am inside the safety of my childhood home, a sound escapes me that is so full of emotion and pain that I can't believe it comes from me. I run up the stairs to my bedroom and dive onto my bed. However, I can still feel him, smell him, and I want it all gone.

I jump up and run to the bathroom then start the water. I strip bare and get in the tiled double shower. Then I stand under the scalding hot water and cry. I cry like I never have before.

I cry for my broken heart; I cry for seven years of dreams now shattered; and I cry because the man I love is so messed up he can't even see what I know is there. Then I cry because, down deep in my soul—past the hurt, past the pain, past the embarrassment, and past the shattered dreams I harbored for years—is a rock solid foundation, and it is built of hope.

As I scrub between my legs almost to the point of pain, I curse hope. I curse it inside my head, and I curse it out loud. I curse it because it curses me.

After my shower, I lie in my bed, playing over the last hour of my life. The literal nightmare and the figurative one. One is devastating to watch, the other devastating to live.

Exhausted, I close my eyes and pray that, when I wake up, this will all have been a nightmare.

Four

Love shouldn't hurt. It should give you life.
— LJ Sexton

I FEEL A HAND ON my forehead, and I have to force my eyes open. They burn so badly.

"Baby girl, it's Christmas Eve. You're still in bed, and it's almost noon. You feeling okay?" Dad sits on the bed beside me.

"Just tired, I guess." My throat is raw, and it sounds scratchy.

"Ava, you sound like…" He pauses. "Well, not like you." He narrows his eyes at me. "Do you have a black eye?"

"I hit the corner of my eye on the bed when I got up earlier," I lie. "And I feel…not like me."

"Gotta be more careful." He leans over and kisses the corner of my eye. "Okay, then sleep. I'll get you some soup and send an email to Santa asking him to make sure he gets you something extra special."

I nod and close my eyes. "Thanks, Daddy."

§

WHEN I WAKE AN HOUR later, he is sitting in the chair next to my bed with a thermos. "Got soup."

I force a smile, and then I force myself to sit up.

He hands me the thermos. "Tessa said the broth should help. She also hopes you can make it tonight. Everyone will be there."

Everyone.

"Maybe I should stay home. I mean, then I should feel better tomorrow."

Dad nods. "I'll stay here with you. Logan, you, and I can—"

"No. Absolutely not. I'm not ruining your Christmas Eve."

"Wouldn't be ruining it, Ava."

Tessa's husband was shot and killed on Christmas Eve; there is no way in hell I'm going to let him stay here with me on an "anniversary" of such magnitude. It would kill him to be away from her, and I know it. I also respect it very much. He loves her and wants to be there for her, but he also wants to be here for me. Little does he know my illness is actually heart sickness.

I get up and open the thermos, drinking some of the broth as he watches me.

"Give me half an hour," I tell him.

§

I STAND IN THE BATHROOM, looking at myself in the mirror. I look like hell—absolute hell—and I am going to see him tonight. I'm going to have to be in the same damn house with the man who broke my heart and shattered my dreams.

When I walk down the stairs in my red dress lined with white fur that hits just above my knees, Dad shakes his head. "You look beautiful, Ava."

The love in his voice, in his words, and the way he looks at me are exactly what I need right now. Still, the pain from Luke's rejection is so raw tears immediately begin to fall.

"Ava?" He walks quickly toward me, and I lunge into his arms. "Oh, baby girl, maybe you shouldn't go."

"No, I'm fine. I ... I just missed you. I love you, Dad." I hug him more tightly. "So much."

"I know, Ava. I know, sweetheart."

I step back and wipe my tears. "I'm ready now."

He looks at me expressionlessly and nods once. "Okay."

Dad insists I ride with him due to my *sickness*, and I agree to keep up the charade.

The entire ride to his and Tessa's house is quiet, and he keeps looking at me out of the corner of his eyes like I'm some ticking time bomb.

Little does he know that the bomb has already gone off. Inside, I am dying, but on the outside, I am still trying to hold it together.

God, I pray I can hold it together.

As soon as we pull in, I spot Luke's white Chevy pick-up. A wave of nausea hits my stomach, and I press against it in hopes of easing the pain.

Dad stops and gets out quickly, walking around the front of the vehicle and opening the door before I am able to.

"You sure about this?" he asks.

I nod.

"Ava, if you feel that badly, we can go back to the house," he says, looking at me curiously.

"Just stay close, okay?"

After I say it, I wish I hadn't. It just slipped out.

"Baby girl, we'll all stay close."

I force a smile and give a nod as I take his hand, and he helps me out.

I reach back into the vehicle to grab my purse and realize I forgot it.

Shit.

"Everything okay?" Dad asks, giving my hand a squeeze.

"Just forgot my bag." I shrug, and he closes the door.

When we walk into the house, Tessa and Harper both greet me and feel my head.

I smile brightly and give a chuckle. "And to think, I'm feeling jet-lagged from an hour flight. I'm fine, really."

Dad eyes me suspiciously, and I notice Tessa watching him.

All eyes are on me again.

"Seriously, I'm fine."

"What happened to your eye?" Harper asks.

"She hit it on her bedpost," Dad explains.

They all seem fine with the answer.

Piper walks up to me and lifts her arms. "Fairy god-Ava."

Without thinking, I pick her up and hug her. "Much more social today, huh, beautiful girl? Have you gotten into the Ross family eggnog?"

She squeezes me tightly around the neck. "It's yummy."

I realize Dad, Harper, and Tessa are still eyeballing me. Then I realize they are probably worried that she could catch my fake illness.

"I swear it's jetlag and probably the sushi from lunch yesterday. I'm fine."

I can do this. I can, and I will.

I position Piper on my hip. "Take me to the eggnog."

She points her chubby, little finger in the direction of the entry hallway that spills into the garage full of people filled with the Christmas spirit. One of those people will be Luke.

The first people I spot are Harper's husband Maddox

and his father Brody. I glance at Harper and wag my eyebrows. She expects it.

For seven years, I have made no secret that I have a lustful school girl crush on the older of the two rock stars. The only reason Maddox has been safe is because he's been Harper's since the two set eyes on each other.

My heart aches for a moment because I have secretly felt the same way about Luke, like he was made for me. I still can't help thinking that maybe, just maybe, someday …

Harper is looking at me, expecting me to follow up with the menacing glance, so I give it to her.

"Brody Hines." I shake my head. "Does that man just get hotter and hotter?"

"Ew," I hear from behind me and turn to see London, Brody's stepdaughter, making a face as if she is going to get sick.

"Sorry, London." I smile and use my free arm to give her a hug. "Damn, look at you."

"What happened to your—"

"Hit it on her bedpost," Dad says, and London nods.

London has grown into a beautiful young woman. She looks like her mother Emma: tall, brown hair, blue eyes, and high cheekbones. She is classically beautiful.

"She got boobs," her little sister Lexi says as she walks toward me to give me a hug. "I wear a bra now, too." She smirks and shows me her bra strap before hugging me.

"Like you need one for your itty-bitties," London huffs.

"I do, too!" Lexington protests, pulling her shirt tightly against herself. "See?"

"Okay, you two," their mother Emma says, shaking her head. "It's Christmas, so could you two possibly take a break from the arguing?"

"Is it present time yet?" Lexington asks Emma.

Brody comes up behind her and scoops her up, throwing her feet over his shoulder and then tickling her.

Her shirt falls down, and she cries out, "Daddy, my boobs!"

"You do not have boobs," he says. "You're a baby and going to remain a baby, you hear me?"

They walk away, her laughing and him telling her she's always going to be his baby. She then tells him babies don't have boobs.

I watch Emma and the way she looks at them. They did not have an easy beginning, but they made it. They made it, and they love each other.

"Food and drinks are in the garage. I'll go with you," Harper says, holding her arms out for Piper; except, Piper is not moving.

"Stay," she says, holding me more tightly around the neck.

"Wow, all right, then." Harper snorts.

We walk out into the garage, and the first person I see is my very best guy friend on the planet, Liam Ross, and a girl. She's tall, thin, blonde, and flat-chested. She's pretty and appears to be very country. When I say country, I mean she's wearing a pair of boot-cut jeans, a flannel shirt, and is totally Liam.

"Hey, Liam." I smile.

He nods then pauses, looking at my eye. "Ava …".

"Hit it on my bedpost," I say, considering wearing a sign around my neck with the explanation.

He nods again. "This is Marta, my girlfriend."

"Nice to meet you, Marta." I hold my hand out to shake hers.

"Cute dress." She smiles. It's forced, but hey, at

least she's trying.

"Thanks. I'm pretty sure it's a dead giveaway that I'm one of Santa's elves, and that's why Piper is hanging out with me," I joke.

I ignore the banter and chatter coming from the left. Every party involves a card game or two. But when I hear a loud baritone laugh coming from that direction, my heart sinks.

"You okay?" Liam asks.

"Yeah, of course. I'm fine. Are you okay?" I giggle, and he nods. "Are you okay, Piper?"

She smiles and nods as she continues to play with the white fur balls hanging from the strings on the dress's neckline.

"Eggnog," I say to Piper.

She points to the right where there is enough food to feed an army.

Piper is clinging to me, but I swear I am doing the same. I realize that she has become my little security blanket. How odd is it that something so small can make me not only want to be strong, but forces me to be?

I sit down at a table with Piper on my lap. Harper sits next to me.

"So"—Harper smiles—"how are things at Woods and Associates?"

"I'm happy to have a job, but not happy that, after seven years, I am not arguing a case in front of a judge and jury. I know I have to prove myself and that it'll take time, but I get a little tired of reading over old rulings."

"You still glad you went into criminal law?"

"I am." I smile. "And you? Tell me what keeps you busy all day besides this little one and her daddy?"

"Maddox and I have been trying to narrow down

where we want to start our charity. We have decided that it will definitely be helping victims of sex trafficking to rebuild their lives. We also have decided that he and I shouldn't be hands-on. We'll do fundraising and awareness for a few years to get things off the ground. But as this little one gets older"—she tickles Piper—"we really don't want her to know everything about his past and the hell he lived or what we went through a couple years ago. We want to let her grow up without a care in the world. Plus, it hasn't been easy trying to find people we trust who aren't family to run an organization and take care of things the way we want them to be taken care of. But we're hopeful."

"And his music?"

"That's where our fundraising efforts are going to be focused. He says he doesn't like the stage, but he's so talented, and obviously, it is a part of who he is." She looks behind her where Maddox stands, his eyes trained on her, and smiles. He doesn't smile, but he lights up for her in a much different way.

She turns and looks back at me. "When are you coming home?"

I laugh and shake my head. "Have you been talking to my dad?"

"No, I miss you," she replies.

"I'm very adamant that I am going to make it on my own. After that, I hope to someday very soon come back here and maybe settle down."

"Are you seeing anyone?"

"I've dated ... a lot."

"Anyone you think maybe ...?"

"No. Can you believe that in a city with eight and a half million people, there has not been one I look at and think, that's the kind of man I want?"

She laughs. "Do you know what kind of man you

want?"

"I think I do."

"Do tell."

"Someone strong and smart. Someone who, when I look at them and they look at me, we know we are meant to be one another's forever. Someone who has lived and knows who they are. Someone who can look at me and know who I am and doesn't want to change me. Someone who feels like they should be family immediately. Someone I can trust to have me emotionally as well as take me to the moon physically."

"And someone your father approves of," Dad says, sitting next to me.

"Pop-pop," Piper says, smiling at him.

"Pip-pip," he chimes back, leaning in and giving her a kiss on the tip of her nose.

"Presents?" she asks him.

He sighs and looks at Harper. "What do you say? I think she's been patient enough, don't you?"

"I think you just want to open gifts, Lucas." She chuckles.

He laughs. "Hell yes, I do."

When they announce that it's gift time, we all walk into the house. It is a rule in this family that no gift cards can be exchanged. The adults—adults being college age and above—draw names on Thanksgiving. I happened to draw Harper's name. She's getting the same shoes I am currently wearing.

After gifts and a few glasses of wine, I feel a little better. Luke has avoided me, and honestly, it doesn't seem weird. Hell, it's normal.

What's not normal is that, after a get-together like this, I used to know he would end up in my bed. When he was home, it was a Christmas tradition.

After everything is cleaned up, everyone heads

back to the garage, and I head to the bathroom. When I come out, Luke is waiting outside.

I look up, and he looks down.

"Excuse me," I say when he stands, unmoving.

"Yeah, sure," he huffs yet doesn't move.

"Is there a problem?"

He looks at me and finally shakes his head then steps aside.

I'm glad he gave me space to get by, but it takes me a moment to move. I desperately want him to say he was sorry, that he woke up ill-tempered or confused. I want him to say something, anything, but he doesn't.

The party is dying down when I go to look for Logan, who has made himself scarce this evening, spending much of the time on the phone, to see if I can get a ride. I want Dad to stay here with his wife.

"Have you seen Logan anywhere?" I ask London as she and the rest of her family are about to walk out the door.

"Wherever he is, he has his phone glued to his ear, and he's avoiding—"

"London," Emma whispers.

"It's true," London gasps.

I can't help smirking. London and Logan are either gonna end up at war when she gets older or married. I have never told either of them that I think that, and I am not planning on it. If it isn't obvious, I don't feel confident about my insight on love right now.

Five

It's better to walk away knowing you tried your best, rather than staying and being bitter from loves failures.
— Phoenix Soy

I OPEN MY EYES AND look at the hot pink alarm clock that I have had since I was sixteen when pink became *cool* again. It's six in the morning, which means I have slept for three hours. I'm exhausted emotionally and, because of that, physically.

I sit up and look around my room. It's much different than my 6th Avenue brownstone apartment in Midtown, Manhattan. My apartment is full of windows and hardwood and marble flooring. Its furnishings are white leather, all very contemporary and sophisticated. It's a place I planned to build my resume and wait for Luke.

My bedroom, on the other hand, is very girly. It's pinks, blues, and everything is soft and warm. My view is trees and the neighbor's house, Luke's house. It's full of hope and childhood dreams.

I fist my hair in my hands and groan, "Daddy didn't raise a quitter."

I throw my legs over the side of the bed and stand up tall—well, as tall as I can. I'm five-two, five-three on a good day.

It's Christmas. Christmas means hope, and dammit, I'm hopeful.

Today, we will spend the day with Tessa, Dad, Piper, Harper, and the rest of the Hines family. Piper, Lexington, and London will obviously be the center of attention, as they should be since they're the youngest. I plan to be myself. Myself without a broken heart.

I walk down the stairs in my bathrobe to find Dad is standing in front of the fireplace, facing away from me. Per the norm, he is in Christmas pajamas, which we will all spend the day in.

The change in my father since he and my mother divorced is obvious. I would have never known he wasn't truly happy in his life. He always seemed it, and maybe he was. Now, though, I see that, with Mom, it seemed like he was never relaxed. He seemed to go nonstop, do more, work harder. I'm sure the man never slept. Now, with Tessa, he seems content, relaxed, and the smile on his face is different. Real.

I don't know if he would have left Mom after Tessa's husband died. I don't think he would have had it not been for discovering Mom was unfaithful to him.

My mother, she's a different story. She lied, cheated, and with the help of my grandfather, whom I have yet to speak to, she stole my father's company away from him. She is my mother, and I love her—hell, even abused kids love their parents, and I am far from abused. Trust her like I do my father, however? Not in the least.

At the same time, I have never walked in her shoes, and if it's true what she says—that Dad always loved Tessa—I'm not sure how I would have managed twenty years of knowing my truth about love was that I was the second choice.

He turns around and smiles. "Merry Christmas, baby

girl. Santa brought your stockings here. I think he took your gifts to Tessa and my place, though."

I can't help grinning. I swear he gets more joy out of the holidays than Logan and I do. Then again, from what I hear, his childhood holidays weren't filled with joy like ours were.

"Merry Christmas, Daddy. That was smart thinking on Santa's part."

He hugs me and kisses the top of my head. "Let's go wake up your brother. You know how much he loves Santa."

§

WHEN WE GET TO DAD and Tessa's house, everyone I expected to be there is. There is also one person I didn't expect.

"Goddess Ava has arrived." T—or Thomas, the British, drummer for Maddox Hines' band, the Burning Souls—is standing in the living room, his arms spread wide for a hug.

"For fuck's sake," my dad grumbles almost inaudibly.

"Lucas." Tessa gives a smile with a dash of warning and mischief. "Can you go and grab a chair from the garage? Thomas is joining us today."

He gives her a glare, and she smiles bigger.

He tosses back a fake smile. "Of course, dear."

I walk toward T's outstretched arms, and Piper runs up and hugs me. I squat down and give her a big hug.

"Merry Christmas, Piper."

"You're not sad anymore," she whispers as she takes a step back and grabs the side of my face.

"I wasn't sad." I giggle. "I was tired."

She eyes me skeptically, which catches me off guard.

"It's gonna be okay. It's Christmas."

"Sure is." T grabs her up and hugs her.

For a moment, I expect her to be resistant, but she's not, not one bit.

"Daddy's best friend." She pats his cheek then slides down, "It's binner time."

"Brunch." Harper laughs. "Breakfast and lunch."

"Right," she says, taking my hand and T's as she walks us to the table.

We sit around the table that is already set. Even the food is out and ready.

Piper has placed me one chair away from T, and she's between us.

I see Maddox look at her, and she grins at him.

"You need your booster seat, Piper," her father tells her.

"Nope," she says, settling on her knees in the chair.

T laughs, and Piper giggles. It's adorable the way she looks at him and equally adorable the way he looks at her. He seems to have this undeniable bond with her. I assume it's no different than the one I share with Piper, her mom being my best friend and all.

T leans back, reaches over, and gives my shoulder a squeeze. "You look beautiful, as always."

I pat his hand and smile.

T and I have a history. It started before Harper and Maddox got married. At an age one shouldn't lie to their parents, Harper and I lied and went to a concert so she could see Maddox when they weren't together. As a matter of fact, Maddox was trying his damnedest to get over her via backstage blow jobs.

After the concert, we stood in line with all the other groupies, waiting for our chance to meet the band.

The guys were both fucked up. At first, Maddox didn't recognize Harper, and T was all like, "Guitar"—pointing to Maddox—"or drums?" pointing to himself. When Maddox finally saw her, he carried her kicking and screaming into the bathroom, and T seriously shot line after line, thinking I was going to buy into his crap. I told him he had a better chance of seeing God than doing anything more with me than rubbing my feet ... so he did.

After we left, my father found us and was chewing me out for lying when the limo pulled beside us, and a shirtless, messed up T hung out of the moon roof and asked me to marry him. Then, when my father was reprimanding me, T threatened the "old pervert," whom he didn't know was my father, and ever since then, my father has not liked T one bit.

We have been known to "make out" on occasion, those occasions being when I was drunk and upset with myself about Luke's and my arrangement, but never more than kissing. If it ever started feeling like more was going to go down, I simply said, "I can't," and T never pushed.

It has been a couple of years since I have put myself in the position to be tempted by his blatant sexuality, hotness, his fame, and the way he treated me. He wants me, which is far different than how Luke ever made me feel. That's also why I knew he was not going to get in my panties. It would be too easy to feel adored and comfortable by him. Love doesn't work like that. It would also be ROCK ...hard. I couldn't imagine bitches—in plural—wanting to sleep with the man I was banging.

I smile to myself, and he squeezes my shoulder again.

"Offer still stands."

"What?" I half-laugh.

"Marriage."

"You're insane." I grin.

"I'll drink to that," I hear my dad say as he lifts his

glass. "Damn, baby." He reaches down and rubs his leg.

Tessa more than likely kicked him.

CJ, Matthew, Logan, and Harper all laugh. T throws his head back and howls with laughter. Piper mimics him, and soon, the entire table is laughing.

Maddox is watching T intently.

When T looks at him, he winks, and Maddox seems at ease.

The day is spent as Christmas should be: laughing, loving, maybe drinking the spiked eggnog, and playing with toys that should not be so fun to play with at my age.

CJ, Matthew, and even Logan try to "out fun" each other for Piper's amusement. She, however, chooses me and even T over the others. Even Dad's nose gets bent, which makes Tessa, who is also drinking, and I laugh.

"Have I told you how much I love you?" she asks me at one point.

"Baby, maybe you should step away from the spiked stuff," Dad whispers.

"Oh, hush up, Links. I'm bonding with my stepdaughter," she scoffs.

This makes T laugh, which makes Dad glare at him, which makes Tessa laugh even harder.

When I go to the bathroom, I hear Logan hissing at someone.

"You're kidding me, right?"

"Oh, are you talking to me?" It's London, and she is full of sass.

"Do you see any other minor in here drunk? Of course I'm talking to you," he snaps at her.

"Well, I wasn't sure if you maybe had that phone implanted in your ear so you could be even less social than you were yesterday, Logan Links," she says with a bit of a slur.

"Listen, London, you are far too young to be getting drunk," he says, trying to sound all adult-like.

"You listen, *Logan*, you were far too young at that football game we all went to, as well, so ..." She stops.

"So, what?"

"Sew buttons on assholes," she says then starts laughing.

I cover my mouth because I am sure I'm going to laugh out loud and get busted for spying on them.

"Oh, yeah, that's mature," he huffs.

"Oh, how about you go pull your phone out of your butt and call one of those *mature* women with the fake boobs, because that's real mature—getting fake boobs." She laughs at herself again.

"You get fake nails," he retorts, sounding completely at a loss for words.

"Loggie," she taunts. "They're real. Just like my—"

"Enough," he snaps. "I'm telling your father."

To this, she burst out laughing, and then she is silenced.

"You're gonna get caught," Logan says.

I peek around the corner to see he has his hand over her mouth, and she is wide-eyed and blushing.

Run, London, run, I think to myself, even though Logan is my brother.

"Who are we spying on?" His whisper hits the back of my neck, and I jump.

T holds his finger over his lips. "Shh, you'll get caught."

I step back, and he does, too.

"London and Logan are arguing, and it's hysterical," I whisper.

"Ava ..." He shakes his head. "Even more beautiful

than last I saw you."

"And T, you're even more charming. I bet that gains you points with your"—I pause—"groupies."

He smiles, and through his light brown scruff, I see a dimple. "Groupies?"

"*Guitar or drums*?"

He shrugs. "It's life."

"How many STIs have you had?" I ask then cover my mouth.

He laughs, and I cover his mouth so London and Logan don't hear us.

He holds his hand over mine, pressing a kiss into my palm before he lets go. "Last tested, just one."

"Just one?" I whisper. "How can you say *just one*? It's an STI, for crying in the night time."

He smirks. "It's incurable. It's one I will never be rid of. I'm pretty certain you gave it to me."

"I ... what?" I gasp.

"I'm confident you were the carrier. You may want to get yourself checked out." He smiles.

"We never slept together," I whisper.

He takes a step back. "They say it's carried through saliva, or"—he scratches his head in thought—"something like that."

I scowl at him. "What are you talking about? I've been checked. I've never had an STI."

"Well, they also said it's only detectable in the male. The female is just the host."

I'm shocked, embarrassed, a bit disgusted, and confused.

I look up at him, and he reaches for my hand that is covering my pounding heart.

"Don't worry yourself over it, Ava. It will never affect you. It never affects the host as much as it does the victim."

"The victim?" I say more loudly than intended.

He looks past me and laughs.

I shove his shoulder. "It's not funny."

"Hello, London, Logan." He smirks. "Were you two playing ten minutes in heaven?"

"Oh, please," London scoffs as she walks past us, "He wouldn't know what to do with a female who didn't come out of a damn Mattel box with plastic enhancements."

"Okay, little lush," Logan snaps, "how about you step away from the punch bowl and check in with your parents?"

She turns around and sticks her tongue out at him.

"See?" He points at her. "She's a child."

"Yeah, well, you're a dick," she whispers "dick" and keeps walking.

"Did you hear that?" Logan asks, pointing at her. "Did you see that she's drunk?"

I suck my lips in and try not to laugh.

"That shit's not funny, Ava. She'll be in college soon. If she walks around, acting like that, she's gonna get … mistreated. I need to tell Emma." He starts to walk past us.

"Let it be." I laugh.

"She's not pissed," T says at the same time.

Logan and I both look at him oddly.

"Pissed"—he nods—"means drunk."

"Well, she's buzzed," Logan says.

"Better she cock up here with family than when she's at school," T says.

"What?" Logan and I both gasp.

He laughs. "Cock up means"—he scratches his head—"mess up, make a mistake."

"She's your best friend's sister." Logan looks at him like he's insane.

"Exactly. She'll be brilliant."

Logan looks at me. "I'm ready to go. You need a ride, or are you sticking around?"

"I'll go with you." I almost laugh. I look at T then back at Logan. "Give me a minute, and I'll be right out."

"Fine," Logan huffs and walks away.

"Okay, you're messing with me, right?"

"About …?" T asks, trying to suppress a grin.

"The STI?"

"Give me your phone." He holds his hand out.

I look at him like he's crazy.

"For but a moment."

I hand him my phone.

"You should charge this, Ava," he tells me as he types something into it. Then he hands it back. "I shouldn't have told you about the incurable disease you've given me today. It is Christmas, after all. Read this tomorrow. If you care to discuss it, text or call me." He turns and walks away.

"Everything okay?" Dad asks, eyeing me skeptically as he walks toward me.

"Yeah. I think Logan's tired. I am, too. We're gonna head home, Skype Mom, and probably go to bed early tonight."

"I can—"

"Dad, your wife needs you here, and we don't need you to tuck us in. Besides, do you really want to Skype your ex-wife?"

He shakes his head. "No, but—"

"We'll see you in the morning, right?"

"Yes." He nods. "Logan and I are going to hit the gym. Then, if you want to do some shopping or a movie, we can do whatever you want."

"Sounds good, Daddy."

You can't experience true love, if you haven't experienced true pain.
— M. Shelley

HALFWAY THROUGH OUR RIDE HOME, Logan refuses to talk about what happened with London. Perhaps it's because I laugh every time he says she's a kid. He's only a couple years older than her. Or maybe because I remind him of what he was doing when he was her age.

I Skype Mom on the way home. She seems happy, which is both annoying and comforting at the same time.

As we talk about … well, nothing, Robert pours her a glass of wine and leans in so we see his big old moon face on the screen.

"Merry Christmas, kids."

Logan holds up his middle finger so that it isn't seen by him or Mom, and I have to bite back a laugh.

Mom gives us a look, as if begging for us to return the bullshit sentiment. And we do like good little children. Less than a minute later, she says good-bye.

As soon as Logan pulls into the garage and shuts off the SUV, he receives a message.

"Is that London?" I laugh.

He glares at me. "It's Jade. They're playing cards and want us to come over," he says, opening his door.

For the past two years, we have been going over after leaving Dad's. It's a little secret tradition. Not a secret because it was wrong to play cards, but Logan and I didn't want Dad to be upset that he wasn't with us. He is where he is supposed to be.

"You getting out, or you gonna sit there all night and make jokes that aren't the least bit funny?"

I grab my phone and realize the battery is dead. Shit!

"Can we drive?"

He looks at me like I'm crazy.

"It's cold."

"I'll grab you a scarf," he says, shutting his door then muttering, "baby."

§

WE WALK INTO JADE AND Ryan's where all of them are sitting around the table, even Luke.

"Perfect! Let's play." Lauren, the youngest of their four kids, smiles.

"Drink?" Jade asks.

"Please." I nod and sit down next to her.

It's not awkward at all, I tell myself the entire two hours I sit across from Luke, pretending like he didn't just crush me yesterday.

Years of practice pays off, and no one except me seems to feel uneasy. No one else even notices because I am that good at making everyone around me smile.

Logan is practically falling asleep, and he hasn't drunk an ounce.

"Go home." Jade laughs at him.

"Good idea." He nods and stands up. "You ready?"

"No, she's staying with us." Riley grins.

"I'll be home soon," I promise him. "Can you make it on your own, Loggie?"

He yawns, looking at Jade. "If she's stumbling when she's done, keep her here, would ya?"

"What are you, the sobriety police now?" I snort, and everyone laughs.

"Good night, sister," he says with a bit of warning.

I know he doesn't want me to say anything about London, and of course, I wouldn't. Hell, I haven't said anything to him about it in all the years I have watched him flip-flop between mooning over her and lording it over her.

An hour after Logan leaves, everyone seems to be yawning. Riley, Jade, Lauren, and I clean up the dishes and take care of the empties while Ryan, Luke, and Jackson clean up the game table.

"You okay?" Jade asks, nearly catching me looking at Luke.

"Yeah, of course. Just tired and—"

"Drunk." Riley laughs.

I hold my hand up with my thumb and forefinger slightly apart. "Maybe just a little."

"Luke, can you walk Ava—"

"No!" I gasp, and they all look at me. I force a smile. "I am seriously fine."

"Come on, Ava," Luke says from the doorway.

My body heats instantaneously. Unwelcome desire and all of those feelings that are called forth when he says my name, regardless of the tone he uses, flood every cell in my body.

I swallow back the thickness in my throat and roll my eyes. "Fine, but it's unnecessary."

I walk to the table to grab my coat off the back of the chair, but Jackson has it in his hands already,

63

holding it up.

I put my arms through my sleeves. "Oh, so you're the ladies' man in the family?" Jackson is by far the quietest of the crew.

"Learning everything I know from my big brother."

I laugh rather loudly then quickly cover my mouth.

Their father Ryan laughs and shakes his head. "You better catch up, then, young buck. Your brother's been around the world, haven't you, son?"

"You ready?" Luke asks as he gives a quick nod to Ryan, seeming almost annoyed.

I throw my hand up and wave. "Good night, everyone."

"You're home for a couple weeks, right?" Jade calls from the kitchen.

"Yep," I say, pushing my feet into my boots, the ones Mom gave me, and then I walk out into the garage as Luke holds the door open. "See you later!"

Once outside, I sigh. "You don't have to—"

"Like hell I don't," he snaps.

I can't stop myself from turning back and looking at him. "Is it necessary to be nasty to me, Luke? After everything, is it really necessary?"

"I'm beginning to think so," he says in a very icy tone.

I turn and look at him. "What happened to—"

I trip and almost fall on my ass, but he catches my elbow and pulls me up.

"And there lies the fucking problem. All of you are oblivious to what the fuck is right under your damn noses."

"Luke, I know you've seen and been through some horrible things in the past few years, but—"

"*Few?*" He laughs callously. "My entire life, I have watched every damn one of you treat me like I'm a fucking ghost. Ryan?" He huffs. "Calls me son? I'm not his fucking son."

"Luke, that's not fair," I say sadly.

"No, fuck you, Ava. What's not fair is that I've had to act like I understand all the fucking shit about my father. I never met the guy, but everyone around here thinks I should get all sentimental when they talk about him. None of them want me to *know* him; they want me to *be* him. Your father"—the way he says it is in disgust—"gives me shit like money for college and offers me a job because that's what my *old man would want*. What about what the fuck I want? How about I be fucking Luke Lane and not some man they think I need to be?"

"Oh, Luke, that's not—"

"The fuck it isn't! Do you know what those people"—he points to his house—"put my grandparents through when I was born? Do you know that Tommy's parents—my grandparents—are the only people who want me to follow my own path? They encourage me to stay in the Army, while all of them and you and your family think I should get out and join the Lucas show. Do you know, Ava, that Tommy died while taking your father to Syracuse because he wanted to get Tessa back from Ben! Ben, the one who is married to Tessa's sister Kendall?"

I shake my head.

"It's all fucking sick. It's a big, incestuous mind-fuck. This whole town is a fucking joke."

"Luke, we all love you, and—"

"No, you all love the memory of Tommy Lane. None of you have a clue who Luke Lane is, and I don't give a fuck what your daddy thinks of me, Ava. Do you know how badly I want to tell him I fucked his little princess for years, knowing damn well I didn't love her and never could?"

My mouth drops open as the reality of what he is saying hits me.

"You and I fucked. It was good. The minute you said those words to me, you fucked up your chance of having a holiday piece of ass handy. Or was it your service to the country that made you fuck me? Or was it the fact that your daddy fucked mine, and you wanted the same—"

I turn and slap him across the face, and he grabs me by the wrist.

"He loves you!" I scream.

"He doesn't even know me. Neither do you, Ava. No more than all the other pussy around the world does!"

"You ... you ..." I stammer, unable to find the words I want to spew at him right now. The words to tell him I love him, but not this version of him.

"What? You what?" He lets go of my hand.

"You have been loved by so many. Truly, honestly, and deeply loved. You, *not* your father." I poke him in the chest. "You!"

"You don't love me," he scoffs, "any more than I love you. We fucked. It was good to get off."

I turn and walk quickly toward my house. Then I hear him coming behind me, so I stop and turn around.

"What do you want from me!"

"I want you to leave me the hell alone."

I shake my head, feeling the finality in his words and his tone.

"Yes. You leave me alone, and you stop looking at me like you need a dick between your legs. Lord knows you're getting it when I'm not here. Love one of them poor fuckers. Maybe then, Ava, you can stop living in their shadows and live your own damn life and not feel like you have to fuck me, because good old Tommy Lane wouldn't like to know his bastard kid is getting fucked by Lucas Links' kid, just like Lucas fucked him all the way up until his last breath."

"You've got yourself a deal, Luke. I will block out any feelings I have for you, but you better make damn sure my father and your family never find out how much we disgust you. From what I hear, your father wouldn't want that for them."

I feel sick to my stomach, like I'm going to get sick, as he turns to walk away.

"Luke!" I call out. "Just so you know, I was in love with the boy who picked me to be on his team so I didn't have to stop being me in order to fit in. That boy was you. I will always love that boy. I loved the man who put his country first. Until you are retired or decide to change careers, I will always say a prayer for your safety. But I am a woman of my word, and I am telling you right now that I am going to do everything in my power to calm the hurt, the pain, and the rejection I feel after how you have treated me. I am going to fill that hole you have created so that, when you pull your head out of whatever darkness it's settled in, there is no room for a do-over."

"Good. Now leave me the hell alone," he snaps.

"And, Luke!"

He turns to look at me.

"Be safe. Please be safe and get some help." That said, I walk into the garage and lean against the door as I lock it behind me. I reach into my pocket to document the time I promised I would never allow myself to fall in love again.

When I can't find my phone, I remember I left it on the charger in the vehicle.

I open the door and grab it, seeing the message T

sent. I read it.

GAD is the disease. Call me when you have some time. Good night, my goddess.

I hit call.

"Ava," he answers.

"What the hell is GAD?" I ask, and for some unknown reason, I burst into tears.

"Ava—"

"I've never heard of it. I don't understand."

"Ava," he tries again, but I can't stop rambling, and when I do try, I sob because I can't catch my breath.

"T," comes out.

"You at your father's home?" he asks. "Are you alone?"

"I'm not a whore. Are you sure—"

"Of course you aren't."

"Well, whores get diseases, not people like me!"

"Ava—"

"They get pregnant at sixteen, and—"

"Ava—"

"No, you listen to me—"

The phone goes dead. He hung up on me.

I hate him. I hate Luke. I hate everyone ... including myself.

I slide down the door and cover my face as I cry. I cry for love lost. I cry for hate. I cry for Tommy, for Jade, for my father, for Luke, and for me. I cry for T because I gave him an STI, and I cry because I know damn well I don't have one. Then, when I am done crying for all of us, I cry for Christmas that is no longer a day of hope.

I don't know how much time has passed, but I am startled when there is a light tap on the window behind me.

Embarrassed at the possibility that Luke heard me and hopeful that he has returned to say he was sorry for all the ugly things he said and for what he actually believes about all of us, I stand and turn around.

T.

I wipe off my face and unlock the door, opening it just enough to ask him, "What are you doing here?"

"Are you alone?" he asks.

I take a shaky breath and tell him, "Logan's asleep."

And then I cry some more.

I step back as he walks in and shuts the door behind him.

"Too much spirit?" he asks, pushing my tear-soaked hair from my face and lifting my chin up.

My lip quivers, and I can't form words.

"Oh, Ava, what have you done to yourself?" he says sadly and hugs me.

"Did I?" I ask then stop because I am still trying to catch my breath.

He steps back, not letting me go, but looks down at me. "It is definitely an incurable disease, Ava, but also a joke. GAD would stand for Goddess Ava Disease, and I am seriously afflicted, so much so that I drove far too fast in buggered up weather to get to you."

"It would be sweet if I weren't a mess."

He smiles and strokes his thumb across my cheek, wiping away a tear.

Lights flash inside the darkened garage, and I look out the window as Luke's truck passes by my house. He's going to see her.

I look up at T as more tears fall.

"Ava," he says sadly, "I wish I knew what to do to make it better."

"Stay." I wrap my arms around his neck and close my eyes.

When he doesn't respond, I open my eyes. He locks eyes with mine and nods once before leaning down and pressing his forehead against mine.

"You're certain?"

"Never more so."

"Lead the way," he says before pressing his lips to my head then taking my hand in his.

Seven

You can Love more than one person.
— Josie Charles

I WALK QUIETLY THROUGH THE house, his hand tightly in mine. As I walk up the stairs, it's with a purpose.

At my door, he stops, and I look back.

"This isn't a good idea," he says in a deep whisper.

"Please don't tell me no." I close my eyes and plead, "Please."

I hear him take a deep breath, and then he slowly lets it out.

I take a chance and walk into my room, meeting no resistance. I then hear the door shut and lock behind us.

I turn, and he lets go of my hand to rub his hand through his messy, dark blond hair.

I step into him and link my hands behind his neck, pulling him down for a kiss.

Deciding to speed up the need to erase Luke's last kiss, I push my tongue into his mouth. He pulls back and kisses my neck softly, gently,... and too slowly.

I take my hands from his neck, grab his jacket lapels, and push it off of him as he kicks off his boots. I take the bottom of his shirt and pull it up as I pull away from him.

"Ava," he says softly, yet his tone is not soft. "Slow it down."

"What?" I ask, still lifting his shirt.

He grabs my hands and pulls them to his lips. He kisses them, and through the moonlight cascading in my bedroom windows, I can tell he's made up his mind.

"Okay, then, why are you here?"

His eyes narrow, and he leans in closer. "My goddess needed me, and I was available."

I laugh uncomfortably.

He doesn't.

He doesn't even move. He just stares at me.

I look up out of the corner of my eye to avoid the intensity, or scrutiny, or whatever he's doing to me that is making me uncomfortable.

"Tell me, Ava, what do you want from me?"

"Sex," I answer without looking at him.

He chuckles, and I finally look back at him.

"Why is that funny?" I'm getting a little upset, and I know it's because I'm embarrassed by his obvious lack of interest.

What was I thinking?

He lifts my chin and kisses my nose. "We have danced this dance for years. We've made out, Ava, and anytime things get too hot, you back off, so forgive me if I don't find this a bit absurd."

"It's different now."

"For you maybe. For me ..."

"For you, what?"

"You are different," he says as if it should be obvious.

"I'm Harper's friend? I'm not a groupie? I'm not someone you want for more than a quick fuck?"

"Ava—"

"I can be a quick fuck, T. And believe you me, Harper never has to know. I just ... I just—"

"You just what?"

I shrug. "I just need this tonight."

The way he looks at me, like I'm some pathetic, needy chick, makes me incredibly ashamed.

"And tomorrow?" he asks.

"I'm not going to go all freaky on you. I won't call or text. I won't expect anything."

Again, he looks at me in a way one would look at a hungry, homeless puppy.

I sigh. "You shouldn't have come. Just leave me to my misery and forget about—"

He wraps his arms around me and grips my ass hard. Then he lifts me so I am eye level with him as he walks toward my bed. My breath is immediately lost as I grip his shoulders.

We are eye to eye, breath to breath.

"If this happens, you can rest assured I will call tomorrow. I won't hide what we will be from anyone. If this happens, Ava, whoever made you cry will be a distant memory, one that I want details of. If this happens, my goddess, you're going to feel like I am your biggest fan. If you give yourself to me, it's a gift I will cherish and one you better make damn sure you're ready to receive because, as insane as it sounds, I have wanted you from the very first time I laid eyes on you. To further show how fucking insane this is, I have stayed away, knowing you are nowhere near ready to take what I have to offer."

I open my mouth to respond, but no words come out.

"Ava, I'm not gonna fuck you. I'm gonna comfort you tonight, and tomorrow, when the dawn is new and your head is clear, you let me know how you want to proceed."

Before I have a chance to process anything more,

my back hits my bed, and he is next to me, holding me, kissing my head, my cheek, my neck, avoiding my lips.

"I don't understand," I whisper as his kisses travel down my throat. "You want me?"

He takes my hand and places it on his chest. Through the soft cotton material of his long sleeved tee-shirt, I feel his heart racing.

"Here," he says as he places a kiss behind my ear. "And here." He slowly slides my hand down his chest, his rock hard abs, and to his jeans where I feel his want. "So fucking badly here."

"I want you, too." I grip him over his jeans. Then, taking his hand, I bring it to rest between my legs.

"Ava," he moans.

"T—"

"Thomas. My name is Thomas."

"Thomas, I want you." I let my hand go back to his jean-covered erection.

"Ava," he moans again as he runs his palm slowly down, pressing against me.

"Please," I say as my breath hitches.

"Christ," he sighs.

He hovers over me, kissing me. His kisses aren't desperate or full of an undeniable need. They are soft, gentle, slow.

I grab his hips and pull him against me, thrusting my hips upward to meet his, rubbing myself against him, seeking release as he continues his slow, torturous kisses.

One of his hands is in my hair, the other moving slowly up my waist before he gently cups my breast. I arch my back into his touch as I continue to press my lower body against his swollen erection.

I grab the raised hem of my shirt and pull it over my

head. Then, as he kisses the top of my breast, I reach between us and unclasp my front closure bra so my breasts are bared to him.

His breath hitches as he raises his hand slowly up my side. When it's at my rib cage, I beg, "Hurry."

He inhales deeply, running his nose across my nipple. The contact is exquisite, and I cry out, thrusting my hips against him.

"Hurry," I repeat, grabbing the long, thick mess of hair on the top of his head and pushing his head down lower, wanting his lips around my aching nipples. "Oh, God, yes," I cry when he licks first my left then my right. "Please," I then beg, pressing into him harder.

He doesn't hurry. He takes his time. Damn him!

I shove my hands down my body, forcing my pajama pants and thong down. I use my foot to push my left and then my right pant leg free. Then I grab his belt and start to undo it.

He pulls back. "Stop."

"What?"

He levels me with a look. "I have all night. I am going to make sure we do this right. If that means I take pleasure in your body's pleasure without taking my own until the dawn breaks, then so be it. You, my beautiful Ava, will be sated and sober, telling me you want me and what I have offered you. Then I'll make love to you tomorrow." He stands up and gazes down at me. "Jesus, you are even more beautiful than I could have ever imagined."

Then why is he walking away? I ask myself.

He holds his phone up, using its flashlight to look around, and then the light is gone.

My bed buckles from his weight as he sits next to me.

"Give me your hands." His voice is thick with desire

and deep with need.

I hold them out, and he takes something silky and wraps my wrists.

"This is just as much for you as it is for me. You're going to miss out on all the things I have planned for you if you keep up this pace. I have already missed out on disrobing you; I won't miss out on what's next." He pushes my entwined hands back so they rest against the headboard. "They stay there, Ava."

"But—"

"You keep insisting I hurry. No fucking way is that gonna happen." He stands and unbuckles his belt, pulling it free from his jeans. Then he walks to the end of the bed and takes my ankle. He wraps the belt around it then loops it over the wooden spindle at the end of my bed. Next, he pulls the scarf I wore from earlier off his shoulder, takes my other ankle, and does the same.

"T, this—"

He interrupts me with a kiss that is much more urgent and needy.

He pulls back, taking my lower lip with him. "I have wanted you for years." His voice is hoarse and strained. "This is my time, Ava. Don't tell me how it will go. When you're naked in a bed, you're mine to do with as I wish. If you want it to stop, tell me now."

He stands, and I shake my head furiously back and forth.

"I am going to take damn good care of you. Better than you have ever had or will ever have." He takes in a breath, seemingly to calm himself down. "Is that okay with you?"

I nod.

"Perfect," he says as he stands over me, drawing his hand slowly down my body and stopping between my legs.

He winces as he slowly rubs between my legs.

"What? Is something wrong?"

He takes in a deep breath. "You're waxed."

"You prefer—"

"That it be done for me, not someone else."

"I do it for me," I say because I do.

He eyes me suspiciously. "Please don't play me for a fool."

I nod.

He climbs on the bed and hovers over me again. His hands are in my hair, and he is looking at me with a tangled mess of desire, need, adoration, and something else I can't quite put into words, but it makes me warm and removes any apprehension I had just moments ago.

He bows his head and kisses behind my ear again. "I'm starting here then making my way down. I want you to close your eyes and focus on how my mouth, my tongue"—he licks down my neck—"my hand"— he slowly moves his fingertips down my side, causing goose bumps to rise in their wake—"make you feel."

"Thomas," I cry out as he clamps down on my nipple and pulls at it.

"Shh," he says, his breath chilling my peaked flesh where it is wet from his mouth.

"Logan's here," I gasp out.

He looks up at me, and I see mischief in his eyes. It's both frightening and titillating.

"If he hears me …" He sucks harder, and I feel it between my legs. I try to close them, but I can't.

"You have to stop," I plead.

He pulls his mouth away and leans up, his lips against mine. "You'll have to try to be quiet." He kisses me, trailing those kisses down my body in a torturously slow pace.

His tongue dips into my belly button, and I am shocked by the pleasure I derive from it. I look down, my mouth opening as his eyes sparkle in the moonlight. I gasp again when he repeats the action over and over, my hips rocking into his body every time.

I am a soaked bundle of exposed nerves of need that are so heightened by the lack of contact that it is painful.

He watches me as I pant as opposed to crying out so my brother down the hallway doesn't hear me. T seems to be driven by the threat it holds to me.

Instead of moving lower, he moves up my body again.

When he finally kisses my lips, I grab his with my teeth and whisper, "I. Need. You."

His tongue caresses my lip, and I release his.

"Patience," he whispers, again kissing behind my ear.

"Please," I beg, squeezing my eyes closed. When I do this, he stops kissing me.

I open one of my eyes to see him smiling and shaking his head.

"What?"

"You're a very greedy girl, Ava. I see this as a challenge."

"Good. Feel free to cave into my charms and take your clothes off."

He sucks his lips in, and his chest heaves in a silent chuckle.

"It's not funny." I scowl.

"Oh, Ava, you have no idea what you are missing. How many men have made love to you?"

"I'm guessing your number is far greater than mine," I say in brutal honesty.

"How many men have made love to you, Ava?" he asks again.

I look away. "Two."

He gasps, and I look back at him.

"What?"

He looks at me in a softer, gentler way. "How many took the time to show you how beautiful you are? Did they fuck you, Ava, or make love to you?"

"T, please, just ..."

I stop when he pulls my arms up and around his head, still bound.

"Change of plans." He kisses me again.

His tongue strokes mine slowly as I grip his soft, thick hair in my hands, and he groans.

He pulls back and kisses my eyelids. "Ask me how many women I've made love to, Ava."

I shake my head.

"None. But that ends tonight." He kisses slowly down my body again. My arms are no longer around his neck, but I still have my hands in his hair.

He's at my belly button again when he looks up as he dips his tongue inside. My mouth opens, and a quiet gasp escapes. He lifts his head, still looking at me. His eyes close for a moment, and when they open, I see something different. Less control.

He runs his nose across my hip bone, inhaling deeply. His teeth lightly scrape from one hip to the other, and then ...

"Oh, God," I gasp as his tongue strokes down my inner thigh.

I hear a soft growl as he inhales more deeply this time. "You smell so fucking good, Ava. I'm gonna love this."

"Teeeee!" I cry as he pushes his tongue inside of me, and I grip his hair as I feel my legs tremble. "Oh, oh, oh."

He moves his mouth to my clit and sucks hard as I fall into a million drops of rain, landing softly on his tongue as he laps at the storm's aftermath, making an almost purring sound as he does.

He doesn't stop, and I am sure I am going to die. I'm going to die from the amount of pleasure his tongue and mouth are giving me. I'm going to die from the way he looks up at me as he licks my most sensitive and private parts. I am going to die from the need he exudes with that look. I am going to die if he doesn't stop, and I'm going to die if he does.

When I am unable to produce a sound, move an inch, or keep my eyes open, he kisses up my body. His lips hit mine, and I can taste myself. I can smell what I know without a doubt is me on his breath. And between my legs, I can feel his erection pressing against me.

His eyes are lighter, softer, sweeter. Even though he has yet to come, the look of relief is written in his eyes. Eyes that don't hide anything from me.

"T?"

"Ava?"

"I want you to feel how I do right now."

He pulls my hands free of the scarf, and then takes one of my hands between us, holding it against his heart. "I'm feeling really fucking good right now."

"T?"

"Ava?"

"Can you let my legs loose?"

"Shit." He laughs. "Of course." He sits back on his heels and unties my legs.

After my legs are free, he rubs from my ankle to upper thigh. Then he does the next.

When he is done, I sit up, my legs still trembling

around him, and take a deep breath as I unbutton his pants.

His hand covers mine, "Ava?"

"I can't make any promises to you. I'm kind of going through something. Everything in my head is kind of a mess, but for the past hour," I shake my head. "Things were good. So good."

He sighs and I look up, "I'm not drunk anymore, T, and I'm not a child, and I want you to feel like I do."

"How's that?"

I shrug and kind of laugh. "Wonderful."

He smiles then closes his eyes as I run my hands slowly up his thighs, watching his chest rise and fall more rapidly.

I reach the hem of his tee and lift it up slowly. He doesn't open his eyes, but he raises his arms.

When the shirt is off, I see the shadow of his bare chest in the moonlight. His body is more muscular than I thought it would be.

I drop his shirt on the bed and run my fingers up the back of his neck and into his hair, pulling him into a kiss. It's slow, unhurried, and deeper than before. Our tongues caress one another's in a dance that feels like...It could go on forever.

I rise to my knees, and he rises to his. I release his hair and unbutton his jeans before pushing them down.

He leans into me, forehead to forehead, eyes to eyes, bare chest to bare chest.

"You're kind of stunning, you know," I whisper as I look in his eyes.

"Thank you, Ava," he whispers back.

I put my hands on his narrow hips and suddenly realize they are shaking.

"You okay?" he whispers.

"Yes, of course. I don't know why—"

"You'll figure it out," he interrupts, saying it with a soft confidence.

I close my eyes and let my hand drift slowly down his body until I have him in my hands.

My eyes pop open when I try to wrap my hand around him, and I look down.

"That's fucking stunning, aye?" he says, and I look up into a smile that is playful and very confident ... for good reason.

"A, B, C—the whole damn alpha—"

He laughs as he kisses me and grabs my ass, hoisting me up against him. Then he leans forward slowly, laying me back down on the bed.

"Trust me?" he asks as he pulls my hand away and grips himself, dragging the head of his very impressive length up and down my seam.

I nod. "Do you have a condom?"

He reaches in the pocket of his jeans that are around his knees and pulls one out. "Hate these things."

"Sorry."

"Ava, don't apologize," he says with the package between his teeth as he rips it open.

"Could you hurry up?"

He smirks as he rolls it on. "Patience is not your strong suit."

"You know how we girls can be." I reach up and help him roll it down then pull him onto me.

"Can I trust you?" I ask as my breath hitches when he taps himself against my clit.

He nods, his eyes sincere. "I will never put you in harm's way, Ava. Never."

I nod as all of the nerves in my body come to life again.

Slowly, inch by glorious inch, he pushes into me. My body stretches, and our bodies tremble.

"You good?" he asks.

"God, yes," I whimper, grabbing his hips and pulling him toward me.

"Don't. Move," he hisses, his eyes fluttering shut.

When he begins to move, I push against him.

"Ava," he warns between his teeth. "You're so fucking tight that, if you don't stop, this isn't gonna last, and I have waited too damn long for this."

"How long?" I ask, needing him to tell me again because no one has ever made me feel so...so... wanted.

"Since." He thrusts in. "The first." He pulls out. "Time." In again.

"Oh, God," I cry.

"I saw you."

He moves steadily in and out at a pace he sets. I don't dare move, not wanting it to stop.

"So perfect," he hisses and bows his head, kissing me then pulling away with a low rumble from his chest.

He's looking at me, showing me how he feels. It's need. It's want. It's patience, acceptance. It's ...

"Damn it," I cry as I thrust toward him when I can no longer hold back, and I come, biting into his shoulder.

"Fuck," he says, rolling to his side and pulling me with him.

He slows the pace and kisses me through my seemingly never ending orgasm.

"T," I whimper after what seems like forever. I'm exhausted.

He pushes my hair back and cups my chin. "What, beautiful?"

"I don't want this to end, but—"

"Tired?"

"Exhausted," I admit.

He rolls to his back, pulling me on top of him. "The

show is yours, Ava."

He grips my hips and sets the pace.

I set my hands on his abs, and he shakes his head. "Behind you. On my thighs."

As soon as I do, he releases my hips and grabs my knees, spreading me wider.

"Ava, look at us." One hand returns to my hip, and his thumb pushes against my clit.

"Oh, God, I can't."

"It's right there." He presses it again. "Take it."

I rock faster, and he groans, "Fuck yes. Fuck. Yes."

"Yes? Yes?"

"Oh, hell yes," he says, and I feel him twitch inside me.

I move faster, grinding harder.

"Stop. Fuck, Ava, stop," he says as I feel him coming inside me. "Ava, damn it," he snaps. "Stop."

I immediately think of Luke and the way he snapped at me. It hurts, and I quickly move off him.

"Ava," he says, sitting up and reaching for me.

I grab my clothes off the floor and walk out the door and into the hallway to the bathroom. I look back to see he is coming toward me naked.

"What are you doing?" I say as he pushes past me and shuts the door behind him.

He pushes me against the wall and kisses me before pulling back. "I tried to stop you."

"What?"

"When this fucking thing broke." He pulls off the condom and tosses it into the toilet. "That was not on purpose."

"Is that why you said—"

"Stop? Yes, of course it was."

I kiss him to shut him up and because I want to kiss him, because... Well, he's not Luke. He's the anti-Luke.

He turns and grabs a washcloth, before running it under hot water and cleaning between my legs.

"Sorry about that."

"It's fine." I nod and smile.

"You didn't seem fine," he says, washing himself off.

"T, I thought you were mad at me."

"Mad at you?" He chuckles. "For making me come? That's absurd."

I smile as he seems to be searching my face.

"Ava Links, you are my goddess." He cups my chin. "Even more so now than before. Let me be the guy who makes you forget your heart was ever broken."

"Who says it was ever broken?" I force a smile.

"You don't ever have to pretend with me."

For some reason, I believe him.

Eight

Love isn't always easy. You have to work at it every day.
— Paige Steele

I LIE IN BED, LOOKING at the clock. I'm exhausted, but I can't sleep. I am giddy because T, hot, hung, and handsome rock star drummer, wants me. And apparently, he wants me for more than today, and I know we could have such fun together.

I also know that means Luke Lane was not the last person I was with and that Luke Lane more than likely saw T's vehicle in my driveway, so Luke Lane now knows I am a woman of my word ... which also makes me feel like a complete and total slut bucket.

As I look at the ceiling, I do it trying my absolute best to make me feel better about sleeping with two guys in two days. Clearly, though, I suck at it.

I roll over to my side, closing my eyes, and reach for Bingo, my blanket that I clearly need because I can smell it. But when I reach for it, it's gone.

I lie across the pillow to reach on the floor for it and realize it's the pillow that has that smell, the one that's home and love and all things Bingo is to me.

Too exhausted to get off my bed and look for the thing, I settle on hugging the Bingo scented pillow and quickly I allow myself to sleep.

Sometime later, there is a knock on the door, and then it opens. "Ava, you have a package."

I roll to my back and look at Logan. "What?"

"It's downstairs."

"Okay, thanks."

He doesn't leave. "Are you gonna open it?"

I close my eyes. "No, I'm going back to sleep."

"Can I?"

My eyes snap open. "Do you need to?"

"It's a big fucking box, Ava, so yeah, I wanna see what's in it."

I close my eyes. "Go ahead."

"Well, at least come down and see what it is."

"For someone who can't stand Christmas, why is a box so damn important?"

He walks over and stretches out his hand. "Come on, Ava. Someone sent you something. Let's hope it's from a man. I don't want you living here alone with ten cats."

I grab his hand and pull myself up. "Why? Do you have plans to fill this house up with little Lond—"

"Don't start with me." He scowls.

"Fine," I grumble as I stomp dramatically out of the room.

When we get to the bottom of the stairs, I see a box, a huge box, and I look at Logan.

"How the hell do you ignore that?"

I walk around it and see a small box that says *Box 1*, another that says *Box 2*, and a *3* is on the large box.

"I need a knife," I tell Logan.

He pulls a pocket knife out of his pocket as he walks over to me. "I got it. You'll cut yourself." He cuts the tape and hands the box to me.

I pry it open and pull out a note card and an iPad mini.

Follow the instructions to a T in order for this act to happen as planned.

Press record on the video recorder.

After cutting box two free, Logan hands it to me and then presses record.

I open the next box and pull out another note card and read it.

Press play on song number one.

I look at Logan who shakes his head.

"Press play," I say, unable to hide my smile.

James Bay's song "I Need the Sun to Break" plays.

"I know this song. *'I'm halfway gone. Sleepless, I'm battle warn. You're all I want, so bring me the dawn'*."

Logan laughs as I sing.

"Don't laugh at me, Logan. I at least get an E for effort."

"Come on, stop messing around." He seems more eager than I am to see what's inside.

"It says, 'Cut the tape free from the sides, let them fall, and open the top, pulling it toward you.' "

"Then do it already." Logan laughs as he holds the iPad.

I cross my eyes and stick my tongue out at him.

"I swear, sometimes I am the most mature person in this house." He rolls his eyes and cuts the sides open. When they fall open, it looks like a green plant.

I pull the top back and laugh out loud when balloons in the shapes of the sun and butterflies come floating out in bright, cheerful, vivid colors.

The box looks like an elementary school painting of two hills and the sun rising between them.

"What the hell is this all about?" Logan chuckles.

I grab the card on the bottom of the box and open it.

Today, I watched the dawn break with you. It didn't

only feel like a new day, my goddess, it felt like a whole new beginning, one full of smiling suns and beautiful nights to come.

My room key is enclosed. I am hopeful you will use it.

I'm here for four more days and three more nights. Then I am going back to my home in the city.

Logan looks in the box and points at the painted drumsticks then reads the cartoon-like blurb coming from them. "*She chose drums?*"

I laugh and cover my face. "Turn it off."

"What the hell is this all about?" Logan laughs. When I don't answer, his eyebrow rises. "Oh, fuck, Dad's gonna love this."

I reach for the iPad and hit the button so it's recording in selfie mode. I blow the camera a kiss then turn it off.

Logan bends down and grabs the key card that fell on the floor. "That's one hell of a booty call." He hands me the card, looking at me with his eyes narrowed. "You like him?"

"If I don't, I'm crazy. He's perfect for me."

"Who is perfect for you?" We both turn to see Dad walking into the kitchen.

Logan smirks at me. "Go ahead and tell him."

I shrug. "T, Daddy. T is perfect for me."

"Like hell, he is," Dad snarls.

"What is your problem with Thomas?" I ask with my hands on my hips.

"He tried to get you to..." He pauses and shakes his head. "That concert...he—"

"Dad, really? That was ages ago." I giggle.

"He takes great pride in forcing his tongue down your throat whenever given the opportunity." He scowls.

"Given the opportunity, Daddy? It's not like he's

forcing himself on me."

"All those women at those shows, Ava ... You can't trust a man who lives that lifestyle," he says as if talking to a child. And although I am his child, I am not ... a child.

"Maddox and Brody live the same lifestyle," I point out.

"Are you in love with him?"

"Oh, my God, Dad. Seriously, we're at a cardboard box and sunshine balloon stage. Jeepers, give it a rest." I throw my hands in the air, and the room key flies out of the card and straight at him.

Of course, Dad being Dad, he catches it and lifts it up. "This, Ava, is not a cute, little cut-out."

"He's got you there." Logan laughs.

"Really? Hey, Dad, where are my box of condoms, pat on the shoulder, and the atta boy he got?" I throw my thumb over my shoulder at Logan.

"Ava ..." He shakes his head.

"Dad ..." I shake mine back.

"You're my little girl," he says with a sincere sadness that I may buy into if he didn't already know about me and Liam giving it up to each other just to be rid of our virginity.

"I became a woman at the Ross family barn my junior—"

He covers his ears. "No! No, I don't want to hear it."

I laugh and walk up to him, take his hands, and smile. "I'm a big girl, Dad. I can take care of myself."

"If he hurts you, I will kill him with the very hands you're holding, and that will land me in jail. So you keep that in mind."

I smirk. "I know a good lawyer."

"Logan, you ready to go to the gym?" he asks.

"You two didn't go already?"

"Nope. Logan messaged me before dawn and told me he was gonna sleep in." Dad walks toward the bathroom. "I'll be right back."

I look at Logan, and he's looking down at me, his eyebrow's perched on that damn high and mighty spot they rest on when he feels he has something on me.

"I believe the words are thank you, Logan, for covering my ass this morning."

"What?" I ask, acting as if he's mistaken.

"And seriously, tell your friend, next time he runs after you to the bathroom, put some fucking pants on," he whispers before turning on his heels and walking to the coat closet.

"Loggie?" I say in the sweetest tone I can muster up.

He looks back at me.

"I won't bust on you about your little crush—"

"I don't have a damn crush. She may, but I don't."

"All righty, then."

Thankfully, a knock on the door takes me out of a very awkward conversation. I walk to the door and swing it open.

Luke is standing there with sweats and a hoodie on. He looks me up and down, at my eyes, my lips, and then I step back.

"Come in."

He walks in. "Your dad and Logan ready?"

"You're going to the gym with them?" I hiss.

He looks back at me, cold and emotionless. "It's been known to happen."

"After what you said—"

"Ava, you caught me on a bad fucking day." He stares at me then squints like he has something to say. I am afraid whatever it is will intensify the guilt I am trying so hard to ignore.

I stare back at him and feel tears pooling in my eyes.

"Don't," he says, his jaw twitching. "It doesn't help shit, Ava. Put the emotions in check, be a good little soldier, and carry on."

One tear falls down my face, and he reaches out and swipes it away.

That one gesture shows more care than he has shown me in seven years.

"Luke."

He shakes his head. "Words have been said. Can't take them back."

"But you can," I insist, wiping away more tears.

He shakes his head again. "You have a good time last night?"

I swallow back more tears.

"It's all good, Ava."

"But—"

He shakes his head again. "Game over. It was already decided." He turns and walks into the kitchen.

"Hey, you showed." Logan laughs, greeting him.

"Said I would, didn't I?"

"Sure did. Check this shit out. Ava has an admirer."

"Cute," he says. "She deserves one."

I walk quickly past them and start up the stairs.

"Where you going?" Dad calls after me.

"Back to bed," I answer.

"You making breakfast for us three when we get back?" Logan asks.

"Yeah, sure," I say, running the rest of the way up.

Once inside my room, I dive onto my bed and bury my face in a pillow. I look over the bed for the blanket, but it's not there. I know it has to be here; I can smell it.

I get down on the floor and look beneath my bed. It's not there, either.

I spend ten minutes tearing apart my bedding and

still I don't find it anywhere.

"Damn you, Bingo," I say as I climb back in bed.

I look at my phone to see what time it is, and I see an unknown message.

I hit the notification and read the message: That bad, huh? It was a gallant effort. It's all new to me, Ava. I'll do better next time. – T.

I kick my feet, trying like crazy to rid myself of some of the guilt I'm feeling, but it's to no avail.

I roll over and hug the pillow, smelling home and love. I cry into it. I cry hard because crying helps. It releases pain and guilt. It seemingly rids me of the emotions I can't sort out, allowing them to boil over. I cry because it's cathartic.

Then I fall asleep.

My eyes sting when I open them and look at the phone that is ringing on the charging dock on my nightstand.

"Hello?"

"Breakfast better include bacon."

"Yeah, sure," I say, throwing my feet over the side of my bed.

"Leaving the gym in fifteen minutes. We need anything at the store?"

"Logan, you've been home longer than I have, so you tell me."

"Sausage gravy," I hear Luke say in the background.

"Anything real and unhealthy," Dad chimes in. "And for God's sake, don't tell Tessa."

"How about you'll eat whatever I make and like it?" I say, and they all laugh. "Logan, am I on speaker?"

"Sure are."

"Nice, jackass." I hang up the phone then run into the bathroom and jump in the shower.

After my shower, I throw on leggings and a sweatshirt

over my panties and bra. Then I pull on a pair of fuzzy socks because my feet are freezing.

I run down the stairs and skid past T's sunshine in a box, bat my way through balloons, and go out to the garage to look in the freezer. I grab a roll of breakfast sausage and a package of bacon. Then I quickly walk into the kitchen and throw them both in the microwave before hitting Google on my phone to get the recipe.

I run around the kitchen that I haven't cooked in since this summer and find pots and pans. I grab flour out of the cupboard and butter and milk out of the fridge. When I measure the milk, there isn't enough, so I shoot Logan a text telling him to pick some up. This should buy me enough time to brown the sausage.

When they arrive, I grab the milk and dump it into the simmering butter, sausage fat, and flour mixture.

"Holy shit, Ava." Logan laughs. "You're cooking!"

"Great observation, Einstein. I do live alone in the city. A girl has to eat."

"That's my girl." Dad kisses my cheek, and I look over at him. "Sausage gravy would send Tessa into a tizzy."

"Because you had a heart attack? Yeah, she probably wouldn't be pleased." I shake my head, smirking to myself.

It's turkey sausage, and he'll never be able to tell the difference.

"What can I do to help?" Luke asks.

Logan snickers. "She's got it all under control."

And he's right; I do have it all under control … until I feel Luke's eyes on me and nearly burn the last four pieces of toast we have in the house.

After they eat, Dad reminds us that we are watching a movie at Harper's house. He tells Luke he hopes to see him there, and Luke agrees to show up. Dad leaves happy after that.

Logan takes off upstairs to find his phone charger, leaving me alone with Luke.

I am doing the dishes when he walks up and starts to rinse them.

I look at him, and he looks at me.

"What?"

"You never hang out here. You certainly never offer to help do dishes," I whisper.

"Well, it's a new day, Ava."

"What's that supposed to mean?"

He narrows his eyes at me. "It means what I said."

"It's a new day, Ava," I mimic him.

"Told you I was in a bad place the other day."

"You mean the past two days?"

"Seems about right." He looks at me and stares at my eyes for a moment. "Mark on your eye's gone, huh?"

"Oh, my God, is this all because of that? It was an accident, Luke."

"No. Ava, it happens. Men like me don't get careless."

"Luke …" I shake my head. "It was—"

"Careless and stupid. Pissed me off. Said some things. Won't take them back. Those things needed to be said."

I turn away and start washing the dishes again.

"You're good. I'm good," he states, and I look back at him. "Dangerous game we were playing, Ava. Can't do it anymore."

I look away and start scrubbing the same pan I have been since he stepped up to the sink.

"I do appreciate you not saying anything to my family or yours about what I said."

"I wouldn't want to hurt them."

"I know that."

I look up at him again. "I don't want to hurt you, either."

"Know that, too."

"Luke," I sigh. "You need to tell me what you want."

"I want to go back to that night in the pool and take it all away."

His words sting, and I am sure he sees that.

"I was good to you then. We were"—he pauses—"buddies. I overstepped. If I could take it all back, I would."

"But—"

"No buts, Ava. If I could go back, I swear I would never—"

"You ready?" Logan asks as he barrels down the stairs.

"Yep," Luke says, looking at me.

"Where are you two off to?" I look between them.

"Double date." Logan grins. "Two chicks at the gym."

I look away and nod. "Have fun."

Luke takes his time putting on his boots while Logan saunters out the door.

"If I could take it back, I would."

"But you can't," I say.

"No, I can't any more than you can take away last night."

"You did that!" I seethe. "You—"

"Shh." He scowls. "Christ, Ava."

He shakes his head as he stands up and walks toward the door.

"Luke," I call out to him, and he looks back.

"No more," he reiterates.

I feel my lip quiver as I nod.

"Good girl." He turns and walks away.

Nine

When you find real love after you've been living in a tornado it's
the best feeling in the world.
— S. Armstrong

WHEN THEY PULL OUT OF the driveway, I sink down
on the kitchen floor, holding the pan I made sausage
gravy in while staring at the balloons floating around
the kitchen.

No second chances.

Easier said than done.

Luke spoke to me more today than he has in years.

Luke wishes he could take it all back, make it go
away.

I can't help thinking that, if I hadn't been such an
idiot, he would have been in my bed last night. More
importantly, he wouldn't look so torn about us.

Us? God, what is wrong with me? I ask as a smiling
sun floats toward me.

I reach for my phone when I get a message alert.

Harper: Piper would love for you to come play.

At this moment, I know that is the distraction I need.

Me: Be there in an hour.

I arrive at Harper and Maddox's home just before
noon and am greeted with a great big smile and the
warmest hug from Piper. Immediately, I feel better.

"Your hugs could save the world."

She takes my face in her chubby little hands and says, "Are you sad?"

I shake my head, and she nods.

"Wanna play?"

"I would love to."

We spend the day in the family room, watching *The Nutcracker* and singing and dancing. She is wearing her pink tutu, and I am wearing her white one, which looks absolutely ridiculous. It almost covers my ass.

Dad and Tessa walk in an hour into our playtime, and Dad laughs as we both leap and twirl and fall. Gracefully, of course.

Lunch is almost ready when Dad pops in and holds out the crown I used to wear.

"You're missing a piece to your costume, Ava."

"This is not a costume, Daddy. We are singing, dancing princesses, right, Piper?"

She is looking at the crown on my head like it is the most amazing thing she has seen.

"Would you like to wear it?" I ask, taking it off.

She smiles. "It's yours."

"You know," I tell her, walking over to my bag and pulling out a pair of sunglasses, "I used to wear this crown every day. It didn't matter if people thought it was ridiculous; I refused to take it off."

"Except for bath time."

I look up to see Logan in the doorway.

"Yes, except for bath time." I laugh. "But I grew up and went to school and then college, and then I got a job. I can't wear it anymore, because"—I pause, trying to choose my words carefully since every girl deserves to believe in fairytales and happy ever afters—"it got a bit too small for my big head."

"You got that right." Logan laughs.

I toss him a glare then look back at Piper. "So now, I think, if it fits you, you should wear it every time you need to feel sparkly."

"Do you think it will fit me?"

"There's only one way to find out." I place it on top of her platinum blonde curls.

Dad gasps, and I do the same.

Her blue eyes widen. "Does it fit?"

"Oh, Piper, it fits beautifully. In fact, I think it was made for you."

"But it was yours," she says as she turns and looks in the mirror.

"But I grew up, and it hasn't fit on any other little girl's head as perfectly as it does yours. So it's now yours. It chose you."

"What will you wear?" she asks me.

I put on my sunglasses and push them up on my head. "Sunglasses are the new crown."

She laughs. "Not the same."

"Maybe not, but I will tell you a secret." I curl my finger toward myself, gesturing for her to come closer. She leans in, and I whisper in her ear, "You can never steal a girl's inner sparkle no matter how old she is."

"So you don't need a crown 'cause you're older now?"

"Exactly. And when you get to be my age, you won't, either."

"Can I have your sunglasses when I get older and the crown doesn't fit my big head?"

I laugh and nod. "Of course you can."

She throws her arms around me and whispers in my ear, "Thank you, fairy god-Ava."

Her words seem to make me a bit emotional. "You're very welcome. Thank you."

"I didn't give you a crown."

"No, Piper, but you gave my crown a chance to shine again."

She smiles as if she gets it. She gets that it's time for me to move on from my naive and childlike ways. Let's hope I can not only talk the talk, but walk the walk.

I stand up. "I'll be back in just a minute."

I walk through the kitchen and see Luke standing at the sink next to Harper as I make my way to the bathroom. A tinge of jealousy hits me, but I have no right. He doesn't love me, and we are done. *No do overs,* I remind myself.

I look in the mirror and realize I look like hell. I need sleep, like a week's worth of it. I love home, but right now, I would give anything to be back in the city where the idea of home makes me miss it, because this trip, home's reality isn't all it used to be.

When I walk out, Piper is twirling in a circle, and I watch Luke watch her. He is smiling at her, and I automatically wonder if he is thinking of when we were younger.

He looks up and nods at me then nods at her. Then Luke Lane smiles at me, and his smile breaks my heart. His smile tells me all I really need to know.

Once upon a time, Luke Lane loved a little, stubborn, delusional girl, and that little girl was me. My fairytale happy ever after always included my black-haired, blue-eyed knight in shining armor, and that knight was Luke Lane. Then I grew up and convinced myself that it wasn't a fairytale after all. It was fate.

I twisted fate to make her story come to life, but fate fought back this week, and now I am looking at a man I still love, but who doesn't feel the same. And now I have to walk away. Not just for me, but for him. And not for the version of him who broke my heart, but for the version who was truly a knight in shining armor to a little girl so many fairy tales ago.

I turn to walk toward the door, needing another minute to myself. A moment in the cold December air to frost over the emotions that keep flooding me.

When I look up, I see T, who immediately looks away.

"Hi," I say nervously in response to the coldness that seems to be coming from him.

"Hello," he says without looking at me.

"Okay, then." I walk past him.

I can't get out the door fast enough. When it shuts behind me and then opens when I have taken the three steps it takes to get off of the back porch, I look back to see T walking toward me.

"Okay, then, what?"

I shrug and smile and then frown and curse, "Damn it." I turn back away and start walking.

"Then my assumption is right?" he yells at me.

I wipe away the tears and keep walking.

When I feel a tug on my elbow, I look back into his angry eyes that soften in reaction to what I guess is the way I look. He shakes his head.

"Don't be mad at me," comes out in a beseeched sound.

"Angry, no. Upset, most definitely."

I shake my head. "What did I do?"

"Ava, I sent you—"

I cover my mouth when the realization hits that I never sent a thank you. "I loved it."

He rolls his eyes and turns his head. "It was childish. I should have—"

"No"—I reach up and grab the sides of his face—"it wasn't. It was perfect. It was so perfect."

"What is the status of your relationship with Luke Lane?"

103

I shake my head. I won't lie, but I won't give him what he is asking for.

"Ava ..." he says in a soft tenor.

"I don't have a relationship with ... him."

"When did it end?"

"There never was a—"

He turns away.

"Wait!"

He looks back.

"We grew up together," I say slowly.

He nods then turns and walks away again.

"T!"

He holds up his hand and shakes his head as he walks back into the house.

I squat down, fist my hair, and scream inside. I can't seem to catch a damn break. Can't he just let it be?

When I look up, Liam is walking down the driveway, so I stand up quickly and turn my back to him as I pull by sweatshirt up and wipe my eyes dry.

He walks up and holds his hand out. "Let's walk."

"You alone?"

"Yep. You wanna talk?"

I shake my head, and he gives me a half-smile, squeezes my hand, and we walk in silence until we get to the pond and the bench that overlooks it.

He uses his gloves to wipe off the bench. "Sit?"

I do, and he sits next to me.

Liam is and always has been calm. The older he gets, the calmer he seems. Right now, I need to borrow it.

He looks over as I look at him and takes in a deep breath. "Luke Lane's home."

"So I've heard," I say.

He chuckles silently and throws his arm around the back of the bench. He uses his hand to pull my head against his shoulder.

"Better?"

"Yeah," I say.

"What's the deal with T?"

I look up at him. "What?"

Again, he smirks and chuckles. Then he leans back and puts my head on his chest.

I close my eyes and wait and wait and wait for Liam's calm to overtake me.

When I feel almost human again, I look up at him. "Love you."

"You, too." He kisses my head. "Now, let's go not face whatever it is we're not facing."

"Do we have to?"

He stands up and holds out his hand just like Logan does. "Yeah, we do."

We hold hands as we walk toward the house exactly like we used to.

Liam was the smart, preppy kind of hot nerd in school. I made him cool, and he made me behave. He is my male Harper.

"Tell me about Martha."

"You mean Marta." He smirks.

"Yes." I smirk back. "Marta."

"We have a lot in common: likes, dislikes, goals, desire to travel—"

I can't help giggling.

"What?"

"Does she make you crazy?" I ask.

"I avoid crazy, Ava."

"Does she get you all worked up?"

"Ava …" he warns.

"Are you happy?" I ask, conceding to Liam's profound dislike for talking about sex.

"I am. Are you?"

I smile. "Aren't I always?"

"I hope so," he says sincerely.

When we walk in, T scowls at me, and my dad notices immediately. His jaw sets, and he shakes his head.

Tessa nudges him with her elbow and pats the spot next to her at the huge table.

After lunch, Piper is heading to take a nap.

"I want Ava."

"Ava is going to stay down here, sweet girl," Maddox says, kissing the side of her head.

"But I want her. She's tired."

I lean over toward Harper. "I really wouldn't mind."

Harper smiles. "She and Maddox are fine."

"No, Mommy, I'm not fine," Piper says, and the whole room gasps. "Ava is not fine. We need a nap."

It doesn't take me but a second to stand. I'm in a room filled with three men I have slept with, and it's fucking exhausting.

"I would have to say I agree that Ava needs a nap if you don't mind, Maddox."

He looks at Piper. "You have something to say to your mommy?"

"Sorry." She looks down sadly.

"Do you have something to ask Ava?" he asks her.

"Wanna take a nap with me?"

"I'd love to."

§

I WAKE TO PIPER WHIMPERING and thrashing, and I don't know what to do, so I hold her.

"Shhh, it's okay."

"Ava?" she says with her eyes still closed.

"Yes, it's okay," I tell her as she shakes in my arms.

"You'll be okay," she whispers. "It's okay."

I look up when both Maddox and Harper walk in the

room.

Maddox slides in next to her on the other side of the bed. "Come here, Piper."

She sighs and rolls into his arms while I slide out of bed and look at Harper who looks concerned.

"She okay?" I mouth.

She nods once, and then I follow her out into the hallway.

"She's been having dreams. Night terrors is what the doctor says they are. Perfectly normal."

"That's perfectly normal?" I gasp.

She shakes her head and shrugs. "It's terrifying."

"How did you hear her? Was she loud? Did I sleep through that?"

She slightly smiles. "Maddox has a monitor on his hip at all times. He heard her." I follow her into hers and Maddox's room, and she flops on the bed. "It's exhausting."

I flop down next to her. "I'm exhausted, and I didn't even know about it."

"The holidays," she says.

I take her hand and squeeze it. Her father was killed at this time of year while saving her life. I know how hard it is for her. "I'm sorry."

"I know," she whispers.

"Everything all right?" Maddox asks quietly as he walks into the room.

"Everything's great," Harper says, taking his hand, and he pulls her up.

I raise mine, and he looks at me, shaking his head. He reaches out and pulls me up, too.

"Thank you, Maddox Hines."

"You're welcome, Ava."

He and Harper then walk hand in hand out the door. Once downstairs, we walk into the living room where Liam is watching Dad look at T. T is looking at Luke, and Luke isn't looking at a damn thing.

Liam then looks at me, and both of us laugh.

All eyes turn to me then Liam.

"Come here, Ava, and have a seat," he says to me.

"Will your girlfriend be here soon?" T asks, and Liam looks at him then me then back at him.

"Not tonight. She's with her family," Liam says kindly.

"Are you in love with her?" T asks before taking a drink.

I want to crawl under a rock. The couch may work.

"We've been dating for four months," Liam answers in the same even tone.

Luke chuckles, and T looks at him crossly.

"And you?"

"I'm in love with my country," Luke says in a far too smug way.

"Interesting," T says back just as smugly. Then he looks back at Liam, "And how long have you been in love with—"

"T," Maddox says, and T looks at him. "I could use some help in the kitchen."

T stares at him, and Maddox stares back at T.

"Now please."

Ten

Love Isn't always lightning bolts and butterflies, sometimes it's gentle rain and the smell of fresh air.
— A. Parke

"WELL, AVA, WHAT DO YOU think now?" Dad asks when the door slams.

I look at him, and he cocks his head in an I-told-you-so style. Then I look at Tessa, who looks down and whispers something.

Luke stands up and walks to the kitchen, and Liam looks over at me and whispers, "You gonna do something about that?"

"About what?"

The door slams again. "That," he says.

"Do you think—"

He nods.

"You go."

He looks at me and shakes his head.

"Yes."

"You owe me." He stands up and walks out the door.

"See, Ava, he's trouble. Even the boys know that," Dad states.

I look at Tessa, whose eyes are closed tightly. God, what must she think of me?

I stand up. "I have to pee."

I stand at the kitchen window, watching as Liam and Maddox stand in front of Luke and T who both have their fists balled. I am embarrassed and angry that my heartbreak and indiscretions are on display.

"What's going on?" Harper asks, standing next to me and then, "Oh. Oh, my. That doesn't look good."

"Would you be upset if I went home?"

"You want to leave?" she asks.

"Yes. Yes, I do." I nod.

"Because of Luke and Liam?"

"Because I feel like shit and because that mess out there will simmer down and because I am completely exhausted."

"Hey, Ava," Harper says quietly. When she talks like that, it's because she doesn't want to say what she needs to. "If something is happening with you and Thomas, just be careful."

"Be careful?" I gasp. "Why? Is something wrong with him?"

She shakes her head. "He really likes you."

"I kind of like him, too. But not right now."

With that, I run and kiss Dad, telling him I will see him in the morning.

Before he can say anything, Tessa grabs his hand and tells me, "Drive safe and get some sleep."

I give Harper a kiss on the cheek before I leave, telling her, "Tell Piper I love her, and I'll see her soon, okay?"

I walk outside where all four men look at me. Three of them, I have slept with. I look away and walk toward the SUV.

"Ava!" Liam yells.

"Have a good night," I say, continuing to walk.

"Ava, you don't have to leave," my dad's voice is

now in the mix, and I am almost starting to run. "She's home for the holidays, and you have her running," I hear him snap.

"*I* have her running?"

I stop and turn around when I hear T's voice.

"Yes, *you* have her running," Dad snaps back.

I look at them, seeing Liam is the only one who notices me. He mouths "go," and I shake my head, walking back to them.

"I came outside. It's these two who—"

"T," I snap, and he looks up. "You drive here?"

"Of course I drove here."

"You been drinking?"

He looks away.

I sigh. "Come with me."

"Ava …" Dad says.

"No, Dad." I shake my head then look at T. "You coming?"

"Is that what you want?" he asks.

I nod. "Yes." I then pull my keys out of my pocket and toss them to Liam. "Can you give these to Harper and tell her I'll be back for them?"

"When will you be back?" Dad asks.

"I don't know, Dad," I tell him before looking at T who is standing beside me. "Keys?"

He hesitates.

"Keys, now."

He huffs and hands them to me.

"Let's go."

"If you hurt her, you and I will have problems," my father warns.

"He's not gonna hurt her," Maddox defends T.

"He better not," Dad snaps.

We walk toward his Land Rover, and I hit the unlock. T climbs into the passenger side, and I get in the driver's seat.

"Can you drive stick?" he asks.

"Of course I can," I say as I grind the gears into reverse.

"She's terribly sorry," he says as he pats the dashboard.

"No, she's not." I purposely grind into drive and floor it so we drive over the bank of snow that was plowed to clear the driveway.

"Ava, please take it easy on her," he says, and I can't help laughing. "Matilda, she doesn't mean it."

I spin the tires, throwing snow behind me as the vehicle fishtails.

"Ava, for fuck's sake!" T pulls his seatbelt down, buckling it. Then he reaches over and tries to grab mine.

I bat away his hand.

"I'm gonna have to insist you put that fucking thing on now, Ava," he says.

I glare at him, and he glares back.

"I'm not fucking kidding."

I grind into second, yelling, "Don't ever do that shit to me again!"

"By shit, I assume you mean questioning Luke and Liam's intentions?"

"It's none of your business, T!"

"I fucking laid it all out to you last night! I asked that you not lie to me!"

"I didn't lie to you!"

"It's obvious that you and Luke—"

"It's not obvious, and it's not something I will discuss!"

"I don't accept that," he sneers.

"Then accept this: when you left this morning, I was ready to look away from my ... past. When you sent that gift, I was more than ready. When my dad questioned me about you, I stuck up for you, for me, for us. I am so sorry that I didn't return your text—I am going through some things—but when I say I'm done, when I said I wanted you, I was sincere. I trusted you! Tonight, you blew that out of the water. You made me feel stupid in front of all of them. And let me tell you, I am going through hell right now, and you, you made it worse!"

He doesn't respond. He doesn't say anything. He doesn't even look at me.

"Fuck you, T. Fuck. You!"

Twenty silent minutes later, I pull into the Statler Hotel. I grind the gears, putting the vehicle in park and killing the engine. Then I turn and look at him.

"My key is at Maddox and Harper's," he says matter-of-factly.

I pull the one he sent me out of my bra. "Take mine."

"I can't. I gave it to you." He lifts his chin in the air. Fucking Brit!

"I don't know how they do things in England, but here, you can ask for another key card at the front desk," I snap.

"I've traveled a bit," he says sarcastically.

"I'm well aware of your travels," I retort.

He turns and looks at me, not saying a word, and then says, "If you would rather be with the farm boy or the toy soldier with the personality of a fucking mop, just let me know. I, too, can find companionship."

"Veterinarian and a fucking career soldier who keeps your ass from speaking German! How dare you?" I toss the keys at him and get out of his vehicle.

His door slams at the same time as mine, and then he is immediately at my side as I walk down the slush-covered sidewalk.

"Listen to me, Ava!"

I look around as people walking by slow down and stare.

"You're causing a scene," I growl at him.

"You're the crazy person walking in the freezing cold, and to where, Ava? Home? It's fifteen minutes from here in a damn vehicle going a hundred and ten kilometers."

"I'd rather freeze than deal with you." I continue walking.

"Deal with me? I'm fucking Thomas Hardy. Women line up to meet me, Ava, just like you did the first time we met!"

Shocked, I look around and see everyone staring.

I slap him across the face. "You go fuck yourself!"

He doesn't even flinch. "Not necessary."

"When I walk away, don't follow me."

"Unbelievable!" he says, raising his hands in the air. "You are unbelievable."

"Yep, sure am." I walk down the sidewalk as people still stare.

"Leave it to me to fall for a crazy woman."

I raise my arm up, and he laughs loudly.

"You aren't in NYC, Ava Links. There are no cabs here!"

A car pulls over, and I flip him off. As I get in, he runs and stops me from shutting the door.

"Are you insane? Do you know what can happen to you, Ava!"

"Is that T Hardy?" Maxi asks.

"Yes, and he's a fucking asshole."

"What did I do?" he asks, his voice full of emotion.

"If you can't figure it out, there is something seriously wrong with you." I look away. "Maxi, can you please take me home?"

"You know her?" he asks.

"We went to high school together. Me, Ava, and Harper—"

"Maxi, please," I plead.

"Right, well, nice meeting you, Thomas Hardy," she says.

"You, as well. Ava—"

"No. No. No. No."

§

I LIE IN BED, AND every time I close my eyes, I see his face: his anger, his jealousy, his smugness, and so many more emotions I can't even begin to understand.

I grab my phone and google Thomas Hardy. The writer and poet and the actor Tom Hardy pop up on Google, and so does T.

I search for his bio, needing to know more about him, more about what makes him tick, but there isn't anything except his time with Burning Souls. You would think someone would have dug in deeper, but apparently, no one has.

T was not himself today, and I can't help blaming myself. But he's not a child. He shouldn't have been rude to Liam, or Luke for that matter.

My phone rings, and Harper's name pops up. I answer immediately.

"Everything okay?" I ask.

"No, T is all out of sorts, and he is never out of sorts. Never."

"What sort of sorts?" I ask.

She laughs. "He's got a disease, and apparently, his ailment is—"

I sigh. "G.A.D."

"Could you call him so Maddox doesn't have to talk him out of moving back to England again?"

"Again?"

"Yeah." She yawns.

"Harper, what's his story?"

"What do you mean?"

I reiterate, "Where is he from? What's his background?"

"Well, I think you should ask him, but not tonight."

"Why?"

"Hold on," she says, and I hear a door shut. "Quickly, before Maddox hears me … He doesn't know his father, and his mother moved to India when he was fifteen. T was basically on the streets from as far back as he can remember. Even when he did have a place to live, he hustled to eat and buy clothes. He and his mom lived in those low-budget weekly rental hostels when there was money. When there wasn't, they slept in a car."

"Are you certain?" I ask.

"He had no one."

I don't know what to say or how to respond.

"That's what I meant when I said be careful with him. He's an awesome guy. Piper loves him, and we trust him explicitly, but he does try very hard to distance himself unless he feels useful or needed."

"That's awful."

"He and Maddox are so close, Ava. They are so similar in so many things, but the difference is Maddox had Brody, Emma, and the girls. T got thrown directly from having nothing to having it all, and he can't always accept that he deserves it. And he does. My God, he deserves so much more."

"He overstepped today."

"Then tell him that," she says softly.

We say good-bye, and I hang up with Harper to dial T.

He answers, saying my name.

"I'm mad at you."

"I'm pissed at you, too," he slurs.

"Last night, I promised not to lie to you, but I didn't promise to tell you everything in my past."

"I told you I wanted to know everything."

"I can't do that."

"Which one do you love?" he demands.

"Love in what sense?"

"Love is love, Ava," he says as if it is an absolute.

"No, love is not love, T. It's not. I grew up with them. I love them both. Liam has been and always will be as loved by me as Harper is. Luke is very different."

"Which one are you fucking?"

"The last person I slept with is you. You, and that was ..." I pause. "T, I can't give you details or answers without breaking promises to myself. I am not in a relationship with either, but I love them both."

"What if I tell you I won't allow it?"

"Then I will tell you that you're missing out because all those things I said last night are true. This morning, I woke to the sweetest thing anyone has ever done for me, and that same person made me feel worse than I already did about ... Well, I told you I was going through some things, and you made those things worse."

"I won't let them hurt you."

"One of them has never hurt me and the other never will again. But you, I believed what you said last night, and the message you sent this morning was heard loud and clear, and I was happy, T. I was happy and excited, but now ... Now I'm tired and am going to bed. I'm sorry you feel like I betrayed you, but you had no right to do what you did today, and you did it in front of *everyone*. Two people know about the things you figured out today. Now I am certain more do. You hurt me today."

"You hurt me, too."

"And I'm sorry for that, but I am tired of hurting. Good night, T. Sleep well."

He doesn't say a word. He simply hangs up.

If there were any tears left for me to cry, I would, but there are none.

Eleven

No two loves are the same.
— M. Bennett

Two weeks later

I WALK INTO MY APARTMENT, dropping my keys and bag on the entry table before sitting on the chair to the left to pull my feet out of my Heritage High boots. I place them on the boot tray so they don't drip and stain the hardwood floor. Tonight, I am having dinner with my mother, and I am secretly praying her new husband Robert doesn't show up.

I walk to the fridge and grab a Greek yogurt to tide me over until I leave again in an hour and a half.

Since I have been back to my home in the city, I have been exhausted emotionally and physically. Thomas took a red-eye out of Ithaca hours after our phone conversation. He didn't text, didn't call. He simply left. I tried to call, and I tried to text, but they were never answered or returned.

Harper told me to give it time. I told her I wasn't giving it anything. I was chalking it up to yet another mistake on my part.

Luke seemed to have flipped a switch. He seemed

... happy, comfortable, like he was actually enjoying his time home for the first time in seven years. On New Year's Eve after Dad's birthday dinner at Harper and Maddox's and Piper had gone to bed, we all went to Jade and Ryan's. All of us laughed as we watched old videos of our families at parties, on vacations. And, of course, there was me in a pink tutu and a crown, and Luke was as much a man as he is today.

He has always had that way about him: always the protector, always seeming to think of others. The difference between then and now is the light. The sparkle that was once in his blue eyes, the one that drew you to seek him out, is now gone. I couldn't help thinking I had something to do with that.

I tossed aside the crown and tried to grow up too damn fast, and when I did, it took his light with it. That feeling—that reality—broke my heart just as much as he broke mine on Christmas.

When Logan and I left that night, I hugged Luke as I always did, and he hugged me back more tightly this time—I think, anyway. I don't know what is real and imagined in the story of Luke and me anymore, and that is one hell of a pill to swallow.

I broke us. I broke that little girl who was as much a princess in her head as she was treated by all around her, and in doing that, I broke that sweet, protective knight. I will never forgive myself for it. Not ever.

He left on New Year's day, heading to Fort Bragg, and then he was off on another mission in the Middle East. I pray for him, and not the version of him I had imagined would be mine someday, but the version of him that was truly mine from as far back as I can remember.

In allowing myself to imagine us together forever, I stole the beauty in the reality of what we were: a knight and a princess, friends, and yes, family.

I sit in the window overlooking the city, thinking about the truths about love for the millions and millions of people in just this small area of this world, and it crushes me.

I set the yogurt down and grab the journal Jade gave me, deciding I would write the truths about love today.

Love is brutal. Love is beautiful. Love is broken. Nine words and my tears have found their way back to me. Three truths, and I can't eat. How can one word mean so many things?

T was wrong! Love is not just love. With him, I could have gotten through this. He was wrong about not hurting me, too. Damn him.

I reach up, tempted to pull the deflated smiling sunshine balloon I hung in my window down. It serves as a reminder of the last time I felt true joy in my heart, even when I was at the lowest point in my entire life.

Hope.

I decide to leave it since the sun hasn't shined in days. I am sure I lack in good old vitamin D. I can pretend it's the real sun, just like I pretended my love for Luke was real love.

I get up and toss my half-eaten yogurt in the garbage and sob. I sob because of who I am, who I was, and who I convinced myself I could be. I sob so hard I make myself sick.

After throwing up, the dry heaves begin, and after they stop, I climb in my bed and fall asleep.

§

MOM'S CALL WAKES ME. SHE is in her car outside of my apartment.

I throw my hair up in a bun as I shove my feet in my

boots. Then I grab my coat and purse and ride down the elevator as I use my phone's selfie mode to wipe the smudges of mascara from under my eyes.

I look like hell as I get in the car, and when I see Robert, I feel sick again. God, how could she go from Dad to that son of a bitch?

"60 East, 65th street," Robert tells the driver.

"Ava, you look well," Mom says, her nose stuck in her tablet. When she looks up, she looks like she could die.

"I feel lovely," I say, sitting back in the leather seat.

She looks at Robert. "How about we head to the Spotted Pig?"

As she says it, I look in my mirror at my splotchy face, wiping makeup off my face. I can't help laughing.

Over the past few years, my mother has changed in a big way. Her cracks don't mean a damn thing to me, but mine, they send her to the … moon.

"The Red Moon on West 54th has amazing sushi," I say, smiling brightly.

Her lips turn into a straight line.

Logan had a few months where it was very hard for him to deal with my mother's new life. He was the one who came up with moon face. He also asked that she not breed—and yes, he said "breed"—with Robert because he didn't think he could possibly love or even pretend to love something that resembled him. She was so angry at him she didn't talk to him for a month.

Dad laughed for a good five minutes about it before Tessa asked him to help her in the kitchen. When they came back, he asked Logan to try to be accepting of his mother's new life and her new husband. We both know Tessa put him up to it, and they both knew we knew it, too.

"I've never heard of it, Ava. Ashley, it might be nice

to try a new spot," Robert says.

"The Spotted Pig sounds lovely, Robert." I smile, and he is none the wiser.

When the car pulls up to the curb, Mom says, "Robert, be a dear and grab us a table. Ava and I will be there in a moment."

Once the door closes, she looks at me. "Are you feeling all right?"

"I'm fine, just tired."

"Is that why you're being irritable?"

I can't help laughing. "Spotted Pig, Mom? Who's being irritable?"

"I've heard good things about it," she says as if she has no idea what I'm talking about.

"Great. Let's go, shall we?"

"Just one minute." She stops me from opening the door. "We received word on New Year's day that the Republican party is backing Robert in his bid for United States senate. Robert and I would love for you to be part of the team, Ava. It would look wonderful on your resume—"

"I have a job, but thank you," I say, not wanting a fight.

"Ava, I am asking you to consider. I am also asking you to tell him you'll think about it when he asks you. And do act like I didn't tell you in advance."

"So you're asking me to lie?"

"I'm asking you to consider," she says.

"There is no way in hell I will take a job with him or you after what you did to Dad."

"That company was as much mine as it was his. More so, actually."

I laugh snidely. "Because Landon said so?"

She narrows her eyes. "Landon knows how hard I worked for the company."

"Landon is my father's father," I remind her. "You and he both fucked my father, who built that company from the time he was a kid, Mom!"

"Clearly, he doesn't think so, or he would have taken it to court," she says smugly.

"Trust me, I've begged him to," I snap.

"You what?" she gasps.

"You fucked up, Mom."

"Ava!"

"No, you did, and he hasn't come after you because he doesn't give a damn about money or fighting for what is his. Material things mean nothing to him. Love and family mean everything!"

"No, Tessa Ross means everything to him. Don't you dare think any differently. And don't you judge me until you have walked in my shoes, young lady." She gets out of the car and looks back at me. "Tell him you'll consider, Ava. That's all I ask of you."

At that moment, I despise the woman who gave birth to me. Walk a mile in her shoes? *Pft.*

I walk into the Spotted Pig behind her, feeling sick for another reason now. I have to act a part for her. I can't believe I even try.

Here's another truth about love: love changes, even the love of a daughter for her mother.

I sit in the corner booth across from old moon face and a woman who resembles my mother. I am miserable, moody, tired, and his face makes me sick to my stomach. As I watch him talk, I smile and nod, and when he asks me to be part of his team, I do what is expected of me: I tell him I will consider it.

I wish Logan were here for me to kick under the table when he was being obnoxious and too … Logan. Or to pass inside jokes and insults back and forth with no one being the wiser.

I wish all my friends who let fate lead them, the ones who went off to college and enjoyed the experience instead of trying to twist fate in the direction they wanted it to go, weren't so busy "adulting." I'm truly happy for them that they have found happiness. I'm happy for Liam, Harper, Maxi, and everyone else. Their happiness is true and real, but seeing it, my loneliness and my failure shine so brightly they burn me from the inside out.

"Ava?" Robert says.

"Sorry, what was that?"

He points to the waiter, and I pull my hands away so he can set my plate on the table.

"Sorry."

"Are you okay, dear?" he asks when the waiter leaves. His question and the sincerity in it shocks me.

I look up at him and nod. "Excuse me, please."

I rush toward the bathroom, afraid I may cry or get sick in the middle of the restaurant, but a crowd of women is blocking the restroom's entrance.

"Excuse me."

None of them move.

"Excuse me," I say, making a V with my hands and begin pushing through the crowd.

Sputters, curses, and groans from unhappy patrons are heard, but I don't care.

A man's back is to me, and it's clear by the crowd in front of him that he is the cause of the restroom being blocked. I can't get past him, so I tap on his shoulder.

"Excuse me!"

He looks over his shoulder with a smile, and I immediately feel a hundred times more emotional.

"Ava," he says with a sadness in his voice. He turns around and looks down at me. "You look beautiful."

"I need to get in there." I point to the bathroom.

His face hardens before he nods and steps aside.

"Thank you, T." I push past the women and into the tiny, two-stalled bathroom.

Thankfully, one is unoccupied, and I run in just in time to throw up everything in my belly. Then I flush the toilet, close the lid, and sit down. I peel some toilet paper off the roll and wipe my mouth.

I hear the door open then shut and almost apologize to whomever it is that had to experience that, but my mouth is filling with saliva, and I am starting to sweat.

I hang my head down, hoping I will feel a little better, but the smell of the bathroom, although clean, makes me even more nauseous.

"Damn it," I whisper as I stand and open the bathroom door.

Against the wall stands a drummer in cargo pants, a gray Henley, and a gray knit hat. His frown is heartbreaking, and his gray-green eyes are filled with so many emotions I can't even begin to sort through them. His arms are crossed over his chest, and when he straightens himself, he looks as if he's going to reach out and hug me, but he doesn't. He shoves his hands in his pockets, instead.

"I need to get out of here, T," I say apologetically.

"Let me call you a cab." He nods as he turns and opens the restroom door.

His hand is on my lower back as he guides me through the crowd. He stops at the table he was next to, and I look back at him. He leans down and tells a beautiful and very sophisticated woman sitting in the shadows that he will call her tomorrow. I take that moment to quickly walk through the crowd toward my mom and Robert.

"Mom, I'm not feeling well. I'm going to take a cab home." I grab my coat and bag. "Thank you for the dinner."

"We can take you, Ava," Robert says.

"I'll see that she gets home," T says from behind me.

"Ava?" Mom asks.

"It's Thomas, Maddox's best friend, Mom. I'm going to catch a cab and—"

"I'll see that she gets home," T says again with more authority.

"You're on a date; don't be silly," I say as I turn to walk to the door.

He reaches in front of me and pushes the door open, and I walk outside.

He walks past me and stands at the curb, raising his hand. Two cabs stop, and he walks to one while I walk to the other, getting in quickly.

"Enjoy your date," I say as I shut the door behind me and give the cab driver my address.

I look back as we pull out on the street, and he is getting into the cab as women stand there, waving as the cab pulls out.

When we pull up to my place, I pay the driver and get out. I shut the door behind me as another cab pulls up and T gets out.

"What are you doing?" I ask in confusion.

"Seeing that you get home like I said I would," he says, shutting the cab door behind him.

The cab pulls away, and he walks toward me, not making eye contact. "Which place is yours?"

"Thomas, go back to your date. I can manage just fine." I hold my hand against my still nauseous belly that is now filled with butterflies.

"I wasn't on a date." He walks closer. "I was with a publicist."

"A publicist or yours?" I ask with a tinge of jealousy

that is unwanted.

The way he looks at me shows me he sees it.

"It's not funny, T," I say, stunned that he actually seems to take some sick pleasure in this.

He smiles. "It's fucking adorable."

"Whatever." I look down, trying not to smile.

How is it that his compliment can have the effect it does? I'm not starved for attention. I don't have daddy issues or low self-esteem. I'm a fucking mess right now, but I haven't always been.

He pushes my hair back and out of my face. "You're blushing, Miss Links."

"I'm not feeling well," I admit, looking up with my eyes only.

"I kind of got that when you threw up in the bathroom at the Spotted Pig." He searches my eyes, my face, my lips, my entire being.

I feel a chill go up my spine, and I shiver.

"You're cold."

"It's January in New York; everyone is cold."

"Then let's get you inside," he says, looking away. "Which place is yours?"

"I'm fine. I can walk all by myself."

He sighs and looks up. Then he smiles and points. "That's your place."

I look up and want to crawl under a snow bank.

The sun balloon.

Twelve

If you find love, hold on to it with everything you have. Life without love is harder than you think.
— R. Knight

HE FOLLOWS ME INTO MY apartment quietly.

"Thank you for seeing me home," I say, expecting him to stop, but he doesn't.

He toes off his boots and walks to the window, touching the balloon before standing motionlessly.

I take my boots off then my coat and hang it up before walking to the bathroom.

After I brush my teeth and wash my face, I walk out to find him still standing in the window. But now he's holding my journal.

"Please don't read that."

"I won't," he says, setting it down. Then he turns and sits in the very spot I sit and reflect every night. "Would you mind if I talked to you for a while?"

I walk to the fridge and grab two bottles of water. Then I walk over and hand him one before sitting down. I don't say anything, knowing in my head, I have a million things to say, to explain. However, whatever comes out of my mouth is going to sound as ridiculous out loud as it does inside.

"I don't like how I felt at Maddox and Harper's

home." His words come out slowly, like he is trying to make sense of the senseless, too. "I don't like that you don't feel for me the way I feel for you."

I open my mouth to respond, but he holds his hand up, stopping me.

"I don't like that no matter how hard I push the thought of you aside, you are still there. I don't like that those *boys* had your body and your heart. I don't like how these feelings"—he holds his hand over his heart then fists his shirt—"are so alien to me that I get very confused by them.

"I don't like that I feel so possessive of you that it took me going to England to stop myself from hunting you down and fucking you until you had come so many times from my mouth, my hand, my dick that you could think of no one else but me. I don't like the thought that it may not have worked out because the mind, the heart, and the body have to connect to make that happen.

"I don't like having to read about women in order to figure you out because I have no idea what I have to do to make you mine. I don't like planning to make you mine when it may be impossible.

"I don't like that your father despises me. And I don't like that I know, in order to truly win you, I have to win over all of the people who have known you for years because, in all honesty, they don't mean shit to me. You do."

"T—"

He holds his hand up again. "I don't like needing to know your past, but I need to in order to get to know you more deeply than anyone else does. I *need* it. I don't like you getting angry at me, and I don't like hurting you. Ava, I don't like saying what is in my heart because, if I do, it exposes my weakness for you. But I can't avoid telling you how I feel because it makes me weak.

"I am not weak. I face every day knowing who I am, where I came from, and what I have done in my past to survive. I am not weak. I am every bit as strong as anyone around you. Stronger, in fact, because I am standing here and I am going to tell you that, even though you love them, I can love you better. And, Ava, make no mistake about this: love is love. It is that simple, and I am without a doubt in love with you."

"T …" I whisper as my breath leaves me. I wish it were true. But not for me. Not for me.

"You are my goddess. I told you that from day one," he says with more conviction and vulnerability. "Let me show you *wonderful* outside of the bedroom. Let us show each other love, Ava."

"I—" My words catch in my throat.

He walks over and kisses me. His kiss is different this time—more possessive, deeper, longer, harder—and during this kiss, he pulls me up. Then we are walking and kissing, our hands and bodies are shaking, and nothing has ever felt so … right.

He pulls away, his face full of angst and pain, and I lean in, wanting and needing more.

He steps back.

"What are you doing?" I ask as I watch him reach behind him and open the front door.

"Fate brought us together tonight, Ava."

I feel my face harden. Fate? I detest Fate.

"There is no other explanation, but I am not always trusting of Fate, either. But hope? Hope springs eternal. When you are ready for what I have to offer, I am less than twenty-five minutes from you. Take the FDR, cross the East River over the Brooklyn Bridge, and you'll find me at 190 West Ave."

"Thomas, don't you dare—"

"Sleep well. I love you, Ava. When you have made a decision to open your heart to me and understand that I need everything I asked you for, come to me." With that, he walks out the door, and I am left with my heart in my throat, tears of joy in my eyes, and millions of butterflies in my belly.

I must stay in that same spot forever, because when I finally move, I do so out of pure need to lie down and sleep.

§

I WAKE TO MY ALARM, feeling rested. It's Friday, and I have to work. I wonder how it will look to my coworkers when I walk in with a stupid school-girl grin on my face.

When I am dressed and almost ready, I send Thomas a message.

Morning, sunshine.

He replies, I am breaking my self-imposed "do not text Ava until you see her at your doorstep" rule by sending this.

I laugh, replying, I'm breaking my "it's too soon to start a relationship rule," but hey, rules are meant to be broken.

The best way to get over a broken heart is to allow yourself the opportunity to be loved, Ava. And I'm impatiently waiting for the opportunity.

Be my friend, Thomas, and be patient with me.

I have no idea what I am doing. I don't want to screw it up. Jumping in with both feet sounds amazing, but do I dare?

He doesn't reply.

Work is busy, but it feels like the day is going by so slowly it's making me crazy. I keep trying to tell myself that it's an awful idea to go to him. But the truth is, I do care about T, and I love the way he says he wants to love me.

Along with that, I told Luke no do-overs, and I am a woman of my word. I have also told myself to stop lying to myself and trying to twist Fate the way I want her to go. I wasn't twisting.

I take a cab to 190 West Avenue, Brooklyn, New York. There was no reservation about this decision all day. There was none on the car ride here nor when I got out of the cab. However, I am a nervous wreck—sweating, shaking, and the nausea is back.

I reach in my purse and grab a stick of peppermint gum, hoping it will do something to stop all the saliva from pooling or, at the very least, kill the awful taste that may be in my mouth because of it.

After a few deep breaths, I start to walk toward his warehouse building, sending him a text.

Whatcha doing?

As soon as I hit send, he walks out the building's entry, his arms around not one but two women's shoulders, and they are all laughing.

Fuck. That.

He stops when his back is to me and reaches in his pocket for his phone. He reads a message, probably mine. Well, I think so, anyway.

Now he is still looking at his phone and typing. Then he shoves it in his pocket and continues walking.

Ava, no more rule breaking.

And I send: Hey, T, go fuck yourself!!!

He stops and reaches in his pocket, grabs his phone, and then he laughs out loud.

You are the worst kind of boy there is!

Send.

He shakes his head. **Is that so?**

I type a reply. **I hope those bitches give you**

something incurable, you asshole. Then I turn and walk down the road, hoping he never sees me and telling Fate she's an ugly, nasty, awful bitch.

"Ava!" I hear him laugh, and then I hear footsteps behind me.

"Go fuck your groupies!" I say loudly enough to know they would hear me, and then I flip them all off as I walk faster.

"Groupies?" one of them says as if she's offended.

T grabs my elbow, and I turn around, yanking my arm away from him.

"Groupies, whores, bitches, which do you prefer?"

"Oh, no, she didn't," the taller one says, starting to take her earrings out.

"Want me to hold your hoops, skank?" I snap, walking toward her, knowing damn well I shouldn't.

"Ava," T says, laughing as he grabs me around the waist and lifts me.

"Let. Go. Of. Me!" I kick at him, and the two skanks start laughing.

"That's quite enough." He's still laughing while I continue kicking him and trying my damn best to get out of his evil clutches. "Ladies, I apologize," he says to them.

"Ladies? Pft. I seriously—"

"T, shut your bitch up," the tall one sneers.

"Oh, she's not a bitch." He chuckles. "But she does seem a bit jealous and maybe a tad possessive."

"Never again. Never, T!" I yell, finally getting out of his arms ... for just a moment. Then I am over his shoulder, and he's holding me by my ass.

"Thank you," he says to the two skanks. "And someday, she'll apologize. Tell Teddy to put your drinks on my tab." I kick hard, and his knees buckle. "Aw ... fuck."

One laughs, saying, "Oh, hell no, would I fuck that."

"Not sure he's gonna be able to. I almost felt that kick. Damn, T, I hope she's worth it."

He doesn't answer, and I slide down his body and start to walk away as he holds where the very well-placed kick landed.

"Ava," he groans, grabbing my arm. "Get. Inside. Now."

"Hell no!" I spew, trying to pull my arm away.

"Right. Fucking. Now," he says as he all but drags me into the building.

He pulls me into the cargo elevator, shoves a key in the keyhole, and when the door shuts, he leans forward and groans.

"Ava, never, ever kick me in the balls again."

I say not one fucking thing.

He looks up. "Did you hear me?"

"I don't speak asshole!" I snap.

"Oh, Ava," he says, shaking his head. "You've got a lot to learn about me."

"The hell I do," I say as the elevator comes to a stop.

"Let's go, love." He forces a smile as he opens the door. "After you."

"No."

"Ava, my balls are literally in my stomach right now, and if I must carry you, I will, but I would truly appreciate it if you'd just walk your sassy ass in our home and—"

"You're delusional! *Our* home? Are you out of your—" I stop when he walks over and picks me up again.

"You kick my shit again, and you're getting your sexy little ass blistered," he warns. "Twice."

He sets me on my feet and closes the elevator

door. Then he walks over and opens a stainless steel freezer that sits next to the industrial refrigerator. He grabs a bag out and throws it on the counter. Then he unbuttons his pants, pushes them down, and kicks off his workboats and then his pants. He grabs the bag of peas, I think, and sneers as he shoves the peas down his boxer briefs,

"Have a seat, love." He walks past me, grabbing my hand and marching us to the white leather sectional. He sits and yanks my arm so I am sitting next to him as he leans back and groans.

"T—"

"How was your day, Ava?" He doesn't wait for me to answer. "Mine was fine, thank you. Two women from Sirius XM 140 came over and did an interview with me, promoting the upcoming tour. Then I offered to take them for drinks, and then, well, I don't have to tell you what happened next because you were actually there." He sits up and looks at me like I should apologize.

"You forgot the part where you had your arms around them, walking down the street, hoping to bring them back here after drinks and fuck them," I give a very weak and totally made up story as an excuse for my acting like a total psycho.

His eyes widen. "Is that what I was doing, or was I just being friendly with two women I have worked with a few times and have built a working relationship with?"

"Have you fucked them?"

It takes him a few too many seconds to answer, and I stand up.

"One. One of them a very long time ago, and she is married now."

I sit back down. "The tall bitch wants to get fucked by you, T. Is that the 'one' you fucked?"

The pause is telling, and I start to stand up again.

"Ava, don't make me chase you when my left nut is broken."

"Don't chase me. Stay and take care of your nut." I stand.

"I will ignore my battered nut to take care of the girl I'm nuts about," he says sweetly.

I look down at him, and he pats the couch.

"You crushed my nut, Ava Links."

I sit down and cross my arms over my chest, mumbling, "Sorry."

"You slapped me across the face two weeks ago, too."

I lift my chin in the air. "I'm not sorry about that."

"I'm not, either," he says, closing his eyes.

"Are you serious right now?"

"Dead serious. Jealousy is a bitch, aye?"

"Yes, and if we're going to do this, you better learn to keep it in check," I warn.

He laughs.

"What? It's not a joke."

He looks up at the ceiling and smirks. "It's healthy in a relationship."

"I'm not interested in a relationship where you chase me down the road like a madman."

"Oh, love, I am trying here, please stop." He laughs.

"Stop what?" I'm a bit pissed now.

"You came to me. For that, I could bow down and kiss those lovely feet ... again, so I should not bring up what just happened down there. But in the interest of keeping things real and honest, Ava, my sexy, confused"—he sits up and leans closer—"jealous, little woman—"

"I'm not jealous."

He looks in my eyes and smiles. "You can continue

this senseless debate, or you can kiss me. I've missed your sass, but I have missed those lips more."

I look down, embarrassed, ashamed … turned on.

"I missed yours, too."

He kisses me softly, unhurriedly, sweetly, and then sits back.

"Ava?"

"Thomas?"

"Next time you get angry at me, please think about how many times I've made you come before you batter my balls."

"Does it really hurt that badly?" I ask.

He gives me a look like I must be joking.

"I really want to know," I insist.

He smirks and adjusts the peas. "Let's say you jumped out of a car going a hundred and thirty kilometers, and your body skidded across the pavement before you rolled off a bridge then fell fifteen meters into a belly flop." He pauses and scratches his head. "Yeah, that's about what it feels like."

"I can make it up to you," I say before kissing his cheek then moving down his neck.

"Oh, Ava, this moment is one I have dreamed about; except, my balls weren't bruised and my dick wasn't frozen." He lifts my chin and kisses me.

Thirteen

Love will find you in the most unexpected moments. The one when you aren't searching for it.
— C. Puckett

I WAKE UP ON THE couch, finding it's dark outside. I can't believe we fell asleep. My head is on T's chest, his sweet smelling breath against my face. I inhale deeply, and then I do it again.

Bingo. Thomas smells like Bingo. He smells like home, and he smells like love. And at this moment, I don't trust myself to believe I am right, so I smell him again.

I look up when he moves to see he is looking down at me.

"What exactly are you doing?"

"You smell …" I pause, trying to figure out how to describe it to him without sounding like a complete and total lunatic. I look up again to see he looks mortified, and I can't help laughing when I realize he thinks I just insulted him. "You smell … wonderful. You smell good. I like the way you smell. I like it a lot."

He sits forward, which forces me to sit up. Then he pulls his shirt to his nose and sniffs.

"I forgot cologne. Do you prefer that—"

"No! God, no. I prefer whatever scent it is you are

putting off right now."

He nods. "Okay?"

"You smell like Bingo," I say, thinking it will make sense.

He lifts his shirt up and sniffs it again.

I smile. "Good, right?"

"Sure," he says.

My stomach growls as I lie back down on his chest, listening to his heart beating under my ear.

"Bingo smells like home."

"Should I be jealous of Bingo?" he asks, looking down at me.

I shake my head. "Bingo is a blanket that I've had since I was born. I threw a fit when I thought I lost it when we came back from a weekend in Jersey. Dad went crazy and tore the SUV apart and came in, waving it in the air, and said 'Bingo.' Ever since, my blanket has been Bingo."

"You've had the same blanket since birth?" He smiles, pushing a strand of hair behind my ear.

"So I've been told. They tried to trick me once when the silky trim started to fray and bought a Bingo replica. I knew immediately."

He chuckles. "I wish I knew you back then. I bet you were even sassier than when I met you."

"I wish I knew you then, too."

He looks past me and nods.

"What were you like?" I ask.

"I'm really not sure." he laughs uncomfortably, and I remember what Harper said.

I smile. "I bet you were the sweetest boy around."

His eyebrow creeps up. "I don't think that's the case."

"Well, I bet you were."

He takes in a breath and leans forward. "I'm hungry.

Are you?"

When I sit up so he can stand, he walks to the fridge and opens it.

"I have a little bit of everything. What would you like?"

"Are you going to cook for me, Thomas Hardy?" I ask, standing up and walking over next to him.

He presses his hand to his chest. "I would be honored to, Ava Links."

I walk in front of him and look in his fridge. "Wow, you don't have a little of everything; you have a lot of everything. Wow, do you eat this much food?"

He wraps his arms around my waist and rests his chin on my shoulder, pulling me tightly against him. "If I don't, I throw out the old and buy more."

The way he says it makes me stop myself from scolding him for being wasteful. I was raised in a house where two men prepped their meals on Sundays for the entire week.

"What's your favorite thing to eat?" I ask.

"Ava," he answers with a smile in his voice.

"Well, what can you and I cook together?"

"We can make a baby," he says, and I laugh. "Don't laugh. I bet you will be a wonderful mother someday." His voice is serious, causing me to look back at him. "I'm going to make babies with you someday. Lots and lots and lots of babies."

The thought that someone thinks I would be a good mother makes me smile. The thought that Thomas Hardy, sexy and sweet drummer for Burning Souls, wants to be my baby's daddy is freaking hot.

"Should we start with maybe a chicken salad?" I ask, leaning my cheek against his as I pull out what must be a ten-pound container of organic chicken breast.

I try to move, but he holds me more securely.

"I'm serious, Ava. Someday, I am going to marry you, and someday, we're going to raise a family."

"If you say so." I smile, still trying to dismiss the fact that I am stupidly giddy over the idea of him wanting that with me.

Girls have those dreams and fantasies. Boys don't.

"I'm not trying to start an argument or bring up the past, but neither of them gave you those things, and it would be my honor to do so."

"Well, you are steps ahead already." I giggle. "Liam and I used each other to rid ourselves of our virginity in eleventh grade. There was nothing romantic about it."

"You gave away your virginity just for the sake of ridding yourself of it?" He snickers.

"Sure did," I admit.

Finally, he lets go, and I walk to the island and put the chicken down. Then I walk over to the electric range and turn it to three hundred and fifty degrees.

"Let's hear how you lost yours."

"You sure you really want to hear it?" he asks.

"Of course I do." I smile.

"I was hungry, and I fucked a woman, hoping she would feed me."

I laugh and roll my eyes, thinking he is joking. "Is that so?"

"Yes, it is."

I look over at him, seeing he's trying to gauge my reaction.

"How old were you?" I ask, straightening myself.

"Fifteen."

"How old was she?"

"Older than I was," he answers, still trying to read me.

"How much older?" I pry.

"If I had to guess, I would say at least fifteen years

older."

"Cool," I say, trying to act like it's not a big deal or that it doesn't make me sick that he was hungry or someone took advantage of him like that.

He walks over and lifts my chin. "Is it cool?"

I shake my head.

"Does it disgust you?"

"She disgusts me." I shake my head again. "Not you."

"What else do you want to know?" He pulls up a stool and sits with his legs spread before pulling me between them.

"Only what you want to tell me. I won't pry."

"I stabbed her husband when he came after me," he admits. "Does that disgust you?"

I shake my head. "Was it to protect yourself?"

He nods, looking down. "I slept in the streets for most of my life. Does that dis—"

I again shake my head.

"I've fucked for money and food and let people fuck me for a place to stay warm and a meal. Does that—"

"No," I tell him, narrowing my eyes.

"I've begged on street corners, delivered shit that I have no idea what it was for money. I have done some horrible fucking things for food and shelter, Ava. Does that—"

"No. Nothing you had to do to survive will ever disgust me." I grip his knees to steady my hand.

"You're trembling. Is it pity? Because I don't want pity."

"It's sadness and anger, not pity."

"Good, because I am a better man than that. I just didn't know it then."

"I know that."

"And that's all that matters."

"When I googled your name, nothing about you outside of the band came up, so you couldn't have done anything that awful."

"Do you know Surge and the men who work for Maddox and what they are capable of?" He smiles. "Arrest records can be erased, Ava. Names can be changed, past mistakes wiped clean."

"Are you trying to scare me?"

"No." He shakes his head. "I'm trying to put it all out there. I trust you implicitly, Ava. Do you trust me?"

I nod.

"I've let men suck my dick. I've let them watch me fuck their wives."

I look at him, half-expecting him to be joking.

"How do you feel right now?" he asks.

"Would it be awful if I said intrigued and slightly …" I pause and close my eyes.

"Christ, tell me you're not turned on by that."

I open my eyes. "No, but it piqued my curiosity."

He scowls. "I won't let any man fuck you, and I certainly wouldn't watch one fuck you."

"I wouldn't want that."

"I want to know that you are one hundred percent done with Luke Lane."

"T, I don't want to talk about it." I'm shocked that, after everything I've said and done, it's not clear to him. "What I want to talk about is that I am here because I am and have always been very attracted to you. I am here because you make me feel good when you're not being an ass. I am here because, if what you said at my apartment is true, I want it. But I am also afraid. I'm afraid that you won't be able to look past Liam and—"

"You've explained Liam. I'm fine with Liam. Liam didn't break your heart. I want to know what Luke did to hurt you and why I should let him breathe for damaging something I am going to fix and cherish, because I am the luckiest man alive to be given an opportunity to be with someone who loves as fiercely as you."

"I'm not saying names." I shake my head. "I'm not."

"Fine. Then tell me about the person"—he pauses—"who broke your heart."

The oven buzzes, telling me it's up to temperature.

"Where are your baking pans?"

He stands up and grabs one.

"Do you have more?" I ask.

"Are you hungry, Ava?"

"Yes, and this chicken needs to be cooked before it goes bad. Then it can be frozen, and you don't have to throw it away."

"Are you avoiding?"

"No." I look at him and shake my head. "The person who shattered my heart is me."

He looks confused, as well he should be.

Love is confusing.

Fourteen

Love comes in seasons and for reasons.
— T. Gonzalez

I TELL HIM THE STORY of a little girl loving the little boy and twisting fate. I tell him that story through tears and shame and guilt. I tell him everything except his name, knowing he knows the little boy is Luke. I cannot break my promise to Luke Lane, even after he broke my heart.

Thomas goes through several different emotions—anger, sadness, jealousy—and at one point, he walks away and goes out onto the balcony.

I don't get angry at his reaction. I don't get upset because he walks away. How could I? He feels it. He feels my pain, and I am sure he is just as confused by it all as I am.

The oven timer goes off, and I get up from the couch and take the chicken out. Then I dig through his cupboards because they aren't set up like they should be; there is no flow to his kitchen.

As the chicken is cooling and T is outside doing the same, I start moving things to where they should be. Baking dishes beside the oven, glasses above the sink, and when I am about to move the silverware, he walks in and stands on the opposite side of the island, looking at me.

"Sorry I moved stuff."

His eyes are locked on mine, his eyebrows turned in, and his jaw is set. I have to look away.

"I probably should have asked."

"Why didn't you?"

His reaction catches me off guard, and I look up at him. "I guess I didn't want to have to ask you where things are. I know it's stupid. I'm sorry."

He lets out a deep breath, and his features soften. "I'm fine with it. Better than fine if it means you're making yourself more comfortable here in our home."

"Your home," I whisper, looking down.

"Ava, you won't be with him again."

I shake my head.

"And you want to be with me? You want to be here?"

I nod.

"Then move anything you want." He walks around the island then lifts me up until I am eye level with him. "You allowed your heart to be broken by someone undeserving."

I feel my bottom lip quiver as he sets me down on the island.

"You tried to love someone enough for two people, and it didn't work."

"I know."

"I love you enough for a million lifetimes, but I am not stupid enough to believe I can make it work if you are unable or unwilling."

"I was stupid." I look down and begin wringing my hands.

"No, Ava, you learned of heartbreak later in life. I learned it at a young age."

I sigh and put my hands on his hips, glancing up.

"You ready to live, to love, to be loved."

I nod, and he smiles.

"Good, because we deserve that. You and I deserve—"

He stops when I pull his hips closer, wrap my legs around his waist, reach up, and grab the back of his head then whisper, "I'm gonna love you so hard."

He reaches under me and lifts me by my butt before kissing me. "I can't wait, my goddess." Then he pushes up my skirt and strokes my silky panties, "You're wet."

"You make me that way," I tell him, and he moves my panties to the side then shoves two fingers in me. I gasp.

"Fuck, Ava." He pulls his boxers down and rubs his head against me before pushing inside just enough that I am already done. Totally done.

"Yes," I cry into his shoulder.

"Love you, Ava, so hard." He thrusts in fully, and I fall apart. "Christ," he hisses as he pushes me back against the counter. "Lie back."

"Here? But the chicken—"

"Fuck the chicken. I want your pussy." He pushes the baking sheet to the ground.

"T!"

He pulls out of me then bends down to kiss my waist, my hips, my belly button, my … everything.

"Yes," I cry. "God, yes."

After I have come, he stands up and thrusts into me fully.

"Condom!" I cry.

"No, Ava."

"But, what if—"

"That's the plan."

"T, it's too soon." My words come out broken and breathless.

He stills. "How do you measure forever?"

I don't say a word, not one. I am at a complete loss.

"Tell me yes, Ava," he says as he thrusts slowly in and out of me.

My head nods yes, my heart beats yes, and my body screams yes.

"It'll be a wonderful life, Ava," he groans as he rolls his hips, buried deep inside of me.

"Yes," I gasp. "Wonderful."

§

I am standing in his bathroom, looking in the mirror and smiling like a fool, wrapped in a towel after a shower with Thomas.

My heart is full. I am exhausted, and not from heartbreak, not insecurity, not pain. I am exhausted from the most amazing feelings I have in my head and heart. I am exhausted from him and me and us and no one else.

I watch as he walks out of the shower gloriously naked, beautifully naked. God, I like naked.

"What are you thinking?" he asks, wrapping his arms around me from behind.

I smile. "I like you naked."

"Perfect, because I think we stay in this weekend, order out, and never get dressed. Sleep, eat, explore, make love, and talk." He spins me around then holds my face in his hands. "God, Ava, I never wanted anything like this before. Never thought there was anything as good as women literally falling at my feet, having a full stomach, and never having to worry about where I would sleep. I was … happy. Over the fucking moon happy."

I meet his eyes in the mirror and feel love for him, a love I don't understand.

"Why do you look sad?" he asks with his lips at my ear.

"I don't want to rush this, but I don't want it to ever end."

He hugs me tight. "We're never going to end."

"Promise?"

"I promise that our love will never get old or tired. It will never die. I promise, Ava. I promise you forever."

§

We're sitting on the living room floor, me still in a towel, him in nothing, eating pizza.

My phone alarm goes off, and I look at it. It's an alarm I set to take my birth control pill.

"Everything all right?" he asks.

"Yeah, but ..." I stop and laugh.

He smiles. "What is it?"

"It's a reminder to take my pill, but—"

"Birth control?"

I nod.

"Well, then delete that alarm. You no longer need it."

"In the heat of the moment, it was a wonderful idea to say yes. In reality, I think we should—"

"No planning. No thinking. No going back. We move forward and enjoy our lives. And no damn pill."

"Shouldn't we discuss our goals and dreams and future plans?"

He nods curtly. "Goals obtained. Dream came true." He squeezes my knee. "My future is yours, and yours is mine."

I smile, and he smiles back.

"It's not that easy."

"It is if you let it be," he counters.

"Let's pretend I get pregnant."

He grins. "Yes, let's."

"I want my children—"

"*Our* children."

"*Our* children," I agree. "I want them to be raised knowing everyone at home. I want my dad to coach their football team, and I want Piper to be her best friend. I want her and him to be as happy as I was."

T nods. "I want our children to be raised by two parents who love each other madly. I want them to never wonder what love is. I want them to be full of life, and love, and"—he smiles and lifts a slice of pizza up to my mouth—"pizza."

I take the bite he is offering and nod as I chew. "We could show them that anywhere," I say after I swallow.

He leans back against the couch. "I bought this place a year ago. When I bought it, I imagined you and I and four kids. I imagined us sharing with them the city culture and the love in our home."

"I love it here."

"We can visit your home anytime you want, but this is our home, Ava. This is a place where no one can tell us how to live or how to love. No one can judge us or push themselves between us."

"Thomas, if we are meant to be, no one will ever come between us."

His brows turn in and he looks unsure. I don't want him to feel that way.

"I want to be with you. It doesn't matter where we end up," I tell him.

"We'll be stronger here."

I set down my pizza and climb onto his lap, straddling him. "By the time we have kids, I think we'll know that we can be strong anywhere."

He looks up at me, placing his hands on my hips. "I want you all to myself."

I feel my smile spread from the inside out. "Good."

We spend the weekend in bed, and when Sunday night rolls around, I tell him I need to go home. He tells me I am home. I tell him I have work. He tells me I need to consider quitting.

I laugh. "That's absurd."

He doesn't laugh. He looks at me, deadpan. Immediately, I feel angry.

"Don't."

"Don't what, Ava?" he asks as he walks to the sink and gets a glass of water.

"Don't shut down."

He drinks down his water then sets the glass beside the sink. "I want you here."

"I want to be here, too, but I have to work."

"No, you don't have to work." He turns around and crosses his arms over his chest. "I make enough money to support us very comfortably."

"I went to school to become a lawyer and busted my ass for seven years to do so."

"I'll hire you." He shrugs as if it's no big deal.

"You may have a fight with my father about that. He's tried the same thing for years. I went through school on my own. I have a job that I got on my own."

"Well, I'll have whatever discussion I need to with your father," he says in a very arrogant manner.

"I'd like it if you'd allow my father to get to know you and like you. He's not your enemy."

"Does he know that?"

"T, I'm his daughter. When you have kids, you'll most definitely be as protective of them as he is of me."

"Is he protective, Ava? Does he know about Luke Lane...Liam?"

I walk toward the bedroom and start putting on my

clothes. He doesn't take the hint; he follows me.

"Does he know that he fucked up as your protector by allowing you to get fucked by him? He did a pretty shitty job, Ava."

"Fuck you," I tell him, pulling on my skirt.

He gasps. "Excuse me?"

"Fuck. You," I say more slowly.

"Tell me I'm wrong?"

"You are *so* wrong."

The bitch in me is dying to come out. She is ready to say hurtful, awful things to him and somehow, this … filter … or something is stopping me.

"You aren't leaving," he snaps at me from behind.

"I had a lovely weekend. Best one in forever. Have a great night, T."

He stands in front of the elevator, angry, pissed, brutish, and Lord help me, sexy.

"You walking me out?"

It takes him a moment of searching my eyes to see I am not changing my mind. "I'll try to be nice to your father, even though he obviously hates me and doesn't want us together."

"He loves me, T. He'll be fine." I hold my head up high.

"Don't leave."

"I have to," I say with a put-on smile.

He doesn't say a word to me after that, not until the next morning when he sends the sweetest text.

What time do you leave for work, beautiful?

I smile bigger after reading it.

Twenty minutes.

Have a wonderful day.

You, too.

When I walk outside to hail a cab, there is a black SUV sitting at the curb. A blonde-haired woman in driver attire gets out and opens the door.

"Miss Links, Thomas would like to offer you a ride to work."

I climb in, expecting him to be inside. Instead, there is a hot cup of coffee, a bag of pastries, and a big smiling sun balloon.

I grab my phone and take a selfie of me with the balloon and a crepe, blowing him a kiss. Then I type, **"Better than flowers,"** and hit send.

A reply comes seconds later.

Morning wood has nothing over Ava wood.

Funny, you should send me a pic.

And he does.

I WAS KIDDING! I send back, laughing.

I wasn't. What time do you get out of work?

Five.

I would love to take you on a date.

Will it end with a make-out session at my door?

It will end up with my face between your thighs.

Okay, he has me. I flop back against the soft leather seat and commence swooning as I message him back.

See you at 5.

Fifteen

Love is not easy. But is definitely worth the effort.
— K. Murdico-Marshall

One week later

I NEVER CALL IN SICK, ever. Today, though, I can't get up without feeling dizzy. I think the late nights with Thomas, which have been every night this week, have caused my exhaustion. If that's not the reason, I think I'm dying.

I hit snooze on my phone's alarm. Ten more minutes and I may be all right.

I feel my bed buckle, and it causes me to shift. That shift causes me to move, moving plays hell on me, and I fly up, covering my mouth as I run to the bathroom where I throw up over, and over and over again.

"Ava," T says, pulling my hair back as I lay my head against the sink, waiting for the next wave of nausea to hit.

"You should leave," I say and then throw up again.

He hands me a wet cloth. "Never."

"You'll get sick, T. You have a show in two weeks. Go," I tell him as my legs begin to tremble.

"Shh." He turns on the water and cups some into his

hand before he holds it in front of my mouth. "Drink."

"Uh-uh," I groan.

He leaves the bathroom then, and I am thankful that he isn't here to see me. That is, until he swoops me up and carries me to my bed.

"Thomas, no," I say as he lays me down. "I am going to get sick again."

"Then you'll do it in the pot. Rest, Ava."

"I need to go to work." I try to sit up.

He grabs my phone and hands it to me.

I can't even talk, so I send a message to Sandra, one of the partners.

"Can we get you into the SUV and take you home?" he asks.

I shoot him a nasty look and roll to my side.

"All right, then," he says.

"Go home. I'm going to sleep."

I hear the door shut and close my eyes.

§

I **WAKE TO SOFT MUSIC** and a smell that makes me hate food.

I open my eyes to see T walking into my room with a bag in one hand and a bowl in the other.

"Soup for my goddess," he announces, sitting down beside me.

"Sorry I was short earlier," I tell him, sitting up.

"You are short." He laughs.

"You should stick with the drums," I shoot back, making him laugh.

"Eat." He hands me the bowl and then reaches into the bag, pulling out a thermometer then dragging it across my forehead to my temple. "Ninety-eight point five. Perfectly normal."

"Good," I say then sip the soup.

He pulls out a bottle of ginger ale, and then he smiles and pulls out a pregnancy test.

I nearly choke and then laugh, setting the soup down and lying back.

"It's worth a try, right?"

"It's a bit early."

He looks down.

"T, it's sweet."

"Will you pacify me?" he asks, peeking up at me. It's adorable.

"No." I laugh.

"Please? I made you soup." He pushes his bottom lip out and pouts.

"You made this?" I ask. "It's wonderful."

"I put it in the microwave." He smirks. "Good enough?"

I stand up and kiss his pouty lip. "I'll be right back."

I make my way to the bathroom, and when I try to shut the door behind me, T says, "Ava, amuse me."

"Fine," I relent, knowing if I don't pee on the stick, he may come in and hold the damn thing between my legs.

When I'm finished, I set the stick on the back of the toilet. When I stand, I feel well enough to shower, so I get in the shower and wash my hair and body quickly. Then, when I step out of the shower, I grab a robe and put my hair up in a towel.

Standing in front of the mirror, I brush my teeth and see the reflection of the stupid pregnancy test. I walk over and grab it, and when I see the plus sign, I am overrun with emotions.

No way, I think. I just stopped taking the damn pill. No way.

"Ava." The door begins to open, and something makes me throw the stick in the garbage.

"Hey." I smile. "I thought I would take a quick shower."

He looks at the counter and then at me. "Did you pee on the stick?"

"No, I couldn't. Stage fright, I guess." I walk toward him, turning off the light.

"You need to drink more; you'll get dehydrated."

"I will, but I would really love to lie down and for you to wrap your arms around me. I think I'll get better faster that way."

He smiles. "Anything you want."

"Promise?"

"Yes, Ava, I promise."

I lie in his arms. He is warm and strong, and he loves me.

I close my eyes and allow the thoughts I have been pushing back to flood me.

There is no way that a test would show in this short of time. There is no way I could be pregnant. There is no fucking way. My head is spinning, and I silently sob. Thomas tightens his hold on me.

"If you feel up to it tomorrow, I was thinking about taking you on another date," he says then kisses the back of my head.

"That sounds nice." I roll to my back and look at him. "T?"

"Yes?" he says as he strokes my cheek with his thumb.

"I think you'll get more sleep at your place, and I think I really need a good night's sleep."

He cocks his head to the side. "I'm not leaving you tonight."

"T, please?" I ask, fisting his shirt in my hands and pulling him closer. "Please."

He nods. "If that's what you want, when you fall

asleep, I'll take your temperature once more, and if you aren't feverish, then I'll leave."

"Thank you. Thank you so much." I bury my nose in his shirt, needing to smell him and love and happiness. I need it so badly right now.

"You all right?" he asks, pulling me more firmly against him.

I nod because, if I open my mouth, I'm going to cry again. I haven't cried in a full week. I have had no reason to. I have been loved. But soon, I will be alone.

§

I WAKE UP TO FIND the bed is empty. He's gone.

I sit up and grab my phone. I google pregnancy cycles and due date calendars and conception guesstimeter.

My period ended twelve days before Christmas. I was late, and I didn't even realize it. The likelihood of me getting pregnant this past week is not good. I try to convince myself that fate couldn't be that cruel, but it was. It was, and she hates me.

I throw my phone across the room and sob into my knees. I need a tissue because the cry is that ugly, so I get up and walk to the bathroom where I blow my nose before heading to the kitchen to get a drink.

"Why did you lie to me, Ava?"

I jump when I hear T's voice and quickly turn on a light switch, hoping I am imagining that he is here. I'm not.

He stands up and walks toward me, his fists balled at his sides. "Why?"

I shake my head.

"When is the last time you fucked Luke Lane?"

"T, I …" I shrug.

"Did you fuck him after I fucked you?" He steps

towards me and stops.

"No! Of course not!"

His shoulders relax a bit, and I reach out to grab him. I want him to hold me. I want him to touch me. I want him to tell me he loves me. But he steps back and crosses his arms in front of himself.

"When?" he asks. "And I don't want any more lies, Ava."

"I love you. I. Love. You. And it doesn't matter, T. It doesn't matter, okay?"

I expect him to be happy I told him I love him, but he looks disgusted.

"You think it's his child," he accuses.

I shake my head. "No. No. No."

"Did you sleep with him when you were home for Christmas?"

I cover my face with my hands, hiding from the harsh reality of the truth. "I didn't sleep with him after you, T. I love you."

"Did you fuck him when you were home before you and I fucked?"

"We didn't fuck, T. Stop saying that! You and I made love, and we made a baby, and you love me, and I love you, and we should be happy. We should be—" I try to grab him, but he steps back again. "T, please."

It's an awful time to find words for all the feelings I have for him, but there it is. I love him. I love him so much. It is too much pressure, too much for him to deal with, and I know it because it's too much for me. But he has to be the father. He has to.

"I cannot believe you," he says as he walks toward the door.

"I do! I love you. Thomas, please don't say anything to anyone until I figure out what I am going to do. Please."

He slams the door behind him.

"Oh, God, what have I done!" I scream. "What have I done!"

§

I SPEND THE WEEKEND IN bed alone. I don't bother getting my phone fixed after its run-in with the wall, but I know he hasn't called because my phone is linked to my computer.

I haven't showered, and I haven't eaten anything besides saltines and yogurt. I have vitamins and folic acid delivered to me in one of my many moments that I don't give a damn if I do this alone; I'm going to do it, and I am going to do it well.

Those moments are good ones. Others, not so good.

I made my bed, so I will lie in it.

When Dad calls, I talk to him through my computer and let him know my phone broke. He makes me promise to get a new one. I tell him I will tomorrow, that I'm getting a new one delivered.

Mom doesn't call, but I message her, telling her I think I have the flu and ask that we skip this week's dinner. I get an automatic reply.

On Monday morning, I drink ginger tea, which settles my stomach. Then I wolf down half a dozen saltines and feel better.

When I walk outside, the SUV is there, and the driver, whom I now know is Casey, opens the door.

I am hopeful he is inside until I peek in and see he's not.

I step back and look at Casey. "I'm going to walk today, but thank you so much."

"It's ten degrees outside, Miss Links."

"I could use the fresh air," I tell her then start walking

the five blocks in the bitter cold to work.

When I arrive at work, everyone is gathered in the conference room. I slide in and take a seat, pulling out a notebook, and then listen to them delegate case work to all of us newbies.

I end up on a case a woman is bringing against a large pharmaceutical company whose drug should not have been approved for pregnant women. As luck would have it, I am asked to do some field work that will take me to Lake Placid, NY. I am to interview five women who miscarried after taking the same medication.

I bury myself in my prep work, and by the end of the day, I am exhausted, but at least work has kept me preoccupied. It also gave me insight into what is safe and not safe during pregnancy.

At lunchtime, I made a list of books I want to buy at the Barnes and Noble after work. There are so many, and I want them all.

Every time my mind goes to T or Luke, I block it. I hide in my own little book-filled world of planning and preparation like I did for seven years. These next nine months are not going to be a problem.

As I ride the elevator down to leave work, I am lost in my head, thinking about all things baby.

I am going to be fine. I am going to be a mom. I am going to ... move to east bum-fuck Egypt so I don't have to face anyone, so I can enjoy this baby who ... I have no idea who the father is.

When I walk out, the SUV is there, and Casey is opening the door. I'm pulling my hood up and starting to decline the ride when T gets out.

"Ava, please get in the vehicle."

I shake my head, walking faster.

I can't deal with this right now. As much as I want

him, I need to allow myself to realize that I will be doing this alone.

I hear the door slam, and then I feel him take my hand. I don't pull away, but I don't look at him, either. I just walk as the snow falls down in large, puffy flakes.

T pulls my hand toward a vending cart and orders two hot chocolates, one with whipped cream, one without. He hands me the one with, and I tell him, "Thank you."

We walk a little farther before he asks, "Have you eaten today?"

"Yes."

He feels obligated, pities me.

He doesn't say anything for a moment, and then we stop at a crosswalk where he stands in front of me and looks down at me.

Before he says anything, I tell him, "Please don't say a word. I've had a good day, T. Please don't make me cry."

He looks crushed as he leans down and whispers, "You look beautiful, my goddess."

I shake my head, and he nods his.

Hope is seeping in, and I want it to go away.

"T ..." I nod to the crosswalk as people pass us by to cross the street.

"Do you love me, Ava?"

I nod, unable to speak while my body shakes as I try not to cry.

"How lucky am I to be loved by you?"

I don't know what to say or how to react. Why is he saying this when he was so angry with me before?

He grabs my face and kisses me. His kiss is full of sorrys and hope and love.

I reach up and fist his hair, kissing him back and giving him the same.

"I love you, T. I love you, and this baby is ours. Mine and yours and love's," I say, revealing the hope I have in my heart, making me vulnerable.

He kisses me softly, which is exactly the kind of kiss I need. It's confirmation that those feelings he has are real.

The SUV pulls up to the curb, and we walk to it, hand in hand.

"Home, please," he tells Casey.

§

SLOWLY, OVER THE NEXT THREE days, my belongings start to show up at his place where I go every day after work and sleep while he holds me. I know he is doing this slowly to avoid overwhelming me. I see it and feel it, but that fear caused by doubting those feelings has betrayed me before. It makes me wonder if he really wants this.

We don't talk a lot about us or the baby or anything at all. It's depressing, it's painful, and it's the truth about our truth, his and mine.

Love hurts.

There isn't a doubt in my mind that I love him. I do. But it hurts to see him hurt, knowing I have caused his pain, knowing if fate thinks I deserve more pain and this child is not his, then his happiness will be destroyed by me.

When I get into the SUV on Thursday, I hand him a printout of my itinerary for my trip next week.

His lips form a line, and he gives a quick nod. "I have a show this weekend. I want you to come."

"I really don't feel up to it."

"I thought you'd say that." He leans back, setting my itinerary between us on the seat as he looks out the window away from me.

I know he doesn't want me to work, but I want to, and now I need to be sure I can support myself. I don't want to burden him with my doubt. I won't.

I lean back and look out the opposite window. "I have brunch with my mother on Sunday."

"That's nice, Ava," he says in a way that I know he's only placating me.

§

ON FRIDAY NIGHT, HE DOESN'T come to pick me up with Casey.

"Thomas left for the airport an hour ago. Where would you like me to take you?"

"His place," I say quickly. "Or did he say I should go home?'

She smiles. "He said to take you wherever you wanted to go."

"Then, if you don't mind—"

"I'm at your beck and call, Ava. Wherever you want to go..."

"To my place for a couple hours and then, if you're available, his."

"Of course," she says and closes the door behind me.

Sixteen

Love doesn't see color or race or gender. Love is blind and will be there when you least expect it.
— T. Greseth

"HEY, DADDY." I WAVE AT him through Skype.

He sighs. "Ava, how are you?"

"Is everything okay?" I smile nice and brightly.

"I was going to ask you the same thing."

Tessa leans down and waves. "Hello, Ava."

I wave back, smiling. "Hi!" Then I ask Dad, "What's wrong?" because it's obvious something is not okay. "Is everyone okay?"

He nods, and Tessa peeks back on the screen. "He's following T's Instagram account."

"Tessa," he growls.

"Open lines of communication, Lucas," she says before giving him a loud kiss on the top of the head.

"He's a nice guy, Dad. I promise."

I love my dad, but the fact that this surprises him after the holidays shocks me.

"Are you living with him?" he asks, trying to keep calm, but when his mouth snaps shut and his jaw muscles flex, I know he is anything except calm.

"We're together."

"*Living* together?"

I hold up my phone and show him around my apartment. "I'm still a resident of 6th Ave."

"Ava ..." he warns.

"I stay with him sometimes, and sometimes, he stays here. And then sometimes, I stay here and he stays there, and—"

"Every night, I see my baby girl sleeping in a bed I know I didn't buy. Every morning, I see her sleeping in that same bed."

"I told you I stay with him sometimes."

"I see my little girl standing at the sink with a man's shirt on," he says between his teeth.

"Well, at least I'm not naked," I joke.

Tessa laughs in the background, and Dad ... Well, he doesn't laugh.

"Are you living with him?"

I take a deep breath and smile. "Not yet."

He leans into the camera. "What the hell do you mean—"

"Lucas, chill," Tessa says as I hear cupboard doors shut.

"I love him, Dad, and he has loved me for years. If he asks me to move in, I will."

"Ava, I don't think it's a good idea."

"Of course you don't. You're my dad." I smile at him. "I love you for it, too. When I have kids, Dad, I will be the same way, but I am twenty-five years old. I found a boy who loves me and didn't trample into my life until I had finished school."

"Is he trampling? So help me God, if he is trampling, I will—"

I reach out and touch the screen. "I wish you could see how he treats me. He loves me, Dad, and I love him."

"How do you know it's love, Ava? How do you—"

"He smells like Bingo."

His mouth drops open and then snaps shut.

"Like love and home and hope."

"Are you on drugs?" he asks.

"Yes, we do meth together, and it makes our sex life so much hotter," I say, smiling. Tessa snorts in the background. "No, Dad, I'm not on drugs. I'm on love."

"I need a lawyer," he says. "You need to come home. It smells like home at home, Ava."

"I'll come home when you sue your fuck-stick father," I tell him.

"Ava." He shakes his head disapprovingly.

"I'm happy, Dad. He's caring and kind. Hell, he sends a car to take me to work and pick me up from work every day."

"I'll send a damn fleet," he says.

"Daddy?"

"Ava?"

"I love you more."

He nods. "You bet your ass you do."

"Okay, I need to get going," I tell him.

"He there?"

"No, he has a show this weekend. But you knew that."

"We're going," Tessa says in the background.

Oh, shit.

Dad looks at me, and I look back at him. A smirk starts to form on his face.

"Tessa," I call out, which is the equivalent of going above his head. It pisses him off.

"Yes?" she replies, walking back to the camera.

"Can you make sure he behaves?"

Dad smirks now. He doesn't even try to hold it back.

"I have a lot of prep to do for next week, so don't make me get on a plane, Dad." I point at him.

"If he loves you, he will deal with me." He nods. "Love you, baby girl."

"Love you, Dad," I say, giving him the evil eye.

He laughs and disconnects the call.

§

I LOOK AT MY PHONE and click on the IG app I haven't used in...forever. I search out Thomas Hardy, finding him under @Drums4life.

I scroll through his recent posts. The day after Christmas, he posted a picture of my boots from behind me, and I can safely assume it's when I was walking down the road after dropping him off at the Stadler in Ithaca. The caption reads: **If I could turn those feet around, I would, and she would be walking back to me.**

There are several hundred comments and thousands of hearts representing likes.

They range from, *Let her go* to *nice boots* to *fuck her. There are a million boots just like those."*

The next few posts are of places in London. He was there for two days. Just two days.

A reminder that you are what you came from.

The responses to those are favorable.

Welcome home.

Don't ever change.

Keep banging those drums.

We love you!

This is your home. We are your people.

I know the sadness in that statement. It is heartbreaking.

The next picture is in his loft, and I am standing at the sink. My feet are bare and so am I, but the picture doesn't show that.

The caption: *I am the luckiest man alive. Her feet*

are planted where they belong. Home.

I see a comment from @PsMomHarper.

So happy for you, T. P is, too <3

His response to that one is, *She knew it all along.*

The next several are the ones Dad spoke of...in bed.

It was love at first rub.

Her toes intrigue me.

Nothing more beautiful.

My heart is forever hers.

Sole to Soul.

She loves me.

One response asks, *Is she so ugly you can't show her face?*

His reply to that is, *Her beauty is blinding. I'm not ready to share her. I may never be. She is mine, and I am hers.*

The last picture of me is from last night.

I know I have to leave her. I don't know how.

An hour ago, he posted a picture of a bar.

Meet and Greet tonight. Who's down?

The responses are all *I choose DRUMS!* and, *Why no more backstage Meet and Greets?*

Bitches!

§

I WALK OUTSIDE, AND CASEY gets out of the SUV and walks around to open the door.

"Where to?" she asks.

"Home."

At Thomas's place, I walk into the old warehouse building and close the cargo door before riding up the three floors to the top.

When I open the door to the loft, I feel the day's tension soften as I breathe in...him. This place may not be home. However, every night I spend here, every time I lie in his arms, every morning I wake up to a cup of ginger tea and a piece of toast, every time he says, "Thank you, Ava," in his deep, sensual British accent when I do something as simple as hand him a glass of water, and every time he says "I love you," it becomes more so.

My childhood home is warm and inviting. Its walls are perfect. The carpet and hardwood floors are faultless and pristine. Nothing was ever out of place or out of reach. The pictures showed the story of my life and love and happiness. Outside are ten acres of yard and woods and flowers and gardens. A place I played and lived and was loved and never ever felt like life would be anything but perfect.

The walls here are mostly exposed brick, the floors all appear to be original hardwood, and the ceilings are beams and pipes. The open living space seems even more open due the size of the windows that give you a welcoming view of the balcony that overlooks the East River.

The master suite has walk-in closets bigger than the one at my apartment, and yes, bigger than my childhood bedroom. The bedroom spills out onto a private patio that allows you to watch the dawn break over the horizon. The second and third bedrooms are modern and roomy. One has a built-in bookshelf that I can imagine being filled with fairytales and children's books that we could read to our children … until I realize there is, in fact, a child involved. Then the dream is no longer sweet or one that you can't wait for a quiet moment to imagine.

I walk out onto the private patio where there are flower boxes scattered about and hug myself. Then I sit on the bench built under the wooden arbor.

I pull my feet up, hug my knees, lean back, and look

at the sky as snow falls down softly. Closing my eyes, I imagine that spring is here as tears fall. I can picture it perfectly.

A girl who had wasted her youth dreaming of a life full of love and happiness, a love more beautiful than she ever saw in a movie or read about in a book, and a boy who never dared dream because his reality wouldn't allow it. Both broken, both unloved until they found each other. And in each other, they found a love that was even more beautiful than her most vivid dreams.

It's beautiful. They are beautiful and happy and in love.

I picture T and myself planting flowers and watching them bloom and them growing as the baby grows inside me. I picture us happy. So happy.

The pain in my chest causes me to press my hand against it. It hurts to think I could have had it all if only love wasn't so complicated … if only there were no possibility of Luke being the father of this child.

When I become too cold to sit outside any longer, I walk in, close the door behind me, kick off my boots, take off my coat, and climb in his bed, allowing myself the luxury of smelling him on his pillow before falling fast asleep.

I wake up to a loud, rumbling sound, and it's dark out. The rumbling is my belly.

I sit up and notice my feet hanging out from under the covers. I take my phone off the base on the nightstand and take a picture. Even though he hasn't texted me, I send him the picture. I want him to know I have seen the posts. I want him to know I think about him, too. I want to know he's not with someone else. Deep down, I know he's not, but I can't stand even the thought of it.

Two minutes later, I'm standing in front of his refrigerator when my phone rings.

"Hello."

"Ava," he says with a smile and not a sigh.

"T, how's your trip?"

"I miss you." He sounds as torn as I feel. I want to hear a smile in his voice.

"Me or my feet?"

He snickers, and I laugh in response.

"You've seen, then?" he asks.

"Your ode to my feet on social media? I hadn't until my father pointed it out to me today." I can't help laughing.

"So he's a fan?" he asks, and I can imagine him smiling.

"Something like that."

"You're home?"

"I'm ..." I pause and look around. "Yeah."

"How are you feeling?"

"Hungry," I say, opening drawers in his refrigerator.

"There should be plenty of fresh food in the icebox, and I filled the cupboard with those crackers you like."

"There is, but there's no chocolate, and right now, I want a Snickers bar so damn badly I may go out and get one ... or twenty."

"I'll have them delivered," he practically rushes to say.

"No, I'll be fine until tomorrow." I continue to search for something that looks good, asking, "How was your meet and great?"

"It went well," he says sweetly, but I think I hear longing in his voice, and I hope it's for me.

"So, you aren't doing backstage meet and greets anymore?"

"Yes, of course. VIP ticket holders."

I immediately feel jealous and decide I have no right to feel that way. Not really, anyway.

"Well, I hope you have fun."

"I will." He uses the same clipped tone I did.

"T ...?"

"Yes?"

I don't want to talk and to feel jealous. I want to sleep.

I shut the refrigerator. "Good night."

"Did you eat?" he asks.

"I will."

"I can stay on the phone," he offers.

"That's okay. I'm sure you're busy."

"No, not really."

I sense his annoyance and wonder what he's thinking. If he's thinking that he would be busy if he didn't have to deal with my mess. Or maybe he's just waiting for me to let him off the hook.

"I'll just talk to you later, okay?"

He doesn't answer, so I hang up. Then I get a message.

I love you, Ava.

Seventeen

Love is not always easy and it's not always kind, but it's always worth it.
— Ivy Love

I WOULD LIKE TO THINK I couldn't sleep because I had taken a five-hour nap, but it wouldn't be true. I have been sleeping nearly twelve hours a day since last weekend. Even before I found out I was … pregnant.

I grab my phone and look at Instagram. He posted the picture I sent him of my feet.

She sent me this. What am I going to do with her?

I want to post: Tell her you don't want her; she'll get the hint. Tell her, see you in nine months when she knows whose kid's growing inside her. But what I want the most is for him to post that he loves me and still will regardless. However, I know that is probably the biggest fairytale lie I have ever told myself. As he said, he doesn't know what to do with me. It's there in black and white.

Three more weeks before a doctor even wants to see me to do bloodwork to confirm my pregnancy. I know I am. I took two more tests, both positive. Then I googled paternity tests during pregnancy, and the two that popped up were amniocenteses and Chorionic Villus Sampling. Both tests are invasive and can cause a miscarriage. I hold my hand protectively over my stomach. The path of putting my child at risk is not one I want to take.

Then I see one that is a simple blood test that can be done at eight weeks for two thousand dollars. I feel both joyful and nervous. Both emotions cause me sleeplessness.

I get up and walk over to my bag sitting on the dresser and pull out my journal before sitting by the window.

Once upon a time, there was a boy who loved a girl and a girl who loved the boy, and they made you. He is handsome and makes her feel beautiful.

I pause because this love story doesn't have a pretty ending, no matter how much I want it to.

Before love was realized, she fucked up. She fucked up bad, and she is sure he regrets having loved her. He probably thinks she's fucking ugly, too, because all he does is take pictures of her damn feet! She is sorry to him, and most of all, she is sorry to you. Hell, she is just plain sorry.

I throw the book across the room then walk back to the bed and climb in like the sorry piece of crap I am.

I wake in the morning pissed. Just plain pissed.

I shower then look in the mirror, wishing I was at my place because I would pull out a pair of scissors and cut off all this stupid hair so my outside looks just as ugly as my inside feels.

Then I look at Instagram and see pictures of T with a dozen stupid girls.

Bitches.

Fuck him and his smile. Fuck them and their no doubt wet panties. Whores.

I wish my dad was there early to see that shit. He would kick his ass. Then I would be pissed at him because I don't want anyone to kick T's ass. I want them to love him. Well, except those bitches.

I would love to blame my mood swings on my pregnancy, but I'm not going to lie to myself or use it as an excuse. I'm a mess because love is messy.

I toss my phone on the floor.

I need answers, and I need them soon.

§

I WAKE UP TO THE sun rising. It's dawn, and all I can think of is that box and the happy sunshine balloons and butterflies, which makes me sad again.

God, what did I ever do to make this become my life? I know I have made mistakes, but I have tried. I have tried with everything I am and everything I have to make everything and everyone around me happy. I have kept secrets. I have been loyal. I have fought for those I love.

I look for my phone, finding it on the floor where I tossed it. I get up and grab it. It's dead, so I put it on the charger and lie back down. I kick the bed in frustration and roll over onto my stomach, trying to talk myself into relaxing, but I can't. I can't until I get some answers.

§

I SPEND THE ENTIRE DAY stressing about what T is doing, whom he is doing, if he wants me, and totally forget to stress the imminent danger—my father and T being in the same place together.

It's ten o'clock at night when I get out of the cab from Dulles Airport to Verizon Center at 601 F Street in Washington DC. I am in a black miniskirt, deep red thigh-high boots, and a red leather jacket over my

Burning Souls short-sleeved hoodie.

I didn't tell either T or my father I was coming. Hell, I didn't tell anyone. I even told Casey that she was wasting her time sitting outside and waiting for me to need her when I was going to read and sleep the entire day and night just so I could surprise him.

It's a necessary trip. Dad with his bagful of blatant disdain and T with his ... well, either "take her please", or "she's mine and it's time she grows up" attitude. Either would send Dad into orbit. Then I can just imagine T letting him know his little girl wasn't "properly protected" by her father and is now knocked up and we aren't sure if it's T, the guy you hate, or your godson Luke's kid she's carrying.

I wasn't worried about getting into the show. I have a "Golden Ticket" from Harper Hines. It's like a lifetime membership card to get into any Burning Souls or Brody Hines Band concert.

I flash it and a big smile at the ticket counter and am handed a VIP all-access pass specifically for Verizon Center's show.

I stand at one of the entries into the stadium's floor seating areas and watch them. Maddox sings with both Brody and the band he started, but so does the bass player, Zack Taylor. They are hot, but the drummer makes me wet everywhere, including my eyes.

I seriously need to get a grip.

"Miss, you need to take your seat," one of the security men scolds me.

I flash my pass then wipe away my tears.

He just nods and walks by.

I stand in the back the entire time, watching the band, the crowd, the entire scene. It's even more impressive from back here.

I normally would have marched my ass up front or

backstage and watched in the wings, but I am so glad I didn't miss this view.

They close with a drum solo. The crowd goes nuts as T throws his shirt off, and I notice he has more ink than he left with. From this distance, I can't make out what he has covering his left side.

When he's done, he throws his sticks into the crowd, and then they walk off stage. When the crowd continues their "encore" screams, the band runs back onstage, and they start my favorite song ever—"Stained."

This time, when they finish, the lights in the stadium come up, and people start to exit. After the floor is clear enough to move, I see the line forming. As I get closer, I notice the entire line of VIPs is of one gender: female. It rubs me the wrong way.

I pull the hoodie up and let my hair fall into my face, disguising myself because, right now, I want to see what T Hardy, hottest drummer ever, is going to do with all of these women who spent the last two hours getting worked up in a sexual frenzy now that he's "in love."

When I show security the badge, I make sure not to flash the one that is recognizable, although I could easily bump ahead. Instead, I show them the same one all these other women have. However, the longer it takes to get through the line, the worse I feel about the decision.

I see Maddox outside of the dressing room, signing autographs, but I don't see T or Zack. I also see my dad and Tessa farther off to the side with Harper. I hope they don't recognize me.

When I get up toward the front, Maddox gets distracted by his wife. It's clear he no longer wants to entertain the fans with pictures and small talk.

The way he seeks her out makes my heart dance.

Their love wasn't easy, but it was worth fighting for. That's their truth.

I am the last in line, and I let the guard know I am here for the drummer. When I see him go talk to Maddox, I turn so Maddox doesn't see my face, but after he signs the posters of the three women, he makes his way to Harper.

Out of the corner of my eye, I see him whisper something in Harper's ear then point. After looking at me for a couple minutes, she smiles.

I draw my hand across my throat, telling her to kill the excitement, and she gives me a very casual thumbs up.

When I walk into the dressing room, Zack makes an exit.

T's back is to me when he says, "Gonna have to make this quick, love. To show my appreciation for your understanding, I am going to sign this poster and give you a towel from tonight's concert, signed."

I reach back and dim the lights.

He laughs. "Not going to happen."

His words breed expectation that I want to allow, but I need more. I need to know they are not just words.

I walk up and reach around him, rubbing my hands up his abs.

"Gonna give you just a second to not make an arse of yourself and walk out of here with some dignity before I call security," he warns.

"Your solo made me all kinds of hot and bothered," I whisper, trying to disguise my voice a tad.

"Well, I appreciate it," he says, trying to pull my hands free of his body. When he can't, he snaps, "That's enough," and I quickly lower my hand and grab him through his pants.

"I chose drums, and so help me God, if you want

me to walk away, I understand, but—"

"Ava," he groans.

"*But*," I say, knowing I'm going to lose my nerve if he turns around. "You need to let me finish."

He covers my hand with his and pushes it harder against him. I feel him begin to harden, and rather quickly, under my touch.

"I want you and me. I want sunshine and butterfly balloons. And, T, I pray this is our baby, but I need you to accept that it may not be and that I made a mistake, but that mistake was not you, and regardless of who the father is, it's not this baby's fault. If you can't accept that, you need to tell me so I can try to figure out a way to not feel like you're home. So I can stop believing that you and I and this baby can be a family, regardless. So that I can stop being sad and lonely, even when the person who has made me happier than any other ever has is right next to me. Tell me and—"

"Don't fucking stop," he says as he takes my hand and places it on his side. He flinches, and I look down.

"What is that?" I ask, looking at what is obviously a freshly inked fairy in front of a sun.

"It's Aine, the Irish sun goddess," he answers then shrugs, pointing to my name tattooed underneath the dark-haired fairy-looking princess now on his skin forever. "Or Ava, my goddess and my sun."

I hear a zipper come undone, and I look up at him. When we are eye to eye, he says it again, "Don't you ever stop."

"I love you," I say as I sink down to my knees.

"Oh, Christ, Ava, you don't have to do this." He palms my cheek as his thumb rubs over my lips.

The way he looks at me makes me want to do this, makes me need to do this.

"I might not be good at this."

"First?" he asks, his eyes lighting up.

"Yes."

"Fuck, Ava," he says as he pulls my hair back into a ponytail.

He is thick and hard, and it's standing straight up. There's a thick vein going straight up the center of his underside, and I want to trace it with my tongue.

I look up at him, seeing his jaw is locked shut and his nostrils are flaring a bit.

I grip him hard at the base and open my mouth as I watch him watching me lick him from root to tip.

A deep growl rumbles in his chest, and his head falls back, his eyes squeezed shut as he whispers, "Killing me, Ava. This won't last long. Fuck. I have dreamed about this for so long."

I'm on my knees in front of the man who has made me happier than any other ever has, and I want to make all his dreams come true. Although I know I can't really give him the life he may have dreamed about with me—the one that may have a forever reminder of this pain we both feel—I can and will give him this.

I open my mouth then scrape my teeth across his tip. He groans again. It's a pleasure-filled, erotic, sensual sound that makes me want to do this even more. I know how his mouth on me makes me feel, and I want to give him the same.

I open wider, descending down him. His fist tightens in my hair as he whispers my name, making me feel like I'm the one being adored when, really, I am worshipping him.

I take every inch of him, and it's not without a *very* large amount of effort. And as I slide my mouth up and down him, the praises and sounds reverberating from him turn me into liquid heat.

"Gotta stop, Ava. I'm gonna come."

I don't stop. I fist him harder, move faster, and suck like I am in a desert and there is only this one drop left in the one well for a thousand miles.

I need this; he needs this; we … need this.

"Fuck," he says as his thick, heavy, rock hard cock jets off in my mouth, and I swallow every bit he gives me before licking him clean while watching his eyes flutter shut.

He reaches down and lifts me up under my arms, takes my hands, and then walks backward to the couch where he sits down and pulls me onto his lap.

"Never," he says, burying his head in my neck, "had that so good."

I lean back and take his face in my hands. "I love you, T. I love us. Please don't leave me again."

"Ava," he says as if he feels hurt. "I never want to, not ever. But if this is his baby—"

I stand up quickly. "Then you'll leave me?" My voice breaks, and I step back as he flies up and grabs me.

"You'll leave me," he says with hurt and sadness protruding from every inch of him.

"No." I grab his face in both of my hands. "No, never."

"Promise me that, if this child is his, you won't leave me, Ava, and I can promise you that I will not leave you until God himself takes me away from you."

"I promise." It is a promise filled with truths, a promise I know I will never take back. And in his eyes, I see acceptance of that promise.

I smile, he smiles, and we hug so tightly I am sure, if someone were to see us at this moment, we would be one person physically as well as spiritually and emotionally.

"Marry me," he says, the words coming from somewhere so deep it's like they are rooted there.

They can and will never be taken back, and because of this, our love will never be taken away.

If we get married, his name will be mine; his name will be this baby's; and everything will be as it should be, as I want so desperately for it to be.

"Yes." I nod.

"Yes?" he asks, holding my face and looking into my eyes, searching, seeking, needing, wanting … me.

I nod again. "Yes."

"Are you out of your damn mind!"

Both of our heads turn to the door we didn't hear open because, well, our love is deafening, and there is my daddy.

I laugh, Dad scowls, and T puffs out his chest.

"There is way too much negative energy in this room," I say, pushing myself up on my toes and kissing T's lips. Then I walk over to Dad and kiss his cheek before looking toward the door where I see Tessa smiling. I look back at the men facing off.

"I love you both," I tell them. "You both love me. Keep in mind that I am stubborn, determined, and that making me happy is important to both of you. Figure out how to make that continue, and please don't kill each other." With that, I walk out, and Tessa takes my hand.

I start to shut the door behind us, but she stops me. "You love him. Don't shut the door."

I laugh, and she sighs.

"You sure about this?" Tessa asks.

"One hundred percent," I answer, smiling.

I look back to see T smiling at me.

He runs his hand through his hair then looks at my Dad. "Tell me what you need me to say to you, promise you, show you, and if it doesn't involve taking my balls away and becoming a bitch, I'm sure you and

I can come up with a way to put you at ease."

"Swoon." I smile, and Tessa wraps her arm around my shoulder and gives me a squeeze.

Eighteen

Love doesn't have conditions.
— A. Stockford

One month later

    The week after I made the sun return to T's eyes, my life with him and love, even with nausea and the stress of work, became everything I could have imagined and more. The time I was away from him, I missed him more than I ever thought I could miss a person. But the case I was working on demanded everything I could give it.

    It was heartbreaking, and poor T had to listen to me rant every night about the injustices that had been done to these women and their unborn children.

    Each of the five days, I interviewed another woman who had miscarried late in their pregnancies due to taking a prescription medication that was deemed safe for pregnant women. One of them, Anna Thompson, started a thread on an online message board where people posted questions. She had a dozen women throughout the United States who had not miscarried but had given birth to children with birth defects and long-term health issues.

When I called Sandra to tell her of this finding, she told me I needed to interview them, too. I didn't want to be away from T, but this was more than just a case. I felt like I was fighting a cause, that I was making a difference.

When I told T on Wednesday that I may be traveling more, he asked if I would be opposed to him coming with me and hanging out at the hotel. I didn't even have to think about it; I simply told him yes.

That night, there was a knock at my hotel door, and when I opened it, he stood there, holding a beautiful bouquet of not flowers, but Snicker bars. We lay in bed, me babbling on and on as he fed me Snickers and, yes, made love to me.

When we come back to the loft on Friday, everything I own is there. He cleaned out my apartment in the first three days I was away.

He shrugs. "I was bored."

I dive on him, and he laughs. I laugh, and we make love on the floor in the middle of the living room.

We're lying there, breathless and panting, afterward when a thought hits me like a gut punch.

"What?" he asks, obviously sensing my head is in a far off place.

"You can't take this the wrong way," I say as a precursor to what's to come.

"O ... kay?"

"Sex before you ..." I say slowly and cautiously as I watch for a reaction, sensing a little trepidation. "T, before you, I thought I had the best sex ever. Now I don't know how I could have thought that." When he doesn't say anything, and I can't read him, I ask, "Should I explain?"

He nods once.

"Well, I think, because sex was twice a year, maybe I

kind of got off on the thought, and that's why I thought it was"—I hold up my fingers to air quote—"'Magical.'"

He sucks his lips in, trying not to laugh, which makes me laugh.

He nods again, telling me to continue, yet he doesn't say a word. His big, plump pillow lips are all sucked in his mouth, and he looks ridiculous and sexy.

"Like my love for ..." I pause.

"Your knight," he finishes, not seeming angry.

"Sure, him. It was all up here." I point to my head. "All a fairy tale. And we all know fairy tales are not real."

"Are they not, Ava?" He takes my hand and covers his heart. "Mine feels real."

I can't help the smile that forms in my heart then spreads across my face.

I take his hand. "Dark fairytales aren't real."

He makes a silly face as if he's terrified. "Grimm's tales."

"Those ones," I agree and laugh as I place his hand over my heart. "But you, Thomas Hardy, are here and real and taking me for who I am, regardless of what I have done. And maybe I believe in sunshine and butterflies and happily ever afters, after all."

"I will until my last breath, my goddess Ava," he says, smiling.

"I promise the same. As long as you promise." I pause and smirk.

"Do go on." He rolls me to my back and hovers over me.

"I just want to say, for the record, we better be making lots and lots and lots of babies."

He presses his forehead against mine. "I plan on it." He reaches between us and adjusts himself against

193

me. Then he pushes in slowly.

I moan, "Good, because sex with you is better than ... Snickers ... every time."

"Better than Snickers, huh?"

"Yes, it really satisfies me."

He laughs, smiles, and makes love to me for hours.

When we finish, I go in search of my journal, the one Jade gave me, but I can't find it anywhere.

He is at the stove, cooking pasta, when I come out and look over his shoulder.

"Do you think you've made enough?"

He nods. "We can throw it out if it doesn't get used."

I bite my tongue instead of scolding him. I understand that he was hungry once. I understand it, but I can't imagine it.

I kiss his cheek then ask, "Have you seen my journal?"

He glances quickly at me then away, looking very suspicious. "Um ..."

"T, did you read it?"

"Not much to read." He sets the wooden spoon on the spoon rest and turns, crossing his arms as he scowls at me. "It was one of those Grimm's tales. We are past that, Ava. If you are mad at me, you have to get over it, because our love is not dark or hidden. It's bright and ..." He stops as he walks away, waving me off dismissively.

I follow him into one of the spare bedrooms that has an entire wall of bookshelves and his desk. He sits down and opens the drawer, pulling out a new journal and handing it to me.

The cover is a picture of us kissing at Maddox and Harper's wedding.

"This is love, Ava." He stands up and pulls the chair

back. "Sit and read while I make you dinner."

I can't stop staring at the cover. We both look so incredibly happy.

I nod as he walks out the door. Then I open the book and look at his handwriting, which is elegant and beautiful.

Page 1

Love is love.

There is a hand-drawn picture of two hearts—his and mine.

Page 2

Love is her feet that brought her to me.

Another picture of feet.

Page 3

Love is her smile and the way in which it effortlessly makes mine feel whole for the first time in my life.

A picture of a smile.

Page 4

Love is the pain you feel

when their heart is aching.

Another heart.

Page 5

Love is the sun breaking through the rain and clouds and storms, giving you strength to carry on.

There is a heart with sunbeams shining from it.

Page 6

Love is the clarity you receive in even the worst moments.

There are two hearts under the word Love that is drawn in the shape of an umbrella.

Page 7

Love is in the kindness she shows others.

There are hands linked together with hearts surrounding them.

Tears spill from my eyes again, and I wipe them away.

"Ava," T says, walking toward me.

"These are the best kinds of tears." I laugh. "I'm okay."

"Yes, you are, Ava. And you are loved." He hugs me.

"You'll never stop being loved. God, T, why did this whole thing not start back when we met? I feel like we wasted so much time."

He kisses my head and lets go of me to grab a pen and the journal.

"Page eight. *Love is timeless*," he says as he writes it out, and then he draws a clock with no hands. He then closes the book, opens the drawer, and takes out a small, shiny metal box. He pushes the chair back and kneels in front of me, "Ava Links ..."

"Yes," I say with conviction, making him smile more brightly than I have ever seen.

"So, you'll marry me?"

"Yes!" I laugh and hold my left hand out. "Yes. Yes. Yes!"

He slides it on my finger, and I don't even look. When he stands, I can't keep my hands off of him long enough to register that I have a rock on my hand because the man, the one who loves me, is my everything now and forever, because our love is ... timeless.

"I'm not broken anymore," he whispers so softly I am not sure I was supposed to hear him.

"I love you," I tell him as he lifts me up, and I wrap my legs around him.

§

AFTER CLEANING UP THE MESS we made by ignoring the boiling pasta on the stove, we order pizza.

He sits on the floor, his back against the couch, my back against his chest, and his arms wrapped around me as he literally shoves pizza into my mouth.

"Monday ..." he sighs, and immediately, the carefree mood I was engulfed in is gone. He senses it, leans forward, and kisses my shoulder. "I planned to ask you Monday after we go to the doctors to prove to you that, if there were any doubt in your head, there is none in mine."

"But you said, 'What am I going to do with her?' You said it, and I thought—"

"You thought wrong. Now you know better. We both know better. Fuck, Ava, I just listened to you talking about fucking another man." I start to object, but he doesn't allow it. "I didn't get upset, Ava. It was you telling me something real, and for that, I am grateful. For you loving me, I am even more in love with you."

I relax, believing everything he's saying. I believe it, feel it. The feeling is emanating from him to me and back again.

I stand up quickly before he has the chance to stop me and run into the room where the journal was left. I take it out and grab a pen.

"Page nine. *Love is at its truest when it is mirrored: his to hers and hers to his, theirs together.*"

I look up when he walks closer.

"T, I love this book," I say like it's a surprise.

He grabs me, pulls me into a tight hug, and laughs. He gets me.

§

WE SIT IN THE DOCTOR'S office, me on the exam table and him on the chair he has pulled up next to me. I look down, focusing on his hand holding mine. It is tight and fills me with tension. When I look in his eyes, I see they are soft and accepting, as well as full of love and understanding.

He leans forward and kisses me softly, sweetly, and then whispers, "I love you."

As I am about to say the same in return, the doctor

walks in.

"Good morning, Ava. I'm Dr. Kennedy," she says, looking down at my chart. "The urine test came back positive, so you're pregnant. The first day of your last period was on the twelfth of December. It says you have a normal twenty-eight-day cycle, and that"— she pauses and looks up at me—"we've drawn blood from both you and Mr. Hardy to do the paternity test. It should be back"—she looks again—"in twenty-four hours since you paid for rush."

We both say yes, our tones mimicking those of teenagers who have been called into the principal's office.

She starts to ready her things for the exam, and I look over at T, who's wide-eyed.

He looks back at me and whispers, "Is she going to—"

"I'm going to do an internal exam." Dr. Kennedy nods. "I'll check her uterus and take a few samples."

"Thank you," I say as she pulls out the stirrups.

I look at T again. He is now looking intently at every tool she picks up from the tray of sterile instruments.

"Relax your knees," she says, and I about die.

What was I thinking to let him be in here?

He looks at me, his brows furrowed, and nods once. "You okay?"

I nod, and he looks away.

He's like a watch dog. He is hardly blinking, as if he's afraid he will miss something.

I wiggle my toes, and he looks back at me.

I smirk. "Are *you* okay?"

His mouth drops open as if to say, *I can't believe you just asked that*, and it makes me giggle.

He doesn't look at me, fixated on her movements and the damn tools of her trade.

Dr. Kennedy glances up at me, and I straighten my smile. I swear she wants to smirk, but she doesn't. She is very professional.

"Ovulation is dependent on the woman's cycle. From the length of it and because you were on the pill, the computation says that ovulation should have occurred anywhere between the twenty-third and the twenty-eighth." She glances up as if that may help answer the awkward question looming over our heads, but we don't say anything, and she continues, "The male sperm can live for up to three days, and the female egg is fertile between twelve and twenty-four hours."

She glances up again, and I see T nod in my peripheral.

When she is done with the exam, she sits back, pulls her gloves off and quickly tosses them, and then washes her hands. Then she turns around and looks at us.

"There is only a twenty percent chance that a woman becomes pregnant in any given month, and only twenty percent of those pregnancies are viable past twelve weeks. You're at nine weeks. Congratulations, you are almost at the safe—"

"What do you mean *almost at the safe*?" T asks worriedly.

"Mr. Hardy, there is no need to worry. Just..." She looks at me as if she is questioning his involvement. I hold up my ring finger, and she nods. "Enjoy life as usual with your fiancée and try not to stress anything."

She focuses back on me. "Another thing you should know is your HCG levels are very high, which means there is a possibility of twins, but it could just be how your body reacts to pregnancy. Oh, and your due date is September 17th."

The word "twins" makes my heart leap in my chest. All I can think about is how Luke had uncles who were twins. They died in a car accident when they were young. It was tragic.

I look at her, and she seems to know what I am concerned with.

"Twins are determined by the female."

I take a deep breath and nod.

Thank God, I think. *Thank God.*

Nineteen

It's never cut and dry.
— J. Ingrid Espino

IN OUR BEDROOM, I BEGIN to pack. Tomorrow, we fly to Chicago where I will meet seven women whose children have disabilities that will forever affect them.

"Why?" I ask myself out loud.

An arm snakes around my waist and pulls me back until I hit a warm hard body. "Why what?"

I turn and hug him. "Those poor women."

"Page ten, *Love shows in her empathy.*"

I look up at him and smile slightly.

"Page eleven, *Love is in the compassion she carries.*" He smiles, making me smile.

"Page twelve," I tell him, "*her love is because of his.* Thank you. Thank you for today, thank you for yesterday, and thank you for tomorrow."

He cups the side of my face and kisses my forehead. "No, Ava, thank *you.*"

"Are you scared?" I whisper.

"No. Things won't change, Ava. We won't let it. Regardless."

"When are we going to get married?" I ask as quickly as I feel it. It sounds needy, and honestly, it is. I need to be his wife.

His smile … God, his smile makes me love him even more.

"Tonight," he answers, and I laugh. His eyes widen. "We can."

I look at him, hoping he sees the thoughts and words I can't even begin to put into a sentence, because it wouldn't make sense. It's yes. It's I want my family to be present. It's I don't care if they are if it will make him at all uncomfortable. It's all weighted down by the doom and hope that hovers over both of us.

"Let's get packed and get through this week," he says. "Then maybe we can take a trip upstate."

I feel the weight of our world lifted off my shoulders, and I can't do anything except lean into him as he rubs my back and kisses my head.

"Thank you, Thomas."

§

"IT'S TOO EARLY," I WHINE as he kisses the back of my neck and chuckles as the alarm goes off at four in the morning.

"You booked the flights," he points out, pulling me until I am on my back, looking up at him.

I smile and lean up to kiss him, and then nausea suddenly rears her ugly head.

I roll off the bed and run to the bathroom, covering my mouth.

He snickers as he pulls my hair back while I throw up in the sink again.

"I was hoping we were past this."

"Two more weeks," I tell him, blindly reaching for the faucet, but he is there, already rinsing the white porcelain sink out.

"Love you," I mumble as I push myself up.

He hands me a washcloth. "Yes, you do." He winks.

I don't know if it's the fact that I should still be in bed for another two and a half hours, that I just threw up, or that he didn't say it back for the very first time ever, but I shoot daggers at him.

He literally steps back as if he thinks I am a demon possessed. "Okay, what was that?"

"You didn't say it back." I turn my back on him.

"Page thirteen, *Love needs not a word. It's in the way we treat each other*, Ava."

I look up and see him smirking at me in the mirror. I roll my eyes.

"Page fourteen, *Love's moods are dependent on physical feelings, so forgiveness is necessary until the second trimester*," I retort.

"Yes, and page fifteen, *Love needs no excuses*."

"That can be taken in a couple ways," I tell him after rinsing my mouth out with water.

"Beautiful girl, then you take it in whichever way pleases you."

I close my eyes and press my hand to my belly, hoping it will ease the feeling that the water I just drank wants to come up.

I feel his fingers lightly pinch the middle of my ear. He doesn't move when I look at him questioningly.

"I've been doing some research. This is supposed to be a pressure point to help stop nausea."

I lean back and sigh.

§

WE WALK HAND IN HAND out of security at Chicago's O'Hare Airport. He is wheeling my carry-on with his bag slung over his shoulder. I smile to myself, picturing T carrying a pink frou-frou diaper bag.

He squeezes my hand, and I look up to see the question in his eyes.

I shake my head. "It's stupid."

He winks. "Perfect, let's hear it.

"You carrying a pink diaper bag."

He grins and pulls me closer to him before releasing my hand and throwing his free arm around my shoulders, kissing my head. "Can't wait."

"But we have to." I smile sadly up at him.

He looks at his watch for the time. The doctor will be calling us with the test results at any moment.

"Not that it changes the fact that I will be carrying a bag full of diapers, but we only have another hour, Ava."

I sigh. "I don't think it was smart to give myself only an hour to absorb the information before going into today's meeting."

He winks. "I can be quicker than an hour."

I laugh and shake my head.

He presses his lips to the top of my head. "It's ours, Ava … regardless."

I nod as I take in the tingling sensation caused by the adoration he has for me, for us, for our love.

"I know. I know it is."

Traffic is horrible, which makes me anxious. T isn't bothered by it at all. He is sitting next to me in jeans with a gray long-sleeved tee under his black vest, tapping some beat with his fingers against mine.

As the car comes to a stop, he sighs. "Traffic," he states, pulling out his phone.

I gave the nurse his phone number. He is stronger than I am; it's obvious. And yes, it makes me feel horrible that I can't bear the burden of being the one to tell him if it is him or Luke who is the father of the baby. How selfish of me. How selfish of me to put that on him.

Self-awareness trumps selfishness in this case. I

can't break his heart. I can't, and it's possible I will.

I lean in closer, which isn't close enough. It will never be close enough.

Unlike Luke, T is a love I can touch and feel and depend on to hold me up.

Am I asking too much of him?

I allow the thought to cloud the reality of what we are. He holds me, kisses me, and hugs me every time the thoughts get to be too much. The fact that we are stuck in traffic after we planned out the flight time, travel to the hotel, and the doctor's call with the results to a T ... This messes with our plans. We were supposed to be in our room when we received the call.

"Talk to me," he whispers.

"Page sixteen, *Love is vulnerable.*"

And as if fate knew when to hit me at my lowest again, his phone rings, and I hold my breath for what seems like forever.

The ringing in my ears and the way my heartbeat is so loud drown out his conversation. Instead, I watch him.

His face is red. He is rubbing the back of his neck. His gaze bounces from me to the ceiling. He lets out a held breath. His mouth moves, and I can read his lips. "*Yes.*" He looks as anxious as I feel.

He leans back into the seat and lets out a breath as he sits up. "And what does that mean in laymen's terms?" His shoulders slouch, and he lets out a slow, steady breath. "Thank you." He hangs up his phone and sits back, rubbing his brow.

I want to scream, "Tell me, dammit!" but I can't. I can't do that. If he needs time, I will give it to him. At this moment and for the rest of my life, I will give him anything he needs.

He lets out a silent chuckle, and I feel like all hope

is deflating.

As the car starts moving, he opens his eyes and releases my hand. He wipes his palms down his jeans to dry them.

"Sorry, Ava." He takes my hand and wipes it down his pants, too. "I was trying like hell to stay calm for you. I wasn't sure if you'd leave me if this wasn't our child."

"I'd never leave you," I reply shakily. "Please don't leave me, T. Please."

He sits up, and a smile starts to form. "Oh, Ava, that is never going to happen." Now his smile is full-on and beautiful. "Ava, our baby likes drums. We're having a baby."

I nod my head, still needing to hear the words even though I see it in his eyes. T loves me, though. He would be happy, regardless.

He grins. "The lab results are ninety-nine percent sure that Thomas Hardy is the luckiest man in the world."

"So it's yours?" I ask, needing affirmation.

"My goddess, my love, my Ava, yes." He smiles and laughs as he pulls me onto his lap. "Yes," he breathes out against my neck, kissing it a dozen times. "Yes," he says again as he holds my face in his hands and looks into my eyes. "Yes," he repeats, his breath hitching.

A tear forms in his eye, and I throw my arms around him, pulling his head against my shoulders.

"Thank you, God," I whisper, hugging him more tightly.

"Thank you, God," he repeats.

§

ALL WEEK, I HAVE HAD meetings in a rented hotel conference room. It has been me, a stenographer named Lizzy, and women who trusted in the FDA's ability to do what they are supposed to do: govern what they were designed to and review test results to determine if a drug is safe for use.

Thomas has met me in the lobby and taken me to dinner every evening. Then he takes me to bed and makes love to me: no hurry; no tying me up, although I hope we can try that again soon; and absolutely no stress.

We are now sitting at a pizza parlor across the road. Eating deep dish pizza seems to be our thing.

"I bought some books about pregnancy today." He smiles after he allows me to wipe the corner of his mouth.

"Good, because we need to make sure I am doing everything right. And God, Thomas," I groan, "I don't even know if I can trust what the doctors say. This common over-the-counter drug used to treat cold symptoms, Sinexes, is a class A drug, which means, after all sorts of tests have been run, the conclusion is that there are no risks to a fetus. It's supposed to be safe. Then our lovely government-run FDA reviews and approves it."

He nods and holds out a fork. I take a bite.

"Then we must see that you don't get sick, which means lots of fluids and rest." His coy smirk is telling.

"Which means I'm in bed a lot."

"Precisely."

I wipe my mouth and stand up. "Then take me there."

He looks up and smiles as if a prayer has just been answered. "Thank you."

Twenty

Love takes commitment and two people willing to understand
everyone has flaws. Acceptance is key.
— C. Santelli Potter

OUR PLANE LANDS IN ITHACA on Friday afternoon.
Knowing I didn't have to be in the office again until
Monday, T changed our flights so we can go tell my
father in person that we are getting married. I decided
we should wait two weeks to let that settle in before
telling him about our little drummer.

T insists I wait until he gets *our*—and yes, he says
our—Land Rover out of long-term parking so that I
don't catch a chill. He's so wonderful to me.

I walk out when I see him pull up to the curb, and
he jumps out and opens the door for me. I can't help
myself. I jump into his arms and kiss him over and over
and over again.

"I'm hard, Ava," he whispers.

"You're insatiable."

He pushes his nose against mine. "I need you so
fucking bad."

The raw tone of his voice makes me want to give
it to him right here. It echoes need. And in his eyes, I
see it all: the insecurity when we are here and the need
for affirmation that I am his and that this place won't

change that.

I get in the vehicle and shut the door behind me while he gets in the driver side, and then he puts the vehicle in drive. I glance over at T to see him gripping the wheel so tightly my heart feels it.

I grab my phone from my bag and snap a picture of him. He glances at me out of the corner of his eye and shakes his head, pulling his knit cap down lower as he lets out a slow breath. The sound calls to me, to every part of me that he has ever loved.

I reach over and place my hand on his tented track pants.

"Fuck," he hisses.

I grip him as best I can and stroke him slowly.

"Fuck, Ava, just like that."

I swallow down my desire, and it's not a desire to be touched. Although I am warm and tingly everywhere, I don't want him to touch me. I want to touch him, to please him, to take care of him like he takes care of me.

I lean over and place a kiss on his neck, his shoulder, his chest, his side where my name is tattooed on him. Then I bend down and kiss his hip, all while stroking him.

I reach inside his pants to find him bare—he always is. Leaning down, I lick the pre-come from his tip, causing his hips to rise slightly. I take just his head into my mouth as he pushes down his pants, fully exposing himself to me.

He's beautiful, I think as I stroke him slowly up and down, licking him, sucking him, tasting him, loving him with my mouth.

He glances down at me in utter adoration as he holds the steering wheel in one hand and cups my face with the other.

I move up and down slowly, making sure to let my tongue caress each and every ridge, every vein, every part of him.

"I don't want it to end," he hisses as I speed up, wet and wanton.

I slow down for him.

"Thank you." His praise is in his words, his eyes, his touch as he caresses my face.

He pulls into my driveway, and I sit up. He is out of the vehicle before I even register that we are not going to Dad's right now. My door opens, and he takes my hand.

At the door, I punch in the code that unlocks the door. Then I let go of his hand so that I can disarm the alarm so Dad isn't alerted.

T wraps his arms around me from behind, sliding his hands down my belly then under my waistband and inside my panties. He cups me as we walk in from the garage to the kitchen.

His fingers on his left hand push under my panties while the other hand pushes under my shirt and squeezes my breast.

I gasp, "T, easy please."

"Which hand, love?" he asks in a low rasp.

"The boobs," I moan as he pushes a finger inside of me, fucking me at a slow, steady pace.

"Drink," I say in a quivering voice.

He walks us to the sink with a finger still inside of me. "Can you get one like this?" he asks, pushing another finger inside my wet center.

"Yes," I cry. "Yes."

My hands shake as I open the cupboard, pull out a cup, and fill it while he moves at a more rapid pace. I drink the water then drop the cup into the sink. Reaching behind me, I grip his neck and pull him down into a kiss.

His kiss becomes more possessive, more filled with need, as my tongue strokes his. He groans, pulling his fingers out of me.

"No," I cry as he turns me around.

He takes my face in his hands and kisses me harder. Then he releases my face, cups my ass, and pulls me free of my pants and underwear before lifting me up and setting me on the sink, kissing me again. He then reaches between us, rubs himself against me, and thrusts in hard.

"Oh, God." My head falls back as I cry out my pleasure.

"That's it, Ava. I'm going to give you a lifetime of orgasms, love," he hisses. "A fucking lifetime."

He grips my ass harder and pulls me firmly to him. "Legs around me," he orders.

I am falling apart as he fucks me faster, harder. One orgasm leads to another then another until I feel him swell inside of me, and he comes, growling my name like he never has before.

I am wrapped around him, his chin on my shoulder and my face buried in his neck.

"Thomas," I pant. "What was that?"

"That was us, Ava. You and me, together for the rest of our lives."

I can't help laughing. "Are you trying to kill me?"

"No, Ava, just trying to love you better."

"Well," I say, leaning back and holding his face in my hands. He is tense and hard and primal-looking. It's hot. So hot. "Damn."

He closes his eyes before a smile forms on his face. "Damn," he whispers.

"I need another drink." I push him back a little.

"I'll give you a drink," he says, setting me on my

feet. His arms are around me as he reaches behind me and fills a glass from the tap before handing it to me.

"Thank you." I smile.

"Anything for you, my goddess," he says, caressing the side of my face. "Anything."

§

WE PULL INTO DAD AND Tessa's to find all the lights off. I get out and look in the garage. Dad's SUV is gone. Then I get back in T's—our—vehicle.

"Probably down the road," I say.

"Maddox's place?" he asks as he puts the vehicle in reverse.

"Yeah." I smile, looking down at my ring.

"Do you like it, Ava?"

"The ring? Of course. It's beautiful," I tell him, hitting the overhead light. "Why would you ask that?"

"Well"—he shrugs—"I thought maybe you didn't like it because it wasn't a traditional solitaire."

"T, it is the most beautiful ring on the planet," I gush over the three stone emerald cut diamonds and the platinum band. Then I sigh when I realize why he is asking. "I haven't properly gushed."

"It's not a big deal." He shrugs as he drives down the lane.

"It is a huge deal. I was just trying not to be such a … girl. But, T, I couldn't have ever imagined getting something like this. Not ever. I love it."

He eyes me skeptically.

"I was also worried maybe you'd … I don't know … take it back," I admit.

"What?" he gasps.

"Don't worry; you'll have to pry this baby off my dead finger before you ever get it back."

At this, he laughs.

I take his hand and kiss it then place it on his heart. "And this, I will fight you for."

He laughs. "Oh, so now that we're home, you're back to sassy badass Ava, huh?"

"No." I laugh. "You'll really have to fight me for it."

"It's yours, Ava. Don't ever try to give it back."

A few minutes later, we walk into Harper's house hand in hand.

"Anyone home?" I yell.

"Ava?" my dad's voice booms, and I laugh.

We walk in to find everyone around the kitchen island. Dad's smile turns from genuine to genuinely pissed off and back to a plastic smile after his wife kicks him under the counter.

"Where's Piper?" I ask.

"Just fell asleep," Harper answers, giving me a hug while Maddox gives T a bro hug.

"I could use a drink." T winks at him, and Maddox laughs.

I walk over and give my dad a big hug. He gives me back a bigger one.

"Ava and I have something we wish to tell you all," T says, and Dad's hug turns into an almost chokehold.

"Daddy," I growl.

"Ava, I am not ready for this." He doesn't even bother whispering it. I guess us making the announcement just made this more real to him.

"Well, prepare yourself, father Links," T says. I can't see him, but I can hear the smirk in his voice.

"Be. Nice," I whisper to Dad.

"I asked Ava to marry me, and she said yes."

"Oh, my God!" Harper exclaims.

"I'm not ready for this, Ava," Dad repeats in a slightly defeated tone this time.

"Shouldn't come as a surprise, Daddy Links," T says.

"I did ask you for her hand in marriage at the concert in Washington."

"You did?" I ask, trying to pull back to look at him, and my father loosens his grip.

"And I said no," he snaps at T.

"Lucky for me, the Links that matters the most said yes." T is smiling. I can hear it, and I want to see him.

"Congratulations, T," Tessa says, giving him the same sincere smile she gave me in DC.

"Daddy, you wanna let go?" I grumble.

"No."

I laugh. "You can't keep me like this forever."

"He thinks I'm not good enough," T says.

"Christ himself wouldn't be good enough for my daughter," Dad says, loosening his grip on me. "If you hurt her, I'm going to jail. You hear me?"

"I'll never hurt her. I'll cherish her. I have since day one," T says sincerely.

I step back and smile at Dad, holding up my left hand and wiggling my fingers so he can see the ring.

"Are you trying to get her killed?" he gasps and scowls at T. "Some piece of shit is gonna try to kill her to steal the damn thing in that city you two are so fond of."

"He takes me to work and picks me up every day," I tell him.

"And I am with her all night. So rest assured, she is safe." T nods.

I shoot him a warning glance because I know damn well it was a jab.

"If you two don't start being nice to each other, I'm gonna run away," I warn them.

"Let me see that ring," Harper says, hugging me again. "I am so happy for you both."

I hear the door shut, and Jade walks in with Ryan

behind her.

"The party started early and no one told us?" Jade laughs.

"Ava and"—Dad points to T—"T surprised us."

That's when I see Luke walk in.

I look at T, and he looks at me. I smile because it doesn't matter. I have let Luke go, and I am in love with T. So in love with him.

"T has asked for Ava's hand in marriage." Dad smiles. It's pretty damn convincing, too.

Jade looks shocked. "Oh, my God." Her eyes shift down to my hand. "Holy shit! Look at that!" She walks up and hugs me.

"Thanks, Jade," I tell her, stealing a glance at Luke who, as per his norm, has no expression.

"Congratulations, Ava." Ryan is the next to hug me.

"Congratulations, Ava," Luke says, forcing a smile.

"Thank you, Luke." I smile back. "Hey, what are you doing home?"

"Our boy rolled his ankle during training, so he's home until Wednesday when he flies into God only knows where to meet his team," Ryan answers with pride. He pats Luke's back. "Last mission, right, son?"

Luke nods. "Last mission." It's what he tells them every time to pacify his family. They accept it, even though we all know better. I suppose there is a chance, but it's highly unlikely.

He looks at me then at T. "Congratulations, Thomas."

T nods, not saying a word.

§

AT DINNER, T SAYS A few words like, "How long will you be deployed?"

Luke tells him six months.

Then T tells him he will miss the wedding, rather pompously, actually.

"When is the wedding?" Tessa asks.

"We haven't set a date yet," I answer.

"But she was okay with getting married the night I asked her," T boasts.

"I'd have a problem with that," Dad sneers, and Luke and everyone else laughs.

T shrugs. "Whatever she wants, I'll give her." Then T drinks his third double-shot of scotch.

"Is it in hostile territory?" T asks Luke.

No one else senses a damn thing, but me, I want to crawl under the table.

I can't be angry at T. He has to take my father's jabs and look at a man I very recently thought I loved. Still, it's not easy.

Dinner couldn't have ended more quickly.

"I think we're going to head back to the house," I announce while helping clear the table.

"Why so soon?" Dad asks.

"She's been working on a big case, traveling all over. She'll be traveling for a few weeks, right, love?"

I nod.

"She's one hell of a lawyer."

"She's worked her ass off to become one," Dad adds.

"And she'll continue if that's what she wants. Although, it is totally unnecessary," T says, narrowing his eyes slightly as he looks at me.

I smile and shrug then go upstairs to peek in on Piper with Harper.

"She's gonna be our flower girl if that's okay with you."

"Of course it is." Harper smiles.

"I'll need a matron of honor, too," I whisper.

"Name the time and the place," she whispers back then looks around and adds, "Sooner than later, though. I wanna look good in the photos." She grins and puts her finger over her mouth. "Shh…"

"Oh, my God," I gasp then cover my mouth. "When?"

"August. Don't tell anyone, including T. He's freaking drunk and very—"

"Over the top tonight." I giggle softly, and she nods. "Yeah, he is, but I can't blame him."

She hugs me. "You deserve to be happy. So does he."

I smile. "And you're going to be a mom of two."

"I know. It's insane. But Maddox has been begging for two years, so I finally said yes and truly didn't expect it to happen so fast."

I want to tell her I'm pregnant, too, but I can't. Not yet.

"You're past your first trimester, so why haven't you told anyone?" I ask.

She smiles and shrugs. "I don't know."

"Wait a couple weeks if that makes you feel better. But call me first, okay?"

"Will you come home?" she asks.

I grin and nod. "Yes. Yes, I'll come home."

"Then we can plan a wedding where I don't have to wear a tent."

I laugh. "You were the most beautiful pregnant woman ever."

"Aw, thanks. I wasn't …" She pauses. "Thanks."

When I walk outside a few minutes later, I find T and Luke standing there, looking at each other, neither saying a word.

"Hey, guys, what's going on?" I ask cautiously.

"Getting some fresh air," Luke replies in a clipped

tone.

"You ready to get home, Ava?" T asks in a cocky, arrogant way that's meant to piss off Luke. It makes me angry.

"What I'm ready for is peace!" I snap.

Luke nods. "I hope you've found it."

"I'm pretty sure I have." I laugh nervously. "T?"

He doesn't budge.

"Thomas Hardy, are you gonna stay here all night? I'm going home."

"You're driving, Ava. Your boy's drunk." Luke chuckles.

Before T can say a word, I point at Luke. "Enough." Then I point at T. "Let's go."

Luke laughs as he walks toward the house. "Good luck."

I take T's hand and yell over my shoulder, "Be safe, Lane." stomping to the vehicle and getting in.

"You wanna take it easy on the gears?" T asks as he gets in.

"You wanna replay of last time we were here, T? I mean, what the hell are you doing starting shit with him?"

"My goddess is pissed."

"Damn straight she is." I grind into first.

"The vehicle is warm, yes, Ava?"

"Clearly," I say, running over a snow bank.

"Because I came out and started it. Your … friend followed me out. So kindly be nice to *our* vehicle," he says with a sigh.

"Why did he follow you out?" I ask, knowing the answer.

Luke has no right to act like a jealous ass. None at all. His actions are contradictory to his words. It's not like Luke to act like that, but it is like T. And as much as it annoys me, I understand, but it needs to stop. I need peace for me, for him, and for this baby.

"Because he likes me, Ava. He wants to be my friend." He snickers.

"Good," I say, not believing that's why Luke followed him out, but I don't give a damn, and I don't want T to, either.

"Can we fly home tonight?" he asks, looking at his phone.

"Yeah, sure," I say.

Twenty-One

To love someone takes work.
— M. Gossett

Six weeks later

"SHE'S, WHAT?" T EXCLAIMS, AND I laugh. "How long have you known?"

"Since we were home," I tell him, feeling a little ashamed of myself.

"And you didn't …" He pauses, his eyes widening. "You lied to me!"

"No!" I cry when he picks me up and acts as if he's going to toss me onto the bed. "Don't you dare! You'll mess up the clothes we're packing!"

"You've had weeks to digest this, Ava soon-to-be Hardy."

I laugh, loving when he says my name like that.

"Let me wrap my head around the fact that our children will be as close as you and Harper and Maddox and I are."

My stomach rumbles, and I cover it with my hand.

"Hungry?" he asks immediately.

I nod, and he sets me on my feet.

"Snickers?" I ask.

"Of course a Snickers. Mini or the larger size?"

"Mini," I answer, knowing it is unhealthy to eat as many freaking Snickers bars as I have been lately. But dammit, they do really satisfy.

When he returns to wherever it is he hides them—upon my request—he has a full-sized bar. He bites half of it off, smirking as he hands me the rest.

"We have a problem, you know." I point at him with the bar and laugh.

"We do. Those damn things are addictive."

Thomas Hardy is my male Harper. He is my best friend. He is my lover. He is the father of the child growing inside of me. And he is everything I ever dreamed of to the tenth power.

I sit down and take a bite, groaning as I chew.

"You know," he says, "I don't think we have a problem at all. In fact, I love the near orgasmic sound you make after taking the first bite."

"So good," I moan, rolling my eyes.

He laughs. "So Memorial Day weekend?"

I nod. "Soonest we can get the venue."

"On a Friday," he says, scrunching up his face.

I laugh and nod because, when we checked into Lake Watch, the same place my prom was held and the same place he and I first kissed at Harper and Maddox's wedding, I was not okay with a Friday night, and he was not okay with waiting two more months.

I lie in bed, and he lies beside me, reading one of the hundreds of children's books he has ordered since we were in Chicago. None are Grimm's fairytales; they are all about love and life and happiness. The one he is reading now is his favorite.

He holds the book in one hand, the other on my belly that is really not all that distended, but I push it out for him because the pride in his eyes and in his heart is as sweet and heavenly as anything on this earth ever has been.

He is going to have a family with a woman who loves him and chose him, a child who will no doubt adore him, and regardless of how my father is acting, he will come around. I know he will because he loves me and he will see that T makes me so happy, so very happy.

We had dinner with mother and Robert last night. She was … cold, and he was as relaxed as could be. He was charming and kind and treated her like a queen. Yet, she was still bitchy. I could have slapped her, but she's my mom.

He closes the book and sighs. "The wonderful thing you will be." Then he leans over and lets his long lashes flutter over my lower abdomen where I felt our child move a week ago and showed him what it felt like by moving my eyelashes across his face.

"Butterfly wings." He smiles. "Wonderful feeling."

Tomorrow, we have an ultrasound scheduled. We chose to do it at a clinic because the office didn't have a time that worked with our flight time. T doesn't care about insurance paying; he is paying out of pocket.

Of course he is. Someday soon, I am going to have to teach him about what the term "waste not, want not" means. Money or no money, throwing away food is a sin. But that little sin makes him feel proud of who he has become. Who am I to take that away from him?

§

WE DECIDED TO FLY HOME to share in Harper and Maddox's joy of telling their families about their little blessing and to hopefully share ours with everyone, as well. The flight is quiet. T appears to be in shock, and I think it is hysterical how the thought of marriage and a child doesn't faze him, yet two babies almost puts him in such a mood. But it doesn't matter, not one bit. I will deal with his change in moods.

"Page seventeen, *love isn't affected by ups and downs.*"

He gives me a questioning look.

"You dealt with all my mood swings, so I can deal with anything you throw at me." I smile, and he gives a silent chuckle, holding me more tightly.

"I love you, Ava."

"I love you, Thomas."

§

TRUTH BE TOLD, I AM unbelievably excited. Tonight, Thomas and I are making dinner at my family home for everyone.

Harper plans to come early. I had to trick her, telling her that I needed her to get a few things at the store. I really want her here to tell her about my pregnancy before we tell anyone else.

When she walks in with Maddox, she looks tired, and I laugh.

"Come sit down. We want to tell you and Maddox a secret."

After removing their coats and hats, they sit down.

I nod to T, and he runs his hands through his hair, taking a deep breath before holding up the little frame we picked up at Tiffany.

"Ava thought it would be cute to put your sonogram picture in here and set it on the table just to see if anyone notices." He hands them the frame and sits down next to me.

I squeeze his hand and smile. He kisses my cheek, smiling back.

"Wait, there's already a picture in—" Harper gasps. "Oh, my God!"

Maddox looks at her and then at the picture, his eyes widening.

"Did you give them the wrong one?" I ask as planned.

"Oh, gee, I must have," he says in a cheesy, 1960's actor voice that makes me laugh.

"You two are having—"

"Twins." I laugh and clap my hands, interrupting Harper.

She looks again. "And you're due a month after I am?"

"Yep. Our babies are going to spend Christmases and holidays together, Harper. Can you believe it?"

"Oh, I am so happy for you." She laughs and tears start to trickle down her face. "I am so happy for both of you."

I notice Maddox and T staring at each other. Then I look at Harper, whose tears now seem more sorrowful than joyful.

It bothers me. I never even thought of how anyone may react. It is hurtful and makes me feel like, if my best friend doubts me, then others certainly will, too.

I smile big and stand up. "Excuse me for just a minute."

I walk quickly to the bathroom before the tears fall. I look in the mirror with self-loathing and self-deprecating thoughts in my head.

The door opens, and T walks in. He shuts the door behind him and immediately hugs me. "Shh...You'll be fine."

"How come I can't just be happy here, T?" I ask him as I wipe my tears away.

"Did she know about him?" T asks.

I nod. "She did, but not the last time I was with him."

"It's possible that was my fault," he says in a self-deprecating tone. "I may have made a scene ... or two. And if she knows, Maddox surely knows. They may wonder if—"

I sigh. "It's ours—mine and yours."

"Ava, does it matter at all what anyone else thinks besides us?"

I pout. "Well, yes ... kind of."

He doesn't say anything for a long minute. Then he kisses my cheek. "You miss home?"

I know he's asking about our place in Brooklyn. I do miss it...very much.

"Yes."

"I'm not saying this to hurt you in any way, but how you feel right now is how I feel every damn time I'm around your father."

"I'm sorry. I really am."

He hugs me more tightly and sighs. "We'll be fine."

"Yeah, once we get back to New York."

He gives me a sad smile as he wipes away my tears. "Let's go tell them about the test."

"Okay."

It infuriates me, but it isn't just me who is going through this. He is, too.

As we begin to walk out the door, I squeeze his hand. "Can we leave in the morning? I want to be home."

He nods. "Yes, anything for you, Ava."

"Thank you."

Harper stays close to me after T tells them about the test, and that yes, he is the father. Both visibly relax, and I know it's not judgment from Harper or Maddox; it's pity, and pity sucks just as much. Sometimes more.

My happy, joyful mood is now put on for show, but as T reminds me, he is here. It may not have changed my mood, but I will bask in that. My smile is for him and for us and our home and our love.

Logan is the first to show up. He's a little annoyed I didn't tell him I'm engaged. He scolds me since it is unlike me not to tell him something before Dad knows. I make sure not to tell him our mother saw the ring before all of them. It would crush him, and he's my little Loggie.

I ask him to fill the glasses with water as I set the table, and he looks at me like I'm crazy.

"People can fill their own glasses, Ava. Damn."

T and I stand back and watch him. He notices and rolls his eyes then goes back to pouring.

He notices the frame and leans in. Then his jaw drops, and I can't help giggling. When he picks it up and sees the name, he looks at me then back at the frame and back and forth again.

"No way," he gasps.

I nod and pat my belly. "And there are two."

He looks bewildered but then smiles, walks over, and hugs me.

"I know you are going to be an amazing mom, Ava. And I hope you know, as much as I love you, I am never changing a diaper."

T and I laugh.

"Don't worry, Logan," T tells him. "I've already volunteered for that privilege."

Logan gives him a quick hug then says, "I need a fucking drink."

I have T at my side, Harper close by, and Logan on my other side. I feel a little better about things now. A little.

Dad, Tessa, Brody, Emma, and London all come in together.

"That's a lot of people," T whispers, causing Logan and me to laugh.

"They occupy the other side of the valley, man. We're safe over here," Logan whispers to him, putting T at ease.

"Safer in the city," T whispers back.

"Love to come visit." Logan chuckles. "Holidays in the city now?"

T holds up his beer, and they clink glasses.

"You're welcome any day."

London walks past Logan. "Hmm … city girls. Now that's a lot of plastic. You'll be in heaven."

"London," Emma gasps while I laugh.

"London, you wanna drink?" Logan smirks.

In the most London-like way, she flips him off. No one notices except him, T, and me.

T smirks. "You can come visit anytime, too, London."

"Let me know when he's not there."

Logan's face turns beet red, and she sticks her tongue out at him.

His jaw tightens. "Yes, please do. I wouldn't want to have to babysit."

I smack Logan as London glares at him.

She walks to the table and sits next to Brody with her arms crossed over her chest. She immediately notices the frame and gasps. She leans in a little and then looks back at me.

I put my finger over my lips to tell her to hush. She seems excited to know something no one else does.

Logan whispers, "I knew first."

She rolls her eyes and mouths, "*Grow up.*"

Within ten minutes, everyone at the table is whispering to each other, and I see Tessa wipe her eyes as she hands Dad the frame. His jaw drops, and he looks at Harper. Before he has a chance to say anything, Tessa hands him the other frame. She is watching him closely, taking in every emotion his face is showing.

He sits back and takes in a deep breath while she smiles at him. God, I wish I could see his face, but the frame is in the way.

He pushes back his chair, stands up, and turns around. He is tearing up, and it makes me do the same.

"This for real, Ava?"

I nod, unable to say anything because I am holding back my emotions.

"Two?" he asks, and I nod.

He closes his eyes and smiles. It's big. It's real, I think.

He walks over, stretches out his hand to T, and T shakes it.

"You have one hell of a young lady here. I hope you know that."

T nods. "I do. Thank you for bringing her into this world."

My dad's eyes get bigger, and then a handshake turns into a hug.

I have to cover my mouth to stop from sounding like an idiot because I am sobbing.

Dad then turns to me, tears falling down his cheeks. "Ava girl."

"Daddy," I whisper.

"I'm so happy for you." He hugs me tightly.

"For us, Daddy, for all of us."

I look at the other side of the table, Tessa, Brody, and Emma are hugging Maddox and Harper.

London walks over and gives T a hug.

"You're going to be a great dad, T Hardy."

He laughs. "Thanks, L Fields."

She steps back and whispers, "Gotta go give the brother from an evil mother a hug."

"Oh, my God, London, really?" Logan snaps at her.

"Seriously, man, lighten up," she says as she walks away, and we all start to laugh.

Logan looks at us like we are traitors.

"Need another drink, Logan?" T asks.

"Yes, yes, I do."

Twenty-Two

You must love yourself and be happy within before you can fully love another.
— M. Meredith

Two months later

"I am big, fat, and pimply," I snarl as I look in the mirror at the zit between my shoulders.

"Ava, you are not," T says, handing me my daily Snickers bar. "Here, eat this. It'll make you feel better."

I unwrap the candy bar and take a big bite then shake it at him. "This is why, you know. You are feeding the fat pregnant chick too much."

"The beautiful pregnant goddess is eating for three, and those two," he says, pointing at my tits, "so that makes five."

I laugh as I chew. "You want me fat, don't you?"

"Ava, you are five months pregnant with twins. The doctor says you have not gained enough weight."

"That's because we changed doctors since you wanted the best for your babies."

"Hell yes, I want the best for you all." He laughs as he walks behind me and cups my very full C cups. "These are so fucking beautiful."

I take another bite. "The new doctor has no idea that I have already gained twenty pounds. The records haven't been received yet."

"I'm convinced it's all right here in my hands." He jiggles my boobs. "Fascinating."

"They won't fit in my dress," I complain.

"They will, and if by chance they spill out a bit, I won't complain at all."

"That's so kind of you." I laugh as he continues watching my boobs jiggle in the mirror. "Okay, T, I need to get to work." I pull away from him, and he groans. "What are your plans today?"

I really didn't have to ask. He has been very busy turning the spare bedroom into a nursery and painting the two walls that are not exposed brick. He is so talented, and not just musically.

"The cribs come today." He smiles and shakes his head as if he still can't believe it. "Ava, we're less than a month away from getting married and four months away from having a baby."

"Two babies." I giggle, and he smiles more brightly than the sun he has painted on the east-facing wall in their room.

"You simply amaze me." He laughs.

"Well, you simply amaze me, too," I say, giving him a quick peck on the cheek. "Now, I simply must go to work."

§

WHEN I RETURN HOME, HE is in the babies' room.

He looks up when I walk in and smiles. "Shit, why didn't Casey tell me you were here?"

I shrug. "Does she always?"

He sets down the screwdriver and stands up to give me a hug. "Bad day?"

I sigh. "Exhausted."

"Snickers?" he asks as he looks down at me.

I smile, and he kisses my cheek then leaves me to go grab one.

"The mini!" I yell.

When he walks back in the room, he holds his hands up. They are empty.

"We're out?" I laugh.

He sighs, looking forlorn. "I have to tell you something."

The playfulness in his put upon sadness is adorable. His head is bowed, and he looks up at me through the thick lashes that frame his beautiful, telling eyes.

"I may have a slight addiction."

I gasp and cover my heart. "No!"

He smirks and nods. "I may have more than one, but both are due to you."

I throw my head back and laugh. "Do tell."

"Snickers and you."

"Snickers and me, huh?"

"Yes," he says, bending down on one knee. "Will you forgive me?"

"Forgive you?" I pretend to consider if I should. "Yeah, I forgive you, and I love you more because of it."

He stands up, gives me a quick hug, and says, "I'll run to the store and grab some."

I laugh again. "You really don't have to. Real food is probably a better idea, and Lord knows we have enough."

He steps back and squints his eyes. "But after dinner?"

"I don't need one." I grin, shaking my head.

"Maybe I do."

"Okay, we'll go together," I say, giving him a quick

kiss.

"No. How about you have a soak, and when you get out, I'll be back and we'll fix dinner together?"

"You sure?" I ask.

"I insist." He hugs me tightly, and yes, I smell him. He looks down and smiles. "I love you, Ava Links very soon-to-be Hardy.

I can't help the smile that spreads across my face. I love the sound of my name when he says it.

"I love you more than Snickers."

At that, he laughs. It's deep and rich and filled with happiness. His happiness is contagious. Every bad part of this day gets erased by it.

He leaves quickly, and I stand and take in the room. It's not just a room anymore; it is a place T has made more beautiful. It is a place that, together, we will show these two babies what true love is.

I walk into the room that his desk is in and grab the journal, bringing it with me. Then I sit down in one of the two rocking chairs he has put together for us in front of the window and open it.

Page 18

Love grows deeper every day.

Page 19

Love is her, and I am so blessed.

Page 20

Love is in the little caramel on the corner of her mouth.

Page 21

Love grows stronger when it's just the two of us.

Page 22

Love's blessings are growing inside of her.

Page 23

Love will grow even more with four.

Page 24

Love is still and peaceful. It's in her slow, sweet breath as I lie next to her with her head on my chest.

Page 25

Love is in everything we do to protect love.

Page 26

Love is love, still.

I open to page twenty-seven and click the pen to start writing, but then I hear something, a sound like metal on metal.

I sigh and set the book down before walking over to the window. I see a car has hit a pole outside our flat. Then I see it back up.

Some idiot is probably drunk and trying to get away without being caught.

"Here's an idea, dipshit, take a cab," I comment, shaking my head.

When I lean over with my phone camera to get a shot of the license plate, because yes, I despise drunk drivers and will report it, I see something. I don't know if it's a person or an animal.

My heart is in my chest as I run to the cargo elevator. I reach for the key we leave on the hook next to it, but it's not there.

"Damn it, T," I say as I make my way to the stairs. I run down the three floors and out through the lobby.

When I look left, I see a crowd has formed and already surrounding whatever it is. I look for T, hoping he's run to the corner store and heard the commotion because I hate blood, and if I pass out, he can take care of me. I don't see him, so I walk up slowly and stand behind the crowd.

"Did someone call an ambulance?" I hear a girl's

voice cry.

"Yes," a man says in a panic-stricken tone.

"There's a lot of blood," someone else cries.

I grab my phone from my pocket to call T, hoping he has his, already feeling light-headed. He doesn't answer, so I try again.

I hear his ring tone, our song, the one that's surrounded by smiling sun shines and soaring butterflies that have now become symbols of our love and our babies.

"T," I say as I walk around, knowing he's here. "T," I say more loudly as I call him again, hearing his phone even more clearly now. "T!" I yell as I see his phone lit up, lying next to the lamp post.

"His eyes opened," someone says with a voice full of hope.

I feel weak in the knees as I grab his phone off the ground and see my number and our picture behind a cracked screen. Reality strikes, and I push through the crowd.

"Oh, God, T!" I fall to my knees beside where he is on his back and reach for him.

I don't see blood, so he's going to be okay. Oh, God, he has to be okay!

"Miss, don't move him," a man warns me.

"T," I say, putting my hands on his face. "An ambulance is coming. You're going to be okay!"

He starts to close his eyes, and I scream at him to keep them open. He does.

"Please, just stay awake. Just stay awake, please."

He opens his mouth and a gurgled, "Love you," comes out … and so does blood.

Oh, God, please! I scream in my head.

"I love you, too. Don't you close your eyes and don't you talk, T. I love you so much that I'm not even going to pass out, and I don't do well with this kind of thing. I love you so much I promise you that I will fight for our love as hard as you are going to in order to heal, T."

His lips curve up on one side. "Forever."

"Of course forever! How could you ask me that!" I yell at him, and his smile doesn't fade.

I look up as I hear sirens approaching, and then I look back at him.

"Open your eyes, T! I need your eyes! The ambulance is here! T, open your eyes."

I hear a sob or a burst of air escape him as I bend over and kiss his chest lightly then his face then his lips. I taste blood.

"T," I whisper, "I can't do this without you. Our babies need you. Please, Thomas, please open your eyes. I need to see you. I need you, T—"

"Ma'am," I hear a male voice behind me, but I won't look away. I don't want to miss the moment that he opens his eyes, because he will. "You need to move out of our way."

"Ma'am, now," says a female voice.

Then arms reach around me and pull me back.

"Let go of me!" I scream. "He needs me! He needs me, dammit!"

My body is shaking uncontrollably now.

"No pulse," one of the paramedics says.

"Fight, dammit, T! I need you!" I sob. "Please, we need you!"

They are putting him on a stretcher, and his hand falls off the side when they lift it.

When they start to wheel him toward the ambulance, something happens to me, and I manage to get it together enough to insist they let me ride with him.

"Up front," the blonde female paramedic insists.

I shake my head.

"Ma'am, we need to work. Get in front, and get out of our way."

My phone rings as I get in the front of the ambulance, and I look down at it.

"Daddy," I answer, "I need you."

"He's gonna be fine, baby girl. They are flying him into Landstuhl, Germany as soon as he's stable. Best medical facility in the world. Just pray, Ava. Pray."

"No, Daddy, we're in an ambulance. Why would they fly him to Germany? What are you—"

"You're in a *what*?" he gasps.

"T, Daddy. God, I don't know what happened, but I took a picture of the car. He's gonna be okay, Daddy, right? Tell me he's going to be okay!" I am sobbing.

"We have a pulse," I hear and sob again into my hands.

"Daddy, they have a pulse. They have a pulse!"

"Ava," he says, his voice cracking. "I'll be there as soon as I can."

"Hurry, Daddy. Hurry and tell everyone to pray. And Maddox. T needs Maddox, too."

"Whatever you need," he says.

"I have to go," I tell him.

"Ava, which hospital?"

"Which hospital?" I ask the driver.

"NYU Lutheran is the closest."

"Daddy, he said—"

"I heard him. We'll be there."

"Okay," I cry as I look back at T. "Hurry, Daddy, I need you."

Twenty-Three

Love is forgiveness, growth, struggle, resilience, laughter and pain.
— J. Ewalani Figueroa

I AM IN THE WAITING room. The police have the pictures I took from my phone and statements from the people at the scene of the accident. I can't even think about justice right now, though. I just need him to be okay.

My mother and Robert are here; Dad must have called them. It has been three hours, three of the most awful hours of my life. Mom keeps telling me no news is good news, and I have to believe it's true.

I can't possibly cry anymore, but I can't stop the silent sobs and the shaking.

I stare at my phone, flipping through all the pictures of T, all of the selfies of both of us. We are forever, just like he said, and forever hasn't ended. It hasn't, and it won't. He will fight for our love, and I will pray for his life.

I stand up and walk to the reception desk.

"Is there a chapel?" I ask.

"Yes, out the door, take a left, and it's at the end of the hall."

"If there is any news on Thomas Hardy, my fiancé,

will you come and get me?"

"Of course, Miss Links."

I turn back to see Mom looking at me.

"I'll be back."

I follow the directions to the chapel, open the doors, and walk in. No one is in here. It's just me, several lit candles, and a cross.

I walk up and lower myself upon the deep red velvet kneeler and light a candle then another and another and another until all of them have been lit.

"God, I've made some mistakes, but please, *please* don't ignore me when I ask that You please save him. I promise I will love him forever. I promise we'll go to church and do good things and raise our babies to know You. I promise with everything I am that I will be the best mother in the world, the best wife, the best friend, the best humanitarian. Whatever You need, I will give to You. Whatever I can't give right now, I will find a way ..." I stop when I get a cramp and hold my hands over my belly. "They need him. They need him because, when I'm with him, I am a better me. You brought him to me at my darkest and made me see him for who he is and who he wants to be. Please, God, please—"

I stop when I feel hands on my shoulders, and I look at one of them.

It's my daddy's hand.

I put my hand on his, and tears find their way back to me.

"Come here, Ava," he says, and I stand up. "Everything's going to be okay."

I don't respond. I just stand in my dad's arms, crying.

"Let's go see if there is any news," he says.

"Then right back here," I tell him.

"Of course."

When we get to the ER waiting room, Tessa comes up and hugs me. "Ava, I need you to give them permission to talk to me, okay?"

Tessa is a nurse, and even though it will annoy my mother, I don't care. I don't care one bit.

I look over at Mom, and she gives a smile that I haven't seen in a few years now.

She gets up and walks over.

"Any news?"

"No, not yet," I answer.

"No news is good news," Tessa says with a nod.

Mom nods at her. "Yes, it is."

I see Maddox standing in the very back of the waiting room. Harper is hugging him. When he sees me, he sighs, and I shake my head. I have no idea what to say or do for him when I can't even breathe right now.

"How are you holding up, Ashley?" Tessa asks my mother.

"Got to be strong for her," Mom answers.

"I know," Tessa says quietly.

"We all do," Mom says.

I look back, and they smile at each other. I am lost in their exchange briefly until Harper hugs me.

"God, Ava, they have to be okay."

Dad clears his throat from behind me, and I look back to see he is shaking his head at her.

"What? Do you know something I don't?" I feel my knees weaken.

"No, baby girl," he says.

"She doesn't know?" Harper asks.

"Know, what?"

Dad sighs and puts his hands on my shoulders, looking me in the eyes. "Luke has been injured."

"What?" I gasp.

"Last night, an IED exploded. He's being flown to Germany."

I shake my head as I say the word, "No."

"We just found out when you called. Jade and Ryan are flying out. They'll let us know when they know anything."

"Is he going to be okay?" I ask.

"Miss Links."

I look over to see a doctor approaching us.

My head spins, my knees shake, and I can't breathe. I gasp for a breath and feel my father picking me up in his arms.

"Ava," I hear Piper and look around. She's lying in Emma's arms with my crown on her head.

I must look shocked, because Harper says, "I'm sorry. She's just been having a … time, and we can't leave her."

I nod as Dad sits down, still holding me.

"You're going to be okay, Ava," she says.

Piper climbs up next to me as the doctor approaches.

"Piper, come with me." Emma smiles at her.

"No." She yawns, leaning her head against me.

"She's fine," I say, looking at the doctor.

"Thomas is in recovery."

I nod my understanding.

"He's in critical condition. His pelvic and hip bones were crushed due to the impact, two collapsed lungs, several broken ribs, one that broke off and punctured his heart. He went into cardiac arrest several times during the initial surgery, and he has lost a lot of blood. We have no idea when or if he will wake up. He is not breathing on his own, so we are using a ventilator, per Mr. Robert's request. His injuries are substantial. We've done everything we can for him."

"So, now what?" I ask.

"Are you praying people?" he asks.

"Yes."

"Then you should pray," he says with a sincerity that nearly scares the life out of me.

Tessa walks up to him as he walks away.

"Can I see him!" I yell.

"As soon as you can, I'll have a nurse come and get you," he answers.

"No! *You.* You come and get me," I demand, pointing at him.

"Ava," Dad says, trying to calm me.

"No," I tell him. "He needs to stay with T."

Piper puts her hand on my knee. "T is okay."

I hug her tightly, burying her face in my chest, not wanting her to see how truly scared I am.

"Pray for him. We all pray for him."

She pulls back and looks up. "T is okay." She puts her hand on my belly and nods. "Yep."

"That's very sweet, Piper," I say, standing up, and I feel crampy again. "I'm going to get a drink."

I drink down the bottle of water Dad gets for me and close my eyes as he hugs me.

"He's going to be okay, Daddy, right?"

"I pray he is. Him and Luke."

I know Dad needs me to say the same, but I am terrified that, if I pray for Luke, Thomas will get less. It makes no sense. None of it makes any sense.

I squeeze him. "Pray, Daddy, pray hard."

"I am."

Twenty minutes later, I follow the doctor to a room. We are told only three people are allowed in, but I don't pay attention to who is behind me; I just need to get to him.

When I see him, I flinch and my stomach turns.

"This is a mechanical ventilator." I glance toward

Tessa and then take T's hand, careful not to pull out the IV. "An endotracheal tube is running from the machine to his lungs."

"Down his throat?" I whisper.

"It has to, Miss Links," the doctor says.

"Doctor, my name is Ava and his is Thomas, or T. We love each other. We're getting married in two weeks and having two babies in September." I feel like I am going crazy, but I know I have to be strong for T. "So please don't call me Miss Links. In my heart and in his, I am Ava soon-to-be Hardy, Mrs. Thomas Hardy. I am the love of his life, and he is the love of mine. Right, T?"

Silence.

"The tube in T's nose is a nasogastric tube," Tessa continues. "The air goes in the endotracheal tube and comes out the nasogastric tube. He's getting oxygen, Ava."

I look up at her and nod. "That's good, T. The machine is breathing for you, and you can concentrate on healing. We need you. The three of us need you." I take his hand and hold it to my belly. "We're right here with you, T. We are right here, praying for you and loving you and waiting for you to open your eyes. Please, T, I need to see your eyes." I pull his hand up and kiss it as I wait.

I know he can hear me. I know he can.

"Please," I beg in a whisper.

§

FOR A WEEK, I LIE next to him, afraid if I leave, he will wake up and I won't be here. The only time I leave is to shower, and Maddox is with him then.

They are all staying at the flat. No one has gone back home. I haven't gone back to our home, either. I can't, not until he is with me.

Every day, the doctor looks at me, and I know what he wants to tell me. He wants to tell me that I need to prepare myself. He won't tell me that again; I can guarantee it.

I have no appetite, and the only time I attempt to eat is when Harper makes me. She sits with me and makes me.

I heard them talk about Luke. He is stable, awake, and a mess. They are trying to get him stable enough to bring him to Walter Reed.

Jade has called my phone a dozen times, but I can't answer it. I won't. Instead, I tell Dad to make sure she knows I'm sending her my love. Never in front of T, though, because I know he can hear me, and I don't want him to be jealous. I want him strong and concentrating on waking up and proving them all wrong. I make sure Dad tells her I love her and that, as soon as T wakes up, I will call her back.

Maddox and Brody are by his side as much as they can be. The publicist T met the night that seems like a lifetime ago at the Spotted Pig has been dealing with the reporters and fans who have gathered outside the hospital to pray for him. I can't look out the window, but I am grateful T is loved by so many and that they are praying for his healing just like I am. I hear them talk about the crowd, but I am one hundred percent focused on him and me and love and hope.

I tell him what I hear and that he has such a support system and love from all over the world. I tell him because he is loved. Regardless of what he felt as a child and young adult, Thomas Hardy is loved by millions and even more so by me and the two we have created.

Maddox sits in the chair, staring at him, but he

doesn't talk to him unless I urge him to. I know he has given up hope. I know they all have. But not me.

God has brought him to me, not fate. Fate is a bitch, and bitches don't bring angels. Fate doesn't bring people who smell like T, like love and home.

I don't cry in front of him or anyone. But in the shower, I cry, I sob, I pray and plead with God to please wake him up soon, because I know ... I know I can't handle it for much longer, and I heard God doesn't give you more than you can handle.

God must know I am strong, so strong that He is waiting for me to promise Him the right promise. When I figure it out, T will open his eyes. T will open his eyes, and we will get married in a week. Here, not home. Here is our home. Home is wherever he and I are.

I am standing under the water now, crying, pleading, begging, and holding my belly.

For two days, T's and my babies have been fighting, too. I can feel them moving. I can feel them, and I know they want him to wake up.

I am naked on my knees, my hands folded as I look up under the shower's water.

"God, please, they need to meet him. They need him."

When my phone alarm goes off, I know it has been seven minutes. I have given myself three to dry off, dress, and get back to him.

When I step out, I slip. I grab the shower curtain, and it falls down, too weak to sustain my weight. I fall on my side, and it hurts. It hurts badly, but it's nothing like the pain T is feeling.

I dry off and get dressed. Our babies are moving, so I know they are okay.

My alarm goes off again, letting me know it has been ten minutes.

I brush my teeth, wanting T to be able to smell me and know that I am clean and taking care of myself and them for him.

When I walk out, Maddox stands. "I'll be back in a few hours."

I walk past him to T's side. "T, did you hear Maddox? He'll be back soon, okay? He has to go see Piper, okay?"

I feel a warm, wet gush between my legs, and I grab my belly that is cramping now worse than ever.

"Ava?" Maddox says as I lower myself to my knees, gripping the sheet covering T.

"I'm okay," I say so T hears me. "I'm okay, Maddox."

"No, Ava, you're not." He reaches past me and hits the call bell. "You're bleeding."

I look down between my legs and see blood.

"Maddox," I say as I feel my head begin to spin. "I don't feel very well."

Maddox lifts me and runs into the hallway.

"Maddox, don't leave him," I say as my eyes get heavier and heavier.

"He'd have my arse if I didn't," he snarls. "I need some help!"

"Ava?" I hear my dad's voice.

"I'm okay," I say. "I'm—"

Twenty—Four

Like a plant, love needs TLC.
— M. Smith

WHEN I WAKE UP, I am in pain—horrible, terrible pain—but I need to get to T. I need to. My body is so heavy, but I try to push myself up, anyway.

"T …" The words are slurred.

I feel hands on my shoulders. "Lie back, Ava."

"I need T, Daddy."

"You need to rest, Ava. You need to get stronger. You have two"—his voice breaks—"tiny, little people who need their mom to be strong."

I drag my hands to my belly and quickly realize that it's the source of all the pain. "Oh, God, why? Why!"

"They are fighters, baby girl. The girl is two pounds, and the boy is two pounds, two ounces."

"It's too soon!" I cry.

"They're in for a hell of a fight, Ava, but they are part you, and I know God is looking out for them."

"They're beautiful, Ava," I hear Mom cry, and I open my eyes.

"I need to see T, Mom. Please take me to see T," I beg. "He needs to see them."

I can't comprehend what has happened. I can't handle everything going on.

"Rest, Ava," Dad says.

I cry, "I don't want to." Then sleep claims me.

§

I WAKE UP AND OPEN my eyes. I am still in pain, but I refuse to let them know that.

I see Harper sitting next to me, my father at the door talking to my mom, and Logan on the other side of me.

"Ava," he says as soon as he notices my eyes are open.

"Logan, when did you get here?" I don't wait for him to answer me. "Take me to T, Logan. Please take me to him."

He shakes his head. "Can't do that, Ava."

"I would do it for you, Logan. I would, and you know it!" I don't know where the strength comes from to sit up, but I do, holding my belly tightly with my hands.

"Ava, don't," Harper pleads as tears escape her eyes.

"Harper, take me to T. Please take me to him."

Dad nearly runs through the room to stand over me.

"Dad, if you make me go to sleep again, I'll never forgive you. Not ever."

"You need rest, Ava. Those babies need you to rest," he says sternly.

"They need to see their father," I snap at him.

Tessa walks over with her phone and holds it up. "Your dad, Maddox, and Brody were allowed to bring them down."

I see my babies on her screen. They are so tiny, so tiny and fragile. They have tubes and wires, just like T.

I cover my mouth with my hands as I watch Maddox take T's hand and put it inside the incubator and hold it there. Then Dad and three nurses carry in some sort of machine and wheel up the other baby, and Maddox does the same thing to that one.

"*Your babies need you ...*" Maddox pauses and chokes back tears in the video. "*Brother.*"

I begin to tremble. I reach up and take her phone.

"Your girl needs you, too. I need you, T. Please, if there is a chance for a miracle, now is the time, T. Open your eyes. Open your fucking eyes!"

Brody takes Maddox by his shoulders. "*Okay, Maddox, let's take a walk.*"

"*No. No, I told her I would stay, and I will. But, T, we need this now. We need it now.*"

The video stops, and I look around the room. I see Maddox sitting against the wall on the floor, his head buried in his knees.

"Maddox?"

He doesn't look up.

I look at Dad and then realize everyone is in the room.

"Who is with T?"

Dad swallows as he sits next to me.

"Dad. Who. Is. With. T!"

"Ava, he met his children. He touched them and—"

"Who is with him!"

Harper begins to sob; Logan is crying; Mom is crying; Dad has tears in his eyes; Brody is holding Emma; and I look at Tessa.

"You tell me. You tell me now ... please."

"Oh, Ava," she says, closing her eyes. "He's gone."

"No. NO. NO!" I push at my father and cry out from the pain inside and outside and all around me.

"Baby girl, we are so sorry," he says.

My hand stings, and I know he has drugged me again.

"Don't. Please don't."

My body begins to fall backward, and he catches me and lays me back.

"Don't ever do that again."

§

I WAKE UP FACING THE window. I see the sun rising, and my heart hurts. I didn't think to insist that T see the sun rise.

I cover my face with my hands and squeeze my eyes tightly. My T, the love of my life, the father of my children, the only person who ever truly got me is gone while the sun is still rising.

I hate the sun. I hate it!

I look around the room to see Brody and Dad are here, asleep.

I hold a pillow tightly to my belly and sit up. I look at the IV and see that they are attached to a pole with wheels. I hurt, and I hurt badly, but I get out of bed and very quietly, very slowly walk out of the room undetected.

In the hallway, I look up to see Dr. Kennedy, the doctor T and I saw when we first found out I was pregnant. She sighs and shakes her head at me disapprovingly as she grabs the empty wheelchair and pushes it toward me.

"I have no idea how you are walking, but I'm telling you it's a very bad idea. Sit, and I'll get you back in bed," she says.

I shake my head. "I want to see T."

"I'm very sorry, but that's not possible." She pats the chair. "But if you'd like, I can take you down to the NICU. You have two beautiful babies who, God willing, are going to pull through."

I can't sit. I don't want to see them. I'm afraid that, if I see them, I won't ever be able to walk away. And if

I pray for them, they will end up just like their father.

"Ava," she says firmly, "sit. I promise you, right now, things may seem hopeless, but down the road, there is hope in abundance."

All of a sudden, I feel weak and have no choice but to sit.

She pushes down the footrests, takes the pole with the IV drip, and starts walking us toward the elevator.

We are alone in the elevator when she walks around in front of me and squats down. "I understand wanting to change doctors, but I hope you know that I take my job very seriously. Doctor/patient confidentiality is part of my job. As I told Thomas on the phone, I would have never divulged to anyone else that he may not be the father of both the children."

"Excuse me?" I gasp, unable to grasp what she is saying.

"If you change your mind and want to have the paternity tests done again, we can remove that doubt."

"He *is* their father."

She nods. "Okay."

"No," I say as she stands. "Not okay. What are you talking about?" I have no idea what she is talking about or why she is saying this to me.

"The same thing I told Thomas. The twins aren't necessarily both his." She pauses, her expression changing to pity. "Oh, sweetheart, he didn't tell you, did he?"

"Why are you doing this to me?" What is wrong with her? Where is her humanity?

"I'm sorry, Ava. I thought he told you. I thought you both knew."

He didn't tell me because he didn't want to hurt me. He didn't tell me because he loves me. He didn't tell me because it's not true. He knew in his heart both babies were his.

The door opens, and she walks behind me and wheels me out into the hallway. "If you'd like the tests run—"

"No. No, and I don't ever want to talk about it again," I whisper to her sternly over my shoulder.

"As you wish."

God, T, what were you thinking? I ask him in my head.

The answer screams back at me. He loves me. He loves me so much he didn't want me to hurt anymore because of Luke.

Twenty-Five

Love isn't all it's wrapped up to be...love hurts.
— D. Holtry

SHE PUSHES ME TOWARD THE glass automatic doors that say NICU, and they open.

My head is spinning from the information she just gave me, topped with the loss of T, the pain I am in, and the fact that I have no idea what I am about to face.

"The female is smaller but stronger. Her lungs are very well-formed for a baby born at twenty-five plus four." My babies are twenty-five weeks and four days old. "We have her on a respirator in case she stops breathing. Your son has a heart condition called PDA. There is a great chance it will heal itself without surgery. We are also concerned that he may have necrotizing enterocolitis. His stomach is distended, and he isn't eating well. When he does eat, he tends to vomit more than we like to see. We are monitoring him very closely. But I will tell you that expressing your breast milk will help him a great deal. NEC can cause a hole to open up and allow the bacteria to the intestines that could leak, and it can be fatal."

When we round the corner, I see my mom and Tessa both sitting next to incubators. They look up and both stand and step toward me. Tessa stops, and I know she is trying not to overstep.

"Ava, how are you?" she asks as I start to stand.

"Ava, sit. This wheelchair is more mobile than you." Dr. Kennedy immediately begins to tell me more about my poor children. "The beds are heated because your children are too small to regulate their body temperature. The lighted probes on their feet are to read oxygen saturation. They have intravenous lines set for antibiotics and feeding."

"You said they were eating," I interrupt.

"Through tubes," she explains.

"When can I take them home?" I ask, wanting them out of here. Out of the place their father died in. Out of the place where they look so helpless.

I cover my mouth and start to cry for them, for mine and T's babies.

"The answer is when they are eating and breathing on their own and when they are healthy, Ava," Dr. Kennedy says, lowering her tone as she pushes me to the one wrapped in pink.

"When will that be?" I whisper back as I look up at her.

"A guess would be their due date," Tessa answers.

"September?" I ask, looking at her.

"Your little girl is so strong, so very strong and doing amazing." Tessa smiles. "She is a miracle, actually."

"And the boy?" I ask, afraid to look at him, not knowing how much more I can take.

"He's a fighter," Mom says. "He's going to be fine. Expect him to act just like Logan did in a few years."

I am afraid to smile or take delight in this. The fear comes from wondering when it will all be taken away like T was.

"Are you sure?"

"Yes," she says firmly. "Yes, I am, because my little girl has struggled enough, and if that man loved you half as much as Harper and Maddox have said over the past week, he is up there right now, making sure of it."

Tessa clears her throat and swallows hard. Her voice breaks when she says, "And Piper said so."

I nod and look back at my mom. "What if I can't do this?"

"Oh, no, that's not my little girl talking. She can and has done anything she puts her mind to from the day she was born. You have got this, Ava."

"And if you feel like you're ready to walk away, you tell any of us. Someone will walk with you while the others fight over who gets to hold these beautiful, little people you created," Tessa says.

"Me and T," I whisper as I put my hand inside the incubator. "Me and T."

Tessa grabs my elbow and pulls it back. "We need to scrub you up, Ava."

After my hands are washed, I ask for gloves, but they tell me that's not necessary. Then Mom wheels me over to my son.

"He's bigger than her, and he has hair," I say when I see his hair from under his blue knit hat.

"You had a lot of hair when you were born," Mom says as she rubs her hand down the back of my head. "Both you and Logan."

I nod and reach in, touching his tiny foot.

"Why do they have blindfolds on?"

"They like it dark, warm, and quiet," Dr. Kennedy answers.

I nod as I count five little toes.

"His belly is big."

"Which is another reason we are monitoring him for NEC."

I look at Dr. Kennedy, remembering she told me it could be fatal.

"I need a pump," I say, squinting my eyes and shaking my head, remembering vividly when T bought a breast pump online and how he tried it out on himself. We both laughed and laughed.

"He's going to miss all of this. Why? Why did he die?"

"Ava, he was never going to pull through. His injuries were too substantial," Dr. Kennedy says.

"But none of us ever gave up hope," Tessa adds firmly, looking at Dr. Kennedy as if to tell her to tread lightly.

I look over at the girl. "Hope. Her name is Hope."

"That's a beautiful name," Mom says. "And his?"

I rub his tiny foot and shrug. "I'm not sure yet."

§

I SPEND A LONG TIME in the room, going between the two of them. It is not without pain. My body hurts. My heart hurts. My soul hurts.

"You need to rest," Mom says, rubbing my shoulder.

"I don't want to leave them."

"Ava, they need you to get stronger, and the only way to do that is for you to take care of yourself. I am telling you this as your mother. You are going to rest."

"And you'll both stay with them?" I ask, looking between her and Tessa.

They both nod.

"And if something happens to me, you'll both take care of them?"

"Nothing is going to happen to you," Mom says with her brows turned in. "Do you understand me? Nothing."

"But if, by chance—"

"Ava, your mother and I are here and will be until you kick us out. And like she said, nothing is going to happen to you."

I nod, but I don't believe for a minute that God—if He is real—could possibly take Thomas Hardy while leaving me here.

§

I WAKE UP TO MY phone ringing and answer it.

"Hello?"

"Ava? Oh, Ava, are you okay? I am so sorry, sweetheart." Jade sniffs. "So, so sorry."

"Thank you," I say quietly.

"How are your babies?"

"Thomas and my children are in for a fight. Mom and Tessa are with them. They made the doctor bring me here to rest."

"You need to rest," she says quietly.

I take a deep breath and hope T can hear my thoughts, that I am only saying this because it's the right thing to do. "How is he?"

"Luke is a fighter." She pauses and sniffs a few more times. "He has two shattered legs, several broken ribs, and both lungs are punctured but healing. He has vision loss in his left eye and"—she pauses—"he's going to be okay."

"Good," I say. It's the right thing to say, but I stop myself from allowing any further thought from entering my mind.

"He wants you to know how sorry he is about T. He asked if you were okay."

"Tell him thank you and that I'm fine."

"And the babies?"

"They have to be okay," I answer. "They have to be strong."

"We would be there if we could, Ava."

"There are a lot of people here now," I tell her instead of telling her that Luke isn't welcome because T wouldn't want him here.

"But we"—she pauses—"would be there."

"Thank you."

"You sound tired, Ava. I won't keep you. I just needed to hear your voice."

"Thank you, Jade."

"We love you, Ava, and you and your children are in our prayers. We fly out of here tomorrow morning and into Washington. When Luke is stronger, we will be there."

"Fly safe, Jade."

"We will."

I hang up then drop the phone on the table, grab my button, and push it, wanting to fall asleep.

§

A WEEK AFTER MY LOVE has passed away, I am discharged from the hospital, but I have no intention of leaving.

T was cremated and his ashes were taken by Brody and Emma to the loft before they flew home. I told Brody— who was a father figure to T, and I could tell he felt the same about T—that he needed to put them in the babies' room by the window so T could see the sun, and Brody agreed.

Logan didn't return to school. Mom, Dad, and I tried to convince him to, but he isn't leaving me and said he didn't care, that until his niece and nephew are home, he will be with me. He can take an extra semester and play another season of football. It's a win-win; except, it isn't. There are no wins in this situation.

Dad and Tessa plan to fly to Washington for two days

to visit Luke. Dad asks me if I can name his grandson before he leaves.

"Chance Thomas," I say without second thoughts. I had never even considered it as an option.

Hope was always there with T and me. My little girl is hope. With our son, every time they thought something could be wrong, but there was a chance he would heal without surgery, he did, so he has become Chance. I know T would have loved it.

Maddox and Harper have no plans to leave, and on occasion, they will bring Piper to visit me.

Piper is such a light in the darkness that surrounds me. She talks about T like he is still here, and she talks about his accident in her dreams.

Harper looks bewildered. "Piper, is that what your dreams were about?"

"T and Luke and they are okay." She smiles big at me and nods. "Right?"

I lean down and kiss her.

I wake in the rocker between my children when an alarm goes off. My first instinct is to reach in and gently pat their feet to startle them so that they remember to breathe.

It's Chance's monitor.

Four nurses rush in.

"Ava, you'll need to move," one says, and I step back as I watch them work on our son.

As soon as the alarm stops, they take more blood out of his poor little body to run a million different tests.

A few hours later, they tell me he needs a transfusion.

I'm terrified, but I tell them to take whatever they need from me. They tell me that Chance is A positive and I am O positive. Curiosity gets the best of me, and I ask what Hope's blood type is.

When I ask the question, I see Dr. Kennedy walk in.

The nurse looks at Hope's chart and tells me, "She is the same as you."

When they leave to get Chance ready for his transfusion, Dr. Kennedy tells me T was also O. She doesn't say anything more, but the woman seems to want to make my life miserable. She is putting doubt in way of healing. I know damn well Chance is T's, as well as I know our love for each other was not perfect, but it was real and true. Unlike mine for … Luke.

"She has the bedside manner of a freaking troll," I tell Logan, and he nods. I roll my eyes. "I may have just made a joke, Logan; the least you could do is laugh."

"These two, Ava, they are little miracles," he says as he rocks Hope who is now off her respirator and feeding from my expressed milk. "And you're doing really well with them."

Twenty-Six

Sometimes the weeds creep in and you need to work to get them out.
— J. Baldwin

SIX WEEKS LATER, I AM leaving the hospital and going to the flat for the very first time. Hope A. Hardy is a miracle. She is up to five pounds, two ounces; eats on her own; breathes on her own; and even has some hair. It's blonde, and her eyes are blue.

When I walk out of the hospital, I take a deep breath as Dad pulls up in his SUV and Casey pulls up behind him. She jumps out and runs over to me, stopping quickly as she gets very close to me.

"Ava," she says, trying to remain calm.

"Casey. Oh, God, I'm sorry," I say as I stand with Hope in my arms and give her a hug. "I must have forgotten to call you, and have you been paid, and—"

"Your father and Brody have kept in touch. Thomas has"—she pauses and clears her throat— "had my pay deposited into my account. I haven't touched it, though. I want to know what you want to do about the vehicle and, well, me. But there is time. I'm just here to see if you need anything or—"

"I want you to do whatever it is you do." I nod. "Casey, this is Hope. Hope, this is Casey, and I really wish she would stay on with us. I'll figure out how to pay you and all that stuff, but I know I'm going to need you. And T trusted you with me, so I know he would trust you with his children."

"You have my number?" she asks.

I nod. "I'll be in touch."

Once in the vehicle, I put Hope into a seat that seems way too big for her. Dad is sitting next to me, helping me buckle her in.

"I don't know if I've said thank you enough for everything."

"Ava, we know, okay, sweetheart? We know."

"I have no idea how I would have made it through without everyone."

"That's why you should move home as soon as Chance is well enough."

I half-laugh at the idea. "We have a home. I will figure it out."

"Ava, you are going to need us. And baby girl, we need you."

"Daddy, did you see what he did for them? I'm not taking them away from it. Not ever."

He looks at me and takes in a deep breath. Then he looks down and kisses Hope's little head before looking back at me. "We'll figure it out, Ava. All of it."

As we pull away from the hospital, I feel a different hell than the one I have been in since the night Thomas was hit. I am leaving one of my children for the first time because the other is strong enough to go home.

"Ava," Dad says, looking back at me in the rearview mirror. "Your mother and Logan are with him."

I nod as my eyes well up with tears.

"He's getting stronger."

I nod again.

"They didn't think he was going to make it, and he

did. He will be with you and his sister soon."

I nod as I look down at my sleeping angel who is holding my finger and sucking on a little blue-green pacifier.

For a week, she couldn't even suck. She couldn't even breathe on her own for a full day, and now, she is going home.

She is hope.

"Brody and Maddox contacted T's lawyer. Apparently, he had already changed everything in his will, leaving you as his sole beneficiary."

"Why did he have a will?" I ask myself out loud. "He's too young to even have had to worry about such things."

"He was also in a rock band and made more money from royalties in a month than I ever did in a year at his age. Those royalties don't stop, Ava. Your children will be taken care of."

I don't respond. I look down at Hope and whisper, "And we would give it all away just to have him here with us, wouldn't we, Hope?"

I look at her, unable to believe she has more than doubled in size since the first time I saw her. Dr. Kennedy tells me it's due to my milk, and she says it with an expectancy in her voice that rubs me the wrong way. I also know it pushes me to continue expressing milk regardless of how much my breasts hurt. Besides, hurt is welcome over pain, and pumping fills the quiet time.

Pain is in those moments.

The pain-filled moments when I think of him, I want to join him. I want to because life on this earth is black and white. The only color I see is in our children and in Piper.

I love my family. I love them. But my love for T, as

well as his for me, is a love like nothing I ever felt. His love for me was euphoric; our home was Utopia; and nothing else will ever compare, not ever.

"Jade called this morning. Luke is coming home," Dad says, but I don't look up. "Ava?"

"I heard you. That's wonderful for them."

"It's wonderful for all of us," he says.

I nod.

§

GETTING OUT OF THE VEHICLE is harder than I could have imagined. However, I force myself for Hope.

"Want to see what your daddy did for you and your brother, Hope?"

In Hope, I find strength, just like I did in her father. Like I still do in his love.

He is with me in my pain, and he is with me in our children. In our children, there is the epic and extraordinary love of two people. I will do whatever I have to for them.

I step out and can't look left. My heart beats in my throat, and my hands tremble.

Pain. Pain lives outside of our home.

"Let's get you inside," Dad says as he leans in and unlatches Hope's seat.

His arm is around my waist, and I am not sure if he is holding me up or if I am. His opposite hand has my Hope in her carrier.

Tessa, Brody, Emma, London, Lexington, Harper, Maddox, Piper, my mother's sisters, Ally, and Alex are in the lobby when we walk in. It's overwhelming.

"We'll give you a minute," Tessa says as we walk past them into the cargo elevator.

"Thanks," Dad says since I am unable.

"I go, too," Pipers says, starting to walk toward us.

"Not yet," Harper stops her.

Hurt shows on her face, and I cannot bear it.

"It's fine." I hold out my hand for Piper.

When Dad closes the door in front of us, Piper lets go of my hand and walks over to the carrier.

"Hi, butterfly," she says as she reaches in and tickles her belly.

Hope's eyes open, and I wonder if she is frightened by all the new surroundings and Piper's little face less than six inches from her.

Piper smiles and giggles. Then she puts her hands up, thumbs facing each other, and makes her fingers dance. "Butterfly hi's, baby Hope, and welcome home."

Hope stares at her and not the light, which is unusual.

Piper giggles again and looks up at Dad and then me. "See? T is okay."

Dad looks at me like he is expecting me to fall apart.

I put on a smile for her, the first in weeks.

"And you're all right, too. See?" She puts her hands up again. "Butterfly hi's."

I nod, grateful the elevator stops, distracting her, because I don't know if I can take it while walking in here.

"Hey, Piper," I say, trying to smile. "I might get sad when I walk in here."

She shrugs. "I know."

When Dad opens the door, I take the carrier from him.

"You sure, Ava?"

I nod. "I'm sure."

"Follow me," Piper says as she skips inside.

"Just a minute, okay?"

"Yep, I'll be in Hope and Chance's room."

I set the carrier on the counter and push the buttons on the side of the handle before pushing back the bar. "Welcome home, Hope," I say as a tear slips down my cheek. I finish unbuckling her and pick her up, holding her tightly against my chest. "Welcome home, sweet girl."

The house is clean, but there are suitcases piled in a corner. I am not alone, still not alone with my grief. I hope I can continue showing that I am strong when, in reality, I'm a mess. I am glad no one can see that I have no idea how to deal with any of what is going on.

As I start to walk toward their room, the bathroom door opens, and Liam steps out.

"Sorry, I was supposed to stay downstairs. I slipped past security to use the bathroom." He walks over and leans over my shoulder. "Hey there, little one. You look like your daddy."

I look up at him. "You think so?"

Despite no one saying that, I have thought it, but I was afraid it was just me wanting to see him in them.

"Eye shape." He smiles. "Facial structure. You definitely look like your father, little one." He gives me a quick kiss on the head. "I'll head down."

"No, stay."

"I will, but you better tell the head of security that you okayed it."

I give him a quizzical look.

"Tessa. She insisted we give you time. She also insisted that we all stay back upstate, and I kind of snuck my way down."

"I'm glad," I say, nodding.

He smiles. "That Tessa is keeping everyone away or that I'm here?"

"Both?" I say because my head is swimming in a sea of overwhelming emotions.

He nods. "Okay, both."

I walk with Hope into the nursery, feeling dizzy, and make my way to the rocker T put together for me to sit in. Piper is next to the one he was supposed to be in, right next to mine.

"It's beautiful, Hope," she whispers and giggles.

Hope looks toward the window, seeking the light. She seems content when she finds it.

"She likes it." Piper also seems content with her summarization of the situation.

After securing Hope in one arm, I pat Piper's head. "Of course she does."

She walks away from me and faces the wall that T drew and painted in bright, vivid colors. She stands in front of it and does the same hand gesture, the butterfly one.

"He's okay, Ava. He's happy."

"How do you know?" I manage to croak out.

She turns around and smiles as brightly as day. "He tells me."

"Pip-Pip, how about we give Ava a minute?" Dad says, peeking his head in. Apparently, I am unable to hide my grief as well as I thought.

He picks her up, and she points to one of the clouds. "Right there. He's happy."

"Okay, little one," Dad says.

"I'll take her." Liam holds his hands out.

She shakes her head. "Pop-pop's girl."

Dad kisses my head then walks toward the door. "I'll be out here if you need anything, Ava."

"Me, too," Liam says, clearly affected by Piper.

"Stay?" Liam has always had a calming effect on me.

He nods once then sits in T's rocker, asking, "Want to talk about it?"

I swallow and shake my head.

"Okay, then."

Piper's giggle and footsteps break the deafening silence.

"Get back here, princess," Dad says. I hear him running after her.

She runs in and stops at my feet. She holds up my sunglasses and, with her finger, motions to me to lean in. I do, and she puts them on my head and smiles.

"Sparkle for your big head."

Dad and Liam both look at me. They look shocked, stunned, and I smile because she's the absolute sweetest thing.

"My big head thanks you." I lean down and kiss her cheek.

"Now kiss her." She grins, pointing to Hope.

So I do.

I look over at Liam as Dad and Piper walk out of the nursery again. He still looks shocked.

"What?"

"She just told you that you have a big head."

"If the crown fits …" I shrug. "She's made this mess almost bearable."

He smiles. "You've got this, Ava. I know it's easier said than done, but you have to believe you do."

I shake my head and shrug. "I have no idea what I am going to do without him, Liam. I love him so much, and he loved me just as much and for longer than I even knew."

"I know, but you don't have a choice, and if you did, I know you'd choose to heal for those babies. It'll make up for the lag in your noticing his love."

"I have no idea what God is thinking, but I am not this strong."

"You are. You just have to allow yourself to believe

it." He stands. "You ready for the troops to arrive?"

"I need to feed her. Can you tell them I'll be out when we're done?"

"Of course."

"Liam."

He stops and turns around. "Yeah?"

"Thank you."

"For?"

"Breaking out of upstate and coming."

He winks. "You wouldn't answer my calls."

"I wasn't answering anyone's."

"I know, Ava."

Twenty-Seven

One of the hardest but rewarding experiences ever.
— M. Gratton

I WAKE UP WITH HOPE in my arms and Mom next to me, awake. Hope doesn't sleep well in her bassinet and fusses. When she is on my belly, she sleeps like an angel, and she smells like T, which is the only reason I have been able to sleep.

Mom and Tessa take turns watching me sleep. I don't mind it a bit. They are helping both Hope and me.

"You okay?" Mom asks, pushing my hair out of my face.

I nod. "I need to wake her up to feed her and get back to the hospital to feed Chance."

"Your brother is there with him," she says, trying like she has for two weeks to convince me that I should take just a day to sleep and let them take care of the babies.

"I know, but the doctors will be making rounds, and I want to be there."

"His heart healed on its own. No more PDA. His NEC is gone—"

"But if it comes back, if he gets it again—"

"Ava, he won't," she says, trying to calm me.

I sit up and pull my shirt up. Then I take the pacifier out of Hope's mouth.

"Sweet girl, wake up. You need to eat, and then you can sleep the day away."

"We need to try to get her on a schedule. Her days and nights are confused."

"So are mine, Mom. At least this way, she sleeps when I'm at the hospital with Chance, and she's awake when I'm home."

"But you need to take care of—"

"I've got it, Mom, and I appreciate the help, but if it's too much for all of you, I'm sure I can manage."

"Ava—"

"No, Mom. No."

"Okay," she sighs. "Okay."

§

AN HOUR LATER, I AM in the SUV with Dad. Everyone else left last night.

Casey is home with Mom so Mom can sleep, and if Mom needs anything at the store, Casey can go for her or help out in any way she needs. I know they think it's overkill, two people for one baby, but it's what I need. It's what Hope needs.

"How're you feeling?" Dad asks.

"Like hell," I admit for probably the first time.

"I know you don't like the idea of moving back home, Ava, but as you can see, there is a much bigger support system there for you."

"As much as I appreciate it, I'm staying here."

"But—"

"Last night, I was able to hold Hope and not worry if shutting myself in the nursery was offending anyone. This morning, I walked through Thomas and my home after a shower and didn't have to fully get dressed in order to move about. Today, I don't have to worry about coming home and eating a much appreciated meal so that people know I am not a cold, cruel bitch, but I'm just not that hungry."

"Ava, no one thinks you're a bitch."

"Well, here's the deal. I am. I am bitter and angry and hurt, and I have not had a moment to grieve the loss of the man who was my everything. As soon as Chance comes home, I may be able to."

"When he comes home, I'll still be there."

"No, Dad, you have a life to get back to."

"You're a mother now, Ava. Tell me how you would feel if they said that to you. Better yet, tell me if you'd listen."

"I would."

He doesn't respond.

"And I have offended you," I sigh. "See? God forbid—"

"Try to offend away, Ava. I'm still here."

There is no sense in fighting with him. None. So I don't.

§

WE WALK INTO THE NICU, and Logan stands up.

"Dad can take you home," I say, giving him a hug. "Get some sleep."

"You sure?" he asks.

"Yeah."

"You wanna take a cab, Logan?" Dad asks.

"No," I insist. "I am fine, okay? I love you both, but look around. There is a ton of people here. I'll be fine."

"Give me a minute with Chance," Dad says over his shoulder as he walks over to the sink and scrubs up.

I bite my tongue and let Dad hold him first. I know they all love them, and they love me, but ten weeks with everyone around is a bit much.

I sit in the rocker, feeding my little man. He is nearly six pounds and nurses just as well as Hope.

"Okay, little rock star"—I rub his cheek to remind him he is eating—"you need to hurry up and heal. Your sister is missing you. I am missing you. And your family—God love them—is driving me nuts."

His eyes open and his lips curve a bit. I know it's gas, but I smile back at him.

"I'll take that as a promise," I coo. "I will. I'll hold you to it."

His eyes are a brilliant blue, and his hair is jet black. Some babies, you can't tell if they are a boy or girl, but Chance already looks like a little man.

"I wish you looked like your daddy, but you're stuck looking like me except that dimple. That's all your daddy's. That's all Thomas's."

His eyes are wide, and it's like he is taking in everything I say. I wonder if it's because he sleeps less than Hope that he seems more alert. That thought hurts me because Chance is awake more since he is poked and prodded all day.

I see the doors open, and Dr. Yoman walks in. He is a neonatologist, and his bedside manner is much better than Dr. Kennedy's.

"Hey, Chance," he says, smiling. "Looking good, little guy, or should I say, big guy. Six pounds at last weigh-in." He gives him an air fist bump. "You know what else is going on? You're breathing and clearly eating on your own. You have had four out of six nights that your apnea machine didn't beep, so that means you're sleeping well. And let's top that with the fact that your NEC scans are clear. The port still needs to stay put for about ten days, just in case, but if your mom here thinks she can make sure to bring you in every other day for scans and blood tests, I see no reason you can't be released in say"—he paused and signs a paper then holds it up—"about ten minutes."

"Are you serious?" I gasp, startling Chance. His little lips quiver around me, and I lean down and smile at him. "You did it, Chance. You did it!"

"Should I give your father a call?"

"Are there car seats here at the hospital? I'd like to do this alone."

He seems to understand and nods. "I'll be back." He sets paperwork on the side table next to me and walks away.

§

I **DON'T LIKE HAVING TO** be wheeled out of the hospital, but it's policy, and if it takes that to get our boy home, I will sit and stew in silence.

The cab pulls up, and I let out a breath as I stand. Suddenly, I am nervous about letting someone I don't know drive our son.

"We can do this, Chance. We can," I say as we get inside, and I strap the base in.

I give the cab driver my address and tell him to please be careful. He looks in the rearview and nods. Then I sit back, buckle my seat belt, and he pulls away from the curb.

When he pulls up in front of our building, he does so in the only place possible to park.

I don't want to get out. I can't.

"Can you drive around and pull up closer to the entrance. We'll get out quickly, I promise."

He nods again and drives around the block before pulling up beside my Dad's SUV. I pay him and quickly get Chance and I out and onto the sidewalk.

I walk in and fish through my purse, grabbing my

key, then board the elevator. Chance is awake and alert, sucking furiously on his pacifier.

"We're home. You are going to love what your father has done for you."

When we get off the elevator, no one is in the open space that is the living area. I take a big deep breath and feel calmness for the first time in over two months.

I set Chance's carrier on the counter and unbuckle him. Then I hear voices, so I pick him up and walk toward the office that has acted as home base for all of our family.

"You tell her to back off, Lucas," my mother snaps. I am not happy that she is back to her old tricks.

"I never should have told you a damn thing, Ash. This isn't about you and me; this is about Ava, Hope, and Chance."

"Ava, Hope, and Chance will be fine. Jade needs to mind her business and leave it alone."

I walk a little closer, wanting to hear everything.

"When she saw Luke for the first time in Germany, he asked if the baby was his!" Dad snaps.

"He was drugged and a mess. Who the hell is she to assume that it's my little girl he's talking about?"

I step back when the weight of the world feels like it's on my shoulders. I close my eyes tightly and shake my head, willing it away. These babies are mine and Thomas's. I will not allow anyone to speculate otherwise. I need to make sure they know it, and I need to do so with the fierce belief that Thomas had in its truth. Clearly, it is true.

"Jade would never do this to Ava without warrant, Ash, and you know it."

"Lucas, she's a mother; she's your friend. She is grasping at straws. Who the hell wouldn't want Ava to be a child's mother? She's got her shit together; she's driven; she's smart; she's clearly strong—"

"You are something else," Dad huffs.

"I'm her mother, and I am telling you that you need to tell that bitch, if she wants to go dragging Ava's name through the mud, I will make her life hell."

"Will you, Mrs. Robertson?" Dad laughs. "Or will you throw up your hands and walk away?"

"You know damn well I will. Do whatever you have to do to get that woman to back down."

"After I ask Ava if it's a possibility, and she tells me it's not, then I will."

"She doesn't need to be part of Jade's head trip over her son who is clearly delusional. She needs you to show her support, Lucas."

"She knows damn well I will support her. I have always been in her corner. You're the one who ran off."

"Well, isn't it interesting that she has made her home here?" Mom says smugly.

"It's her home because of T," Dad says defensively.

"And what was it before, then?" She doesn't give him a chance to answer. "Her mother, Lucas, and the fact that she is bigger than that little town or a young man who runs off at any chance he gets to blow shit up."

Dad laughs haughtily. "You really are a fucking bitch, Ash."

"You helped make me that way," she counters.

I walk back to the door, holding Chance tightly to me. I don't want them to know I heard them. I want to get to Hope and take my babies—mine and T's—far away.

I have no idea what I will say if Dad confronts me. None. But I pray he doesn't.

I hear the elevator begin to move, and I assume that it's Logan. I have to let them know I'm here now before he gets out so they don't know I heard them.

I take a deep breath, kiss Chance, and whisper, "You are ours."

I set him in the carrier and yell, "Anybody home?"

They both come out of the room, looking shocked.

"What …? How …? Ava, do they know you brought him home?"

I smile because I have to. "Yeah, Dad, they do. Chance is home, and he is doing great." I pick him up and smile. "T and my babies are home."

"That's great news, Ava." Mom smiles as she walks toward me.

I now know where I get the ability to fake happiness. It's from her.

"Isn't it, Lucas?" she asks from over her shoulder.

He nods. "Yeah, it's wonderful."

Wonderful.

I remember vividly our first night together and when T's mouth touched me everywhere and the way he made me feel.

"I'm not drunk anymore, T, and I'm not a child, and I want you to feel like I do."

"How's that?"

I told him, "Wonderful."

Logan walks out of the elevator, his hair soaked with sweat. "Holy shit!"

"Go shower. I can smell you from here." I smile at him then turn and look at Mom. "Take Chance a second?"

When she does, I walk quickly to the office, open the desk drawer, and pull out the journal.

I open it to page twenty-seven as I sit and grab a pen.

Page 27

Our Love is forever, Thomas Hardy. Yours, mine, and our children's forever.

I set the journal on the table next to my father's phone charger, knowing he will get curious and read it. Then I get up and walk out.

When I pass the nursery, I look in. Hope's crib has been moved to the window, and she is sleeping soundly with the sun on her back. I bend down and kiss her sweet, little head, and she stirs yet doesn't wake up.

When I turn around to walk out, I am greeted with a father's wish for his children: butterflies and a smiling sun.

I kiss my fingers and reach up, touching the cloud that Piper pointed to and told me he was sitting on. "Our love is forever."

When I walk out, I see Dad warming up lunch, clearly something Tessa cooked for tonight.

"If you don't want to eat, you don't have to."

I hold my hands out and take Chance from Mom. "I'm actually a little hungry," I say, walking over next to him.

"He looks like me, doesn't he?" I ask.

"He does." Dad nods.

"Except this right here." I point to his dimple. "That's totally T. Even Liam said so."

Dad nods again.

"They have matching birthmarks, too," I tell him. "Right on their left cheek."

Dad looks at Chance's cheek and then at me.

I smile. "Butt cheek."

He kisses my head and turns to put the casserole in

the oven.

"And to think, your daddy didn't think you two were his and made me do a paternity test," I say in a sickly sweet tone.

"He, what?" Logan laughs.

"Yeah, men." I look back at Chance. "He said he loved me, anyway, but needed to know. Simple blood test and that stress was gone."

"Hell, I could have told him it was his. If I remember correctly, I saw him Christmas night bare-assed, running after you."

"Shh," I say. "Not in front of the kids."

"Or your father," Dad says in a more relaxed tone.

"Condom broke." I shrug. "Good thing we aren't Indian; that would have been a hell of a name to be stuck with."

Logan laughs, getting the joke. "Broken Condom and Bare Ass. Yeah, that would have sucked."

"It wouldn't have happened." I smile at Chance. "No way would I have done that to you. No way."

Epilogue

Love is hope, love is chance, love is forever.
— MJ Fields

THE POLICE FOUND THE CAR that hit and killed T. It was registered to a ninety-year-old man who had dementia and an alibi. The police think that the car was stolen and that the old man never reported it because he didn't notice it was gone. The plate was registered to a totally different vehicle. They didn't close the case, but because of empty bottles and drug paraphernalia they found inside the car, they were sure they were right.

It didn't help to know that no one was gunning for him. I never thought it to begin with. I had never seen Thomas Hardy unkind to anyone except Luke Lane. It didn't help that they found a motive for why it happened. It didn't help, because it didn't bring him back.

That night, I dream of T, and when I wake up, I am confused.

You know that feeling when you walk into the bitter February cold and you take your first breath, and your breath is frozen? You feel the pain in your throat, your chest, and you think to yourself, *This is what it feels like when you are dying.*

Or that moment you walk into the desert air, and

you feel like your lungs are so full that you can't take a breath when you desperately need one? None comes, and you are dying.

I can't breathe. Death is strangling me. It's bitter cold, it's sufficiently hot, and then there is this.

I look around. I am in the middle of the twins' room. Dad put a bed together for me in here so that maybe they could sleep, and when they did, I would.

I get up and look in their cribs, terrified they are going to be taken away, too. It has become a secret and all-consuming thought.

My dad rushes in the room, and I smile. It's fake, so fake, but I need them to leave. I need to grieve and love and grieve and love repeatedly.

I walk past him, needing to use the bathroom, and quickly hide behind the door.

I grab a towel and sob into it as I climb into the empty tub and sit.

The door opens, and Dad walks in, steps in the tub, sits down, and holds me.

"Talk to me, baby girl."

Everything rushes out, and I can't stop it.

"Daddy, I don't want to live, and I don't want to die, but this pain … This pain is unbearable. I can't do this. I can't do it anymore. I want to die. I want to fall asleep and never wake up. I want our babies in my arms on a cloud high above the world that is so full of death and pain and suffocation. I want to open my eyes and see him. I want to see him and for him to sit on the cloud, pain free and breathing, looking at me the way he did, and for his babies to see him and all the love he has for them! They are his, Daddy. They are, and Jade is wrong! *You* are wrong! I heard you and Mom. Do you know what that felt like?"

"I'm sorry, Ava. I'm sorry I wanted to ask you."

"Do you know what it would be like if they were his? *Do you?* It would be horrible, horrible and awful, and I don't want it. I don't want him. I want T, Daddy. I want him here with me so badly so that I can breathe and love and not think about death and sadness."

"Ava, what are you saying?"

"I'm telling you that T and I did a paternity test when I first found out. Dr. Kennedy administered it. T is my babies' father, and—"

"Could Luke have been, Ava?" he asks, his voice shaking in anger.

"No!"

"Okay. Christ, Ava." He holds me more tightly. "Okay, baby girl."

"It's not okay. Nothing is okay. There is life, and there is death, and there is nothing else." I sob.

"You're wrong, baby girl. You are wrong because you have me. You have us," he says as Mom and Logan come into the bathroom. "You have yours and T's babies. It hurts, and it's hard, but in the midst of death, there is life."

"It hurts," I cry. "It hurts so badly."

"You don't want to die, Ava," he says, and the fear in his voice shakes me.

I shake my head. "No. No, I just want to see him again. I didn't get to say good-bye, Dad. I didn't even tell him I loved him before I was carried out of that room."

"He knew, and he wants you to live, Ava, just like Collin wants Tessa to. When you love someone, you don't want them to be miserable; you want them to be happy. So if not for you, be happy for those babies and T, Ava. Allow yourself to be happy."

§

After that outburst, it takes a week before I can convince them it was due to a dream and that I'm fine.

Dad agreed to go home, but at a moment's notice, he would be back. He made me promise I would go to the Cape for Labor Day.

Mom was easier to convince. She hired a nanny to come in for five hours a day to allow me to rest and help with laundry.

When everyone was gone, I sent Casey home for the night with a promise I would call if I needed anyone. Otherwise, I would see her at eight so we could get Chance to the doctor.

That night, I close my eyes and remember page twenty-seven and all the pages before that. In our journal is all the truth that matters. He left me that without even knowing he would, and on page twenty-seven, I wrote,

Our love is forever, Thomas Hardy. Yours, mine, and our children's... forever.

My promise to him.

"You are the truth about love," I whisper to Hope and Chance as they sleep. "There is no greater love than that."

Love is brutal.

Love is beautiful.

Love is broken.

These are my truths.

The Truth About Love

Just like life, true love doesn't always come to us in the way we anticipate, dream, or expect.

Just like life, losing something we cherish doesn't mean that all is lost.

Just like Ava's father told her, life doesn't end in death. I believe that love in its truest and most breathtakingly beautiful form comes from within and grows when mirrored by those who are able to give it back.

Just like millions of people in this big, beautiful, and somewhat broken world, love lives in hope.

The greatest love in my life came to this world much earlier than expected, tiny and beautiful. Her eyes are blue and full of love, dreams, and kindness.

What I hope I can show her is the beauty in herself, in this world, and in people who are different. And, in differences, there is beauty.

Keep dreaming, hoping, and loving,
XOXO
MJ

Want more?

Expect another book in the Truth About Love series in
October 2016.
(Title to be announced.)

While you wait, follow MJ and Lucas Links on
Facebook to get periodic updates on the Ross, Links,
Hines, Abrahams families.
Feel free to post or message your truth about love.

Want to reads more about these characters?

*LRAH Legacy Series (These families' stories are
intertwined starting with The Love series, they move
to the Wrapped Series, the Burning Souls series, and
end in Love You Anyways. Many more series will spin
off from these characters already written and each
will be a standalone series but for those of us who
love a story to continue I recommend reading in this
order.*

**The Love Series
(Must Be Read In This Order)**
Blue Love (free everywhere)
New Love
Sad Love

27 Truths

True Love

The Wrapped Series
Wrapped In Silk
Wrapped In Armor
Wrapped In Always and Forever

Burning Souls Series
Stained
Forged
Merged

LRAH Legacy Additions
Love You Anyway
Love Notes

Contact MJ

USA Today bestselling author MJ Fields love of writing was in full swing by age eight. Together with her cousins, she wrote a newsletter and sold it for ten cents to family members.

She self-published her first contemporary, new adult romance in January 2013. Today she has completed seven self-published series, The Love series, The Wrapped series, The Burning Souls series, The Men of Steel series, Ties of Steel series, The Rockers of Steel series and The Norfolk series.

MJ is a hybrid author and publishes an indie book almost every month and has over 40 self-published titles. She is also signed with a traditional publisher, Loveswept, Penguin Random House, for her co- written series The Caldwell Brothers.

MJ was a former small business owner, who closed shop so she could write full time.

MJ lives in central New York, surrounded by family and friends. Her house is full of pets, friends, and noise ninety percent of the time, and she would have it no other way.

mjfieldsbooks.com
facebook.com/MJFieldsBooks
@mjfieldsbooks
Instagram.com/mjfieldsbooks
mjfieldsbooks.tumblr.com
Pinterest.com/mjfieldsbooks

SIGN UP FOR MJ'S MONTHLY NEWSLETTER WITH GIVEAWAYS ON WEBSITE

Made in the USA
Middletown, DE
24 July 2016